"HIGHLY ORIGINAL AND SATISFYING ... CLEVER SCIENCE, BIZARRE SETTINGS, LOTS OF PACE AND ACTION IN A TRULY EXOTIC UNIVERSE."
—Charles Sheffield
author of *Proteus Unbound*

Five hundred years after a handful of human starship travelers got lost in a hostile universe, their descendants are still struggling for survival. As hard as life is on The Raft—a platform remnant of the ship's hull—it's even harder in The Belt—a string of shacks circling the iron-rich core of a dead star. Every Belter has heard the story of the legendary starship but most of them don't believe it. But Rees, a lowly mine-rat, does. He wonders why the sky is angry red instead of the blue his parents remembered. Why food from The Raft gets less and less nutritious. Why fewer and fewer stars form every day. In his quest to find answers, Rees travels from boyhood to manhood, from the outermost edges of his world into its mysterious heart. And along the way he discovers there's more at stake than his simple curiosity: Life in his enigmatic universe is about to become impossible. . . .

"Good hard SF of a kind rarely seen nowadays, with exotic science and engineering worked out in loving detail. . . . The people who inhabit Baxter's strange world are well drawn in their pain and confusion, their friendships and enmities."
—Joe Haldeman,
author of *The Hemingway Hoax*

RAFT

Stephen Baxter

A ROC BOOK

ROC
Published by the Penguin Group
Penguin Books USA Inc., 375 Hudson Street,
New York, New York 10014, U.S.A.
Penguin Books Ltd, 27 Wrights Lane,
London W8 5TZ, England
Penguin Books Australia Ltd, Ringwood,
Victoria, Australia
Penguin Books Canada Ltd, 10 Alcorn Avenue,
Toronto, Ontario, Canada M4V 3B2
Penguin Books (N.Z.) Ltd, 182–190 Wairau Road,
Auckland 10, New Zealand

Penguin Books Ltd, Registered Offices:
Harmondsworth, Middlesex, England

First published in the United States by Roc, an imprint of New Ameri-
can Library, a division of Penguin Books USA Inc. First published in
Great Britain by GraftonBooks. An earlier version of part of this novel
appeared in a very different form in *Interzone* magazine, September–
October 1989.

First Roc Printing, January, 1992
10 9 8 7 6 5 4 3 2 1

To my wife, Sandra

I must express my thanks to Larry Niven, David Brin and Eric Brown, who took the trouble to read and comment closely on drafts of this novel, and on the imagined universe it portrays: thanks to their input the quality of this work has been greatly enhanced. Thanks also to Arthur C. Clarke, Bob Shaw, Charles Sheffield, Joe Haldeman, and David Pringle for their words of praise and encouragement. Finally I owe a great debt of gratitude to Malcolm Edwards, my editor at Grafton, for his patience, encouragement, and close attention to the development of this work.

1

It was when the foundry imploded that Rees's curiosity about his world became unbearable.

The shift started normally enough with a thump on his cabin wall from the fist of Sheen, his shift supervisor. Groggily Rees pulled himself from his sleeping net and moved slowly about the jumbled cabin, grinding through his wake-up routines.

The water from the rusty spigot emerged reluctantly in the microgee conditions. The liquid was sour and cloudy. He forced down a few mouthfuls and splashed his face and hair. He wondered with a shudder how many human bodies this water had passed through since its first collection from a passing cloud; it had been dozens of shifts since the last supply tree from the Raft had called with fresh provisions, and the Belt's antique recycling system was showing its deficiencies.

He pulled on a stained, one-piece coverall. The garment was getting too short. At fifteen thousand shifts old he was dark, slim—and tall enough already and still growing, he thought gloomily. This observation made him think with a stab of sadness of his parents; it was just the sort of remark they might have made. His father, who had not long survived his mother, had died a few hun-

9

dred shifts ago of circulatory problems and exhaustion. Suspended by one hand from the door frame Rees surveyed the little iron-walled cabin, recalling how cluttered it had seemed when he'd shared it with his parents.

He pushed such thoughts away and wriggled through the narrow door frame.

He blinked for a few seconds, dazzled by the shifting starlight . . . and hesitated. There was a faint scent on the air. A richness, like meat-sim. Something burning?

His cabin was connected to his neighbor's by a few yards of fraying rope and by lengths of rusty piping; he pulled himself a few feet along the rope and hung there, eyes raking the world around him for the source of the jarring scent.

The air of the Nebula was, as always, stained blood-red. A corner of his mind tried to measure that redness—was it deeper than last shift?—while his eyes flicked around the objects scattered through the Nebula above and below him. The clouds were like handfuls of grayish cloth sprinkled through miles of air. Stars fell among and through the clouds in a slow, endless rain that tumbled down to the Core. The light of the mile-wide spheres cast shifting shadows over the clouds, the scattered trees, the huge blurs that might be whales. Here and there he saw a tiny flash that marked the end of a star's brief existence.

How many stars were there?

As a child Rees had hovered among the cables, eyes wide, counting up to the limits of his knowledge and patience. Now he suspected that the stars were without number, that there were more stars than hairs on his head . . . or thoughts in his head, or words on his tongue. He raised his head and scoured a sky that was filled with stars. It was as if he were suspended in a great cloud of light; the star-spheres receded with distance into points of light, so that the sky itself was a curtain glowing red-yellow.

The burning scent called to him again, seeping through the thin air. He wrapped his toes in the cabin cable and released his hands; he let the spin of the Belt straighten his spine, and from this new viewpoint surveyed his home.

The Belt was a circle about eight hundred yards wide, a chain of battered dwellings and work places connected by ropes and tubes. At the center of the Belt was the mine itself, a cooled-down star kernel a hundred yards wide; lifting cables dangled from the Belt to the surface of the star kernel, scraping the rusty meniscus at a few feet per second.

Here and there, fixed to the walls and roofs of the Belt, were the massive, white-metal mouths of jets; every few minutes a puff of steam emerged from one of those throats and the Belt tugged imperceptibly faster at his heels, shaking off the slowing effects of air friction. He studied the ragged rim of the nearest jet; it was fixed to his neighbor's roof and showed signs of hasty cutting and welding. As usual his attention drifted off into random speculation. What vessel, or other device, had that jet come from? Who were the men who had cut it away? And why had they come here . . . ?

Again the whiff of fire. He shook his head, trying to concentrate.

It was shift-change time, of course, and there were little knots of activity around most of the cabins in the Belt as workers, grimy and tired, made for their sleep nets—and, a quarter of the Belt's circumference from him, a haze of smoke hovered around the foundry. He saw men dive again and again into the grayish fog. When they reemerged they tugged limp, blackened forms.

Bodies?

With a soft cry he curled, grasped the rope and sprint-crawled over the diffuse gravity wells of cabin roofs and walls to the foundry.

He hesitated on the edge of the sphere of smoke. The stench of burnt meat-sim made his empty stomach twist. Two figures emerged from the haze, solidifying like figures in a dream. They carried an unrecognizable, bloodied bundle between them. Rees anchored himself and reached down to help them; he tried not to recoil as charred flesh peeled away in his hands.

The limp form was bundled in stained blankets and hauled tenderly away. One of the two rescuers straightened before Rees; white eyes shone out of a soot-smeared face. It took him a few seconds to recognize Sheen, his shift supervisor. The pull of her hot, blackened body was a distant tugging at his belly, and he was ashamed to find, even at a moment like this, his eyes tracking sweat droplets over her blood-smeared chest. "You're late," she said, her voice smoke-deep as a man's.

"I'm sorry. What's happened?"

"An implosion. What do you think?" Pushing scorched hair from her brow she turned and pointed into the stationary pall of smoke. Now Rees could make out the shape of the foundry within; its cubical form had buckled, as if crushed by a giant hand. "Two dead so far," Sheen said. "Damn it. That's the third collapse in the last hundred shifts. If only Gord built strong enough for this damn stupid universe, I wouldn't have to scrape my workmates off each other like so much spoiled meat-sim. Damn, damn."

"What shall I do?"

She turned and looked at him with annoyance; he felt a flush of embarrassment and fear climb in his cheeks. Her irritation seemed to soften a little. "Help us haul the rest out. Stick close to me and you'll be fine. Try to breathe through your nose, OK?"

And she turned and dived back into the spreading smoke. Rees hesitated for a single second, then hurried after her.

The bodies were cleared and allowed to drift away into the Nebula air, while the injured were collected by their families and gently bundled to waiting cabins. The fire in the foundry was doused and soon the smoke was dispersing. Gord, the Belt's chief engineer, crawled over the ruins. The engineer was a short, blond man; he shook his head miserably as he began the work of planning the rebuilding of the foundry. Rees saw how the relatives of the dead and injured regarded Gord with hatred as he went about his work. Surely the series of implosions could not be blamed on the engineer?
. . . But if not Gord, who?

Rees's shift was cancelled. The Belt had a second foundry, separated from the ruin by a hundred and eighty degrees, and Rees would be expected to call there on his next working shift; but for now he was free.

He pulled his way slowly back to his cabin, staring with fascination at the blood-trails left by his hands on ropes and roofs. His head seemed still to be full of smoke. He paused for a few minutes at the entrance to his cabin, trying to suck clean oxygen from the air; but the ruddy, shifting starlight seemed almost as thick as smoke. Sometimes the Nebula breezes seemed almost unbreathable.

If only the sky were blue, he thought vaguely. I

13

wonder what blue is like ... Even in his parents' childhood—so his father had said—there were still hints of blue in the sky, off at the edges of the Nebula, far beyond the clouds and stars. He closed his eyes, trying to picture a color he had never seen, thinking of coolness, of clear water.

So the world had changed since his father's day. Why? And would it change again? Would blue and those other cool colors return—or would the redness deepen until it was the color of ruined flesh—

Rees pulled his way into his cabin and ran the spigot. He took off his tunic and scrubbed at his bloodstained skin until it ached.

The flesh peeled from the body in his hands like the skin from rotten fruit-sim; bone gleamed white—
He lay in his net, eyes wide, remembering.

A distant handbell rang three times. So it was still only mid-shift—he had to endure another shift and a half, a full twelve hours, before he had an excuse to leave the cabin.

If he stayed here he'd go crazy.

He rolled out of his net, pulled on his coverall and slid out of the cabin. The quickest way to the Quartermaster's was along the Belt past the wrecked foundry; deliberately he turned and crawled the other way.

People nodded from windows and outdoor nets as he passed, some smiling with faint sympathy. There were only a couple of hundred people in the Belt; the tragedy must have hit almost everybody. From dozens of cabins came the sounds of soft weeping, of cries of pain.

Rees lived alone, keeping mostly to his own company; but he knew almost everybody in the Belt. Now he lingered by cabins where people to whom he was a little closer must be suffering, perhaps dying; but he hurried on, feeling isolation thicken around him like smoke.

The Quartermaster's bar was one of the Belt's largest buildings at twenty yards across; it was laced with climbing ropes, and bar stock covered most of one wall. This shift the place was crowded: the stink of alcohol and weed, the bellow of voices, the pull of a mass of hot bodies—it all hit Rees as if he'd run into a wall. Jame, the barman, plied his trade briskly, laughing raucously through a graying tangle of beard. Rees lingered on the fringe of the milling crowd, anxious not to return to his desolate cabin; but the drink and laughter seemed to flow around him, excluding him, and he turned to leave.

"Rees! Wait . . ."

It was Sheen. She had pushed away from the center of a group of men; one of them—a huge, intimidating miner called Roch—called after her drunkenly. Sheen's cheeks were moist from the heat of the bar and she had cropped away her scorched hair; otherwise she was bright and clean in a fresh, skimpy tunic. When she spoke her voice was still scoured rough by the smoke. "I saw you come in. Here. You look like you need this." She held out a drink in a tarnished globe.

Suddenly awkward, Rees said, "I was going to leave—"

"I know you were." She moved closer to him, unsmiling, and pushed the drink into his chest. "Take it anyway." Again he felt the pull of her body as a warmth in his stomach—why should her gravity field have such a distinct flavor from that of others?—and he was distractingly aware of her bare arms.

"Thanks." He took the drink and sucked at the globe's plastic nipple; hot liquor coursed over his tongue. "Maybe I did need that."

Sheen studied him with frank curiosity. "You're an odd one, Rees, aren't you?"

He stared back, letting his eyes slide over the smoothness of the skin around her eyes. It struck him that she wasn't really much older than he was. "How am I odd?"

"You keep yourself to yourself."

He shrugged.

"Look, it's something you need to grow out of. You need company. We all do. Especially after a shift like this one."

"What did you mean earlier?" he asked suddenly.

"When?"

"During the implosion. You said how hard it was to build anything strong enough for this universe."

"What about it?"

"Well . . . what other universe is there?"

She sucked at her drink, ignoring the shouted invitations from the party behind her. "Who cares?"

"My father used to say the mine was killing us all. Humans weren't meant to work down there, crawling around in wheelchairs at five gee."

She laughed. "Rees, you're a character. But I'm not in the mood for metaphysical speculation, frankly. What I'm in the mood for is to get brain-dead on this fermented fruit-sim. So you can join me and the boys if you want, or you can go and sigh at the stars. OK?" She floated away, looking back questioningly; he shook his head, smiling stiffly, and she drifted back to her party, disappearing into a little pool of arms and legs.

Rees finished his drink, struggled to the bar to return the empty globe, and left.

A heavy cloud, fat with rain, drifted over the Belt,

reducing visibility to a few yards; the air it brought with it seemed exceptionally sour and thin.

Rees prowled around the cables that girdled his world, muscles working restlessly. He completed two full circuits, passing huts and cabins familiar since his childhood, hurrying past well-known faces. The damp cloud, the thin air, the confinement of the Belt seemed to come together somewhere inside his chest. Questions chased around his skull. Why were human materials and building methods so inadequate to resist the forces of the world? Why were human bodies so feeble in the face of those forces?

Why had his parents had to die, without answering the questions that had haunted him since childhood?

Shards of rationality glittered in the mud of his overtired thinking. His parents had had no better understanding of their circumstances than he had; there had been nothing but legends they could tell him before their sour deaths. Children's tales of a Ship, a Crew, of something called Bolder's Ring . . . But his parents had had—acceptance. They, and the rest of the Belt dwellers—even the sparkiest, like Sheen—seemed implicitly to accept their lot. Only Rees seemed plagued by questions, unanswered doubts.

Why couldn't he be like everyone else? Why couldn't he just accept and be accepted?

He let himself drift to rest, arms aching, cloud mist spattering his face. In all his universe there was only one entity which he could talk to about this—which would respond in any meaningful way to his questions.

And that was a digging machine.

With a sudden impulse he looked about. He was perhaps a hundred yards from the nearest mine elevator station; his arms and legs carried him to it with renewed vigor.

Cloud mist swirled after Rees as he entered the station. The place was deserted, as Rees had expected. The whole shift would be lost to mourning; not for another two or three hours would the bleary-eyed workers of the next shift begin to arrive.

The station was little more than another cubical iron shack, locked into the Belt. It was dominated by a massive drum around which a fine cable was coiled. The drum was framed by winch equipment constructed of some metal that remained free of rust, and from the cable dangled a heavy chair fitted with large, fat wheels. The chair was topped by a head and neck support and was thickly padded. There was a control panel fixed to a strut at one end of the drum; the panel was an arm's-length square and contained fist-sized, color-coded switches and dials. Rees rapidly set up a descent sequence on the panel and the winch drum began to vibrate.

He slid into the chair, taking care to smooth the clothing under his back and legs. On the surface of the star a crease of cloth could cut like a knife. A red light flashed on the control panel, casting sombre shadows, and the base of the cabin slid aside with a soft grind. The ancient machinery worked with a chorus of scrapes and squeaks; the drum turned and the cable began to pay out.

With a jolt Rees dropped through the station floor and into the dense cloud. The chair was pulled down the guide cable; the guide continued through the mist, he knew, for four hundred yards to the surface of the star. The familiar sensation of shifting gravity pulled at his stomach like gentle hands. The Belt was rotating a little faster than its orbital velocity—to keep the chain of cabins taut—and a few yards below the Belt the centripetal force faded, so that Rees drifted briefly through true weightlessness. Then he entered the gravity well of the star kernel and his weight built up rapidly, plating over his chest and stomach like iron.

Despite the mounting discomfort he felt a sense of release. He wondered what his workmates would think if they could see him now. To choose to descend to the mine during an off-shift ... and what for? To talk to a digging machine?

The oval face of Sheen floated before him, intelligent, skeptical and pragmatic.

He felt a flush burn up through his cheeks and he was suddenly glad that his descent was hidden by the mist.

He dropped out of the mist and the star kernel was revealed. It was a porous ball of iron fifty yards wide, visibly scarred by the hands and the machines of men. The guide cable—and its siblings, spread evenly around the Belt—scraped along the iron equator at a speed of a few feet each second.

His descent slowed; he imagined the winch four hundred yards above him straining to hold him against the star's clutching pull. Weight built up more rapidly now, climbing to its chest-crushing peak of five gees. The wheels of the chair began to rotate, whirring; then, cautiously, they kissed the moving iron surface. There was a bump which knocked the breath out of him. The cable disengaged rapidly, whipping backwards and away through the mist. The chair rolled slowly to a halt, carrying Rees a few yards from the trail of the cable.

For a few minutes Rees sat in the silence of the deserted star, allowing his breathing to adjust. His neck, back and legs all seemed comfortable in their deep padding, with no circulation-cutting folds of flesh or cloth. He lifted his right hand cautiously; it felt as if bands of iron encased his forearm, but he could reach the small control pad set into the chair arm.

He turned his head a few degrees to left and right. His chair sat isolated in the center of an iron landscape. Thick rust covered the surface, scoured by valleys a few inches deep and pitted by tiny craters. The horizon was no more than a dozen yards away; it was as if he sat at the crest of a dome. The Belt, glimpsed through the layer of cloud around the star, was a chain of boxes rolling through the sky, its cables hauling the cabins and workshops through a full rotation every five minutes.

Rees had often worked through in his head the sequence of events which had brought this spectacle into being. The star must have reached the end of its active life many centuries earlier, leaving a slowly spinning core of white-hot metal. Islands of solid iron would have formed in that sea of heat, colliding and gradually coalescing. At last a skin must have congealed around the iron, thickening and cooling. In the process bubbles of air had been trapped, leaving the sphere riddled with caverns and tunnels—and so making it accessible to humans. Finally the oxygen-laden air of the Nebula had worked on the shining iron, coating it with a patina of brown oxide.

The star kernel was probably cold all the way to its center by now, but Rees liked to imagine he could feel a faint glow of heat from the surface, the last ghost of star fire—

The silence was lanced through by a whine, far above him. Something glittering raced down through the air and hit the rust with a small impact a yard from Rees's chair. It left a fresh crater a half-inch across; a wisp of steam struggled to rise against the star pull.

Now more of the little missiles fizzed through the air; the star rang with impacts.

Rain. Metamorphosed by its fall through a five-gee gravity well into a hail of steaming bullets.

Rees cursed and reached for his control panel. The chair rolled forward, each bump and valley in the landscape jarring the breath from him. He was a few yards still from the nearest entrance to the mine works. How could he have been so careless as to descend to the surface—alone—when there was danger of rain? The shower thickened, slamming into the surface all around him. He cringed, pinned to his chair, waiting for the shower to reach his head and exposed arms.

The mouth of the mine works was a long rectangle cut in the rust. His chair rolled with agonizing slowness down a shallow slope into the depths of the star. At last the roof of the works was sliding over his head; the rain, safely excluded, spanged into the rust.

After pausing for a few minutes to allow his rattling heart to rest, Rees rolled on down the shallow, curving slope; Nebula light faded, to be replaced by the white glow of a chain of well-spaced lamps. Rees peered up at them as he passed. No one knew how the fist-sized globes worked. Apparently the lamps had glowed here unattended for centuries—most of them, anyway; here and there the chain was broken by the dimness of a failed lamp. Rees passed through the pools of darkness with a shudder; typically his mind raced through the years to a future in which miners would have to function without the ancient lamps.

After fifty yards of passageway—a third of the way around the circumference of the star—the light of the Nebula and the noise of the rain had disappeared. He reached a wide, cylindrical chamber, its roof about ten yards beneath the surface of the star. Rust-free walls gleamed in the lamplight. This was the entrance to the mine proper; the walls of the chamber were broken by the mouths of five circular passageways which led on into the heart of the star. The Moles—the digging machines—cut and refined the iron in the passageways, returning it in manageable nodules to the surface.

The real function of humans down here was to supplement the limited decision-making capabilities of the digging machines—to adjust their quota, perhaps, or to direct the gouging of fresh passageways around broken-down wheelchairs. Few people were capable of more ... although some miners, like Roch, were full of drunken stories about their prowess under the extreme gravity conditions.

From one passageway came a grumbling, scraping sound. Rees turned the chair. After some minutes a blunt prow nosed into the light of the chamber, and—with painful slowness—one of the machines the miners called the Moles worked its way over the lip of the tunnel.

The Mole was a cylinder of dull metal, some five yards long. It moved on six fat wheels. The prow of the Mole was studded with a series of cutting devices and with handlike claws which worked the star iron. The machine's back bore a wide pannier containing several nodules of freshly cut iron.

Rees snapped: "Status!"

The Mole rolled to a halt. It replied—as it always replied—"Massive sensor dysfunction." Its voice was thin and flat, and emanated from somewhere within its scuffed body.

Rees often imagined that if he knew what lay behind that brief report he would understand much of what baffled him about the world.

The Mole extended an arm from its nose. It reached to the panniers on its back and began lifting head-sized nodules down to a pile on the floor of the chamber. Rees watched it work for a few minutes. There were crude weld marks around the prow devices, the wheel axles and the points where the panniers were fixed; also, the skin of the Mole bore long, thin scars showing clearly where devices had been cut away, long ago. Rees half-closed his eyes so that he could see only the broad cylindrical shape of the Mole. What might have been fixed to those scars on the hull? With a flash of insight he imagined the jets that maintained the Belt in its orbit attached to the Mole. In his mind the components moved around, assembling and reassembling in various degrees of implausibility. Could the jets really once have been attached to the Mole? Had it once been some kind of flying machine, adapted for work down here?

But perhaps other devices had been fixed to those scars—devices long since discarded and now beyond his imagination—perhaps the "sensors" of which the Mole spoke.

He felt a surge of irrational gratitude to the Moles. In all his crushing universe they, enigmatic as they were, represented the only element of strangeness, of otherness; they were all his imagination had to work on. The first time he had begun to speculate that things might somewhere, sometime, be other than they were here had been a hundred shifts ago when a Mole had unexpectedly asked him whether he found the Nebula air any more difficult to breathe.

"Mole," he said.

An articulated metal arm unfolded from the nose of the Mole; a camera fixed on him.

"The sky looked a bit more red today."

The transfer of nodules was not slowed but the small lens stayed steady. A red lamp somewhere on the prow of the machine began to pulse. "Please input spectrometer data."

"I don't know what you're talking about," Rees said. "And even if I did, I haven't got a 'spectrometer.'"

"Please quantify input data."

"I still don't understand," Rees said patiently.

For further seconds the machine studied him. "How red is the sky?"

Rees opened his mouth—and hesitated, stuck for words. "I don't know. Red. Darker. Not as dark as blood."

The lens lit up with a scarlet glow. "Please calibrate."

Rees imagined himself to be staring into the sky. "No, not as bright as that."

The glow scaled through a tight spectrum, through crimson to a muddy blood color.

"Back a little," Rees said. ". . . There. That's it, I think."

The lens darkened. The lamp on the prow, still scarlet, began to glow steady and bright. Rees was reminded of the warning light on the winch equipment and felt his flesh crawl under its blanket of weight. "Mole. What does that light mean?"

"Warning," it said in its flat voice. "Deterioration of environment life-threatening. Access to support equipment recommended."

Rees understood "threatening," but what did the

rest of it mean? What support equipment? "Damn you, Mole, what are we supposed to do?"

But the Mole had no reply; patiently it continued to unload its pannier.

Rees watched, thoughts racing. The events of the last few shifts came like pieces of a puzzle to the surface of his mind.

This was a tough universe for humans. The implosion had proved that. And now, if he understood any of what the Mole had said, it seemed that the redness of the sky was a portent of doom for them all, as if the Nebula itself were some vast, incomprehensible lamp of warning.

A sense of confinement returned, its weight more crushing than the pull of the star kernel. He would never get anyone else to understand his concerns. He was just some dumb kid, and his worries were based on hints, fragments, all partially understood.

Would he still be a kid when the end came?

Scenes of apocalypse flashed through his head: he imagined dimming stars, thickening clouds, the very air souring and failing in his lungs—

He had to get back to the surface, the Belt, and onwards; he had to find out more. And in all his universe there was only one place he could go.

The Raft. Somehow he had to get to the Raft.

With a new sense of purpose, vague but burning, he turned his chair to the exit ramp.

2

The tree was a wheel of wood and foliage fifty yards wide. Its rotation slowing, it lowered itself reluctantly into the gravity well of the star kernel.

Pallis, the tree-pilot, was hanging by hands and feet below the knotty trunk of the tree. The star kernel and its churning Belt mine were behind his back. With a critical eye he peered up through the mat of foliage at the smoke which hung raggedly over the upper branches. The layer of smoke wasn't anywhere near thick enough: he could clearly see starlight splashing through to bathe the tree's round leaves. He moved his hands along the nearest branch, felt the uncertain quivering of the fine blade of wood. Even here, at the root of the branches, he could feel the tree's turbulent uncertainty. Two imperatives acted on the tree. It strove to flee the deadly gravity well of the star—but it also sought to escape the shadow of the smoke cloud, which drove it back into the well. A skillful woodsman should have the two imperatives in fine balance; the tree should hover in an unstable equilibrium at the required distance.

Now the tree's rotating branches bit into the air and it jerked upwards by a good yard. Pallis was almost shaken loose. A cloud of skitters came tumbling from the foliage; the tiny wheel-shaped creatures buzzed around his face and arms as they tried to regain the security of their parent.

Damn that boy—

With an angry, liquid movement of his arms he hauled himself through the foliage to the top side of the tree. The ragged blanket of smoke and steam hung a few yards above his head, attached tenuously to the branches by threads of smoke. The damp wood in at least half the fire bowls fixed to the branches had, he soon found, been consumed.

And Gover, his so-called assistant, was nowhere to be seen.

His toes wrapped around the foliage, Pallis drew himself to his full height. At fifty thousand shifts he was old by Nebula standards; but his stomach was still as flat and as hard as the trunk of one of his beloved fleet of trees, and most men would shy from the network of branch scars that covered his face, forearms and hands and flared red at moments of anger.

And this was one of those moments.

"Gover! By the Bones themselves, what do you think you are doing?"

A thin, clever face appeared above one of the bowls near the rim of the tree. Gover shook his way out of a nest of leaves and came scurrying across the platform of foliage, a pack bouncing against his narrow back.

Pallis stood with arms folded and biceps bunched. "Gover," he said softly, "I'll ask you again. What do you think you're doing?"

Gover shoved the back of his hand against his nose, pushing the nostrils out of shape; the hand came away glistening. "I'd finished," he mumbled.

Pallis leant over him. Gover's gaze slid over and

away from the tree-pilot's eyes. "You're finished when I tell you so. And not before."

Gover said nothing.

"Look—" Pallis stabbed a finger at Gover's pack. "You're still carrying half your stock of wood. The fires are dying. And look at the state of the smoke screen. More holes than your damn vest. My tree doesn't know whether she's coming or going, thanks to you. Can't you feel her shuddering?

"Now, listen, Gover. I don't care a damn for you, but I do care for my tree. You cause her any more upset and I'll have you over the rim; if you're lucky the Boneys'll have you for supper, and I'll fly her home to the Raft myself. Got that?"

Gover hung before him, hands tugging listlessly at the ragged hem of his vest. Pallis let the moment stretch taut; then he hissed, "Now move it!"

With a flurry of motion Gover pulled himself to the nearest pot and began hauling wood from his pack. Soon fresh billows of smoke were rising to join the depleted cloud, and the shuddering of the tree subsided.

His exasperation simmering Pallis watched the boy's awkward movements. Oh, he'd had his share of poor assistants in the past, but in the old times most of them had been willing to learn. To try. And gradually, as hard shifts wore by, those young people had grown into responsible men and women, their minds toughening with their bodies.

But not this lot. Not the new generation.

This was his third flight with the boy Gover. And the lad was still as sullen and obstructive as when he'd first been assigned to the trees; Pallis would be more than glad to hand him back to Science.

His eyes roamed around the red sky, restless. The falling stars were an array of pinpoints dwindling into the far distance; the depths of the Nebula, far below him, were a sink of murky crimson. Was this nostalgic disregard for the young of today just a symptom of ageing . . . ? Or had people truly changed?

Well, there was no doubt that the world had changed around him. The crisp blue skies, the rich breezes of his youth were memories now; the very air was turning into a smoky sludge, and the minds of men seemed to be turning sour with it.

And one thing was for sure. His trees didn't like this gloom.

He sighed, trying to snap out of his introspection. The stars kept falling no matter what the color of the sky. Life went on, and he had work to do.

Tiny vibrations played over the soles of his bare feet, telling him that the tree was almost stable now, hovering at the lip of the star kernel's gravity well. Gover moved silently among the fire bowls. Damn it, the lad could do the job well when he was forced to. That was the most annoying thing about him. "Right, Gover, I want that layer maintained while I'm off-tree. And the Belt's a small place; I'll know if you slack. You got that?"

Gover nodded without looking at him.

Pallis dropped through the foliage, his thoughts turning to the difficult negotiations ahead.

It was the end of Rees's work shift. Wearily he hauled himself through the foundry door.

Cooler air dried the sweat from his brow. He pulled himself along the ropes and roofs towards his cabin, inspecting his hands and arms with some interest. When one of the older workers had dropped a ladle of iron, Rees had narrowly dodged a hail of molten metal; tiny droplets had drifted into his flesh, sizzling out little craters which—

A huge shadow flapped across the Belt. Air

30

washed over his back. He looked up; and a feeling of astonishing cold settled at the base of his skull.

The tree was magnificent against the crimson sky. Its dozen radial branches and their veil of leaves turned with a calm possession; the trunk was like a mighty wooden skull which glared around at the ocean of air.

This was it. His opportunity to escape from the Belt ...

The supply trees were the only known means of traveling from Belt to Raft, and so after his moment of decision following the foundry implosion Rees had resolved to stow away on the next tree to visit the Belt. He had begun to hoard food, wrapping dried meat in bundles of cloth, filling cloth globes with water—

Sometimes, during his sleep shifts, he had lain awake staring at his makeshift preparations and a thin sweat had covered his brow as he wondered if he would have the courage to take the decisive step.

Well, the moment had come. Staring at the magnificent tree he probed at his emotions: he knew he was no hero, and he had half-expected fear to encase him like a net of ropes. But there was no fear. Even the nagging pain in his hands subsided. There was only elation; the future was an empty sky, within which his hopes would surely find room.

He hurried to his cabin and collected his bundle of supplies, which was already lashed together; then he climbed to the outer wall of his cabin.

A rope had uncoiled from the tree trunk and lay across the fifty yards to the Belt, brushing against the orbiting cabins. A man came shimmering confidently down the rope; he was scarred, old and muscular, almost a piece of the tree himself. Ignoring the watching Rees the man dropped without hesitation across empty air to a cabin and began to make his way around the Belt.

Rees clung to his cabin by one hand. The rotation of the Belt carried the cabin steadily towards the tree's dangling rope; when it was a yard from him he grabbed at it and swarmed without hesitation off the Belt.

As always at shift change the Quartermaster's was crowded. Pallis waited outside, watching the Belt's pipes and boxy cabins roll around the star kernel. At length Sheen emerged bearing two drink globes.

They drifted to the relative privacy of a long stretch of piping and silently raised their globes. Their eyes met briefly. Pallis looked away in some confusion—then felt embarrassed at that in turn.

To the Bones with it. The past was gone.

He sucked at the liquor, trying not to grimace. "I think this stuff's improving," he said at last.

Her eyebrows arched slightly. "I'm sorry we can't do better. No doubt your tastes are a little more refined."

He felt a sigh escape from his throat. "Damn it, Sheen, let's not fence. Yes, the Raft has got a liquor machine. Yes, what comes out of it is a damn sight finer than this recycled piss. And everyone knows it. But this stuff really is a little better than it was. All right? Now, can we get on with our business?"

She shrugged, indifferent, and sipped her drink. He studied the way the diffuse light caught in her hair, and his attraction to her once more pulled at him. Damn it, he had to grow out of this. It must be five thousand shifts since the time they'd slept together, their limbs tangling in her sleeping net as the Belt rolled silently around its star . . .

It had been a one-off, two tired people falling

together. Now, damn it to hell, it only got in the way of business. In fact he suspected the miners used her as their negotiating front with him knowing the effect she had on him. This was a tough game. And it was getting tougher ...

He tried to concentrate on what she was saying. ". . . So we're down on production. We can't fulfil the shipment. Gord says it will take another fifty shifts before that foundry is operational again. And that's the way it is." She fell silent and stared at him defiantly.

His eyes slid from her face and tracked reluctantly around the Belt. The ruined foundry was a scorched, crumpled wound in the chain of cabins. Briefly he allowed himself to imagine the scene in there during the accident—the walls bellying in, the ladles spilling molten iron—

He shuddered.

"I'm sorry, Sheen," he said slowly. "I truly am. But—"

"But you're not going to leave us the full fee," she said sourly.

"Damn it, I don't make the rules. I've a treeful of supplies up there; I'm ready to give you what I get back in iron, at the agreed exchange rate."

She hissed through clenched teeth, her eyes fixed on her drink. "Pallis, I hate to beg. You've no idea how much I hate to beg. But we need those supplies. We've got sewage coming out of our spigots; we've got sick and dying—"

He gulped down the last of his drink. "Leave it, Sheen," he said, more harshly than he'd intended.

She raised her head and fixed him with eyes reduced to slits. "You need our metal, Raft man. Don't forget that."

He took a deep breath. "Sheen, we've another source. You know that. The early Crew found two star kernels in neat circular orbits around the Core—"

She laughed quietly. "And you know the other mine isn't producing any more. Is it, Pallis? We don't know what happened to it, yet, but we've picked up that much. So let's not play games."

Shame rose like a bubble inside him; he felt his face redden and he imagined his scars emerging as a livid net. So they knew. At least, he reflected gloomily, at least we evacuated the Nebula's only other mine when that star fell too close. At least we were honorable enough for that. Although not honorable enough to avoid lying about all that pain in order to keep our advantage over these people—

"Sheen, we're getting nowhere. I'm just doing my job, and this is out of my control." He handed back his drink globe. "You have a shift to decide whether to accept my terms. Then I leave regardless. And—look, Sheen, just remember something. We can recycle our iron a hell of a lot easier than you can recycle your food and water."

She studied him dispassionately. "I hope they suck on your bones, Raft man."

He felt his shoulders slump. He turned and began to make his slow way to the nearest wall, from which he could jump to the tree rope.

A file of miners clambered up to the tree, iron plates strapped to their backs. Under the pilot's supervision the plates were lashed securely to the tree rim, widely spaced. The miners descended to the Belt laden with casks of food and fresh water.

Rees, watching from the foliage, couldn't understand why so many of the food cases were left behind in the tree.

He stayed curled closely around a two-feet wide branch—taking care not to cut open his palms on its knife-sharp leading edge—and he kept a layer of foliage around his body. He had no way of telling the time, but the loading of the tree must have taken several shifts. He was wide-eyed and sleepless. He knew that his absence from work would go unremarked for at least a couple of shifts—and, he thought with a distant sadness, it might be longer before anyone cared enough to come looking for him.

Well, the world of the Belt was behind him now. Whatever dangers the future held for him, at least they would be new dangers.

In fact he only had two problems. Hunger and thirst . . .

Disaster had struck soon after he had found himself this hiding place among the leaves. One of the Belt workmen had stumbled across his tiny cache of supplies; thinking it belonged to the despised Raft crewmen the miner had shared the morsels among his companions. Rees had been lucky to avoid detection himself, he realized . . . but now he had no supplies, and the clamor of his throat and belly had come to fill his head.

But at last the loading was complete; and when the pilot launched his tree, even Rees's thirst was forgotten.

When the final miner had slithered down to the Belt Pallis curled up the rope and hung it around a hook fixed to the trunk. So his visit was over. Sheen hadn't spoken to him again, and for several shifts he had had to endure the sullen silence of strangers. He shook his head and turned his thoughts with some relief to the flight home. "Right, Gover, let's see you move! I want the bowls switched to the underside of the tree, filled and lit before I've finished coiling this rope. Or would you rather wait for the next tree?"

Gover got to work, comparatively briskly; and soon a blanket of smoke was spreading beneath the tree, shielding the Belt and its star from view.

Pallis stood close to the trunk, his feet and hands sensitive to the excited surge of sap. It was almost as if he could sense the huge vegetable thoughts of the tree as it reacted to the darkness spreading below it. The trunk audibly hummed; the branches bit into the air; the foliage shook and swished and skitters tumbled, confused at the abrupt change of airspeed; and then, with an exhilarating surge, the great spinning platform lifted from the star. The Belt and its human misery dwindled to a toy-like mote, falling slowly into the Nebula, and Pallis, hands and feet pressed against the flying wood, was where he was most happy.

His contentment lasted for about a shift and a half. He prowled the wooden platform, moodily watching the stars slide through the silent air. The flight just wasn't smooth. Oh, it wasn't enough to disturb Gover's extensive slumbers, but to Pallis's practiced senses it was like riding a skitter in a gale. He pressed his ear to the ten-feet-high wall of the trunk; he could feel the bole whirring in its vacuum chamber as it tried to even out the tree's rotation.

This felt like a loading imbalance ... But that was impossible. He'd supervised the stowage of the cargo himself to ensure an even distribution of mass around the rim. For him not to have spotted such a gross imbalance would have been like—well, like forgetting to breathe.

Then what?

With a growl of impatience he pushed away from

the trunk and stalked to the rim. He began to work around the lashed loads, methodically rechecking each plate and cask and allowing a picture of the tree's loading to build up in his mind—

He slowed to a halt. One of the food casks had been broken into; its plastic casing was cracked in two places and half the contents were gone. Hurriedly he checked a nearby water cask. It too was broken open and empty.

He felt hot breath course through his nostrils. "Gover! Gover, come here!"

The boy came slowly, his thin face twisted with apprehension.

Pallis stood immobile until Gover got within arm's reach; then he lashed out with his right hand and grabbed the apprentice's shoulder. The boy gasped and squirmed, but was unable to break the grip. Pallis pointed at the violated casks. "What do you call this?"

Gover stared at the casks with what looked like real shock. "Well, I didn't do it, pilot. I wouldn't be so stupid—ah!"

Pallis worked his thumb deeper into the boy's joint, searching for the nerve. "Did I keep this food from the miners in order to allow you to feast your useless face? Why, you little bonesucker, I've a mind to throw you over now. When I get back to the Raft I'll make sure not a day of your life goes by without the world being told what a lying, thieving . . . little . . ."

Then he fell silent, his anger dissipating.

There was still something wrong. The mass of the provisions taken from the casks wasn't nearly enough to account for the disruption to the tree's balance. And as for Gover—well, he'd been proven a thief, a liar and worse in the past, but he was right: he wasn't nearly stupid enough for this.

Reluctantly he released the boy's shoulder. Gover rubbed the joint, staring at him resentfully. Pallis scratched his chin. "Well, if you didn't take the stuff, Gover, then who did? Eh?"

By the Bones, they had a stowaway.

Swiftly he dropped to all fours and pressed his hands and feet against the wood of a branch. He closed his eyes and let the tiny shuddering speak to him. If the unevenness wasn't at the rim then where . . . ?

Abruptly he straightened and half-ran about a quarter of the way around the rim, his long toes clutching at the foliage. He paused for a few seconds, hands once more folded around a branch; then he made his way more slowly towards the center of the tree, stopping about halfway to the trunk.

There was a little nest in the foliage. Through the bunched leaves he could see a few scraps of discolored cloth, a twist of unruly black hair, a hand dangling weightless; the hand was that of a boy or young man, he judged, but it was heavily callused and it bore a spatter of tiny wounds.

Pallis straightened to his full height. "Well, here's our unexpected mass, apprentice. Good shift to you, sir! And would you care for your breakfast now?"

The nest exploded. Skitters whirled away from the tangle of limbs and flew away, as if indignant; and at last a boy half-stood before Pallis, eyes bleary with sleep, mouth a circle of shock.

Gover sidled up beside Pallis. "By the Bones, it's a mine rat."

Pallis looked from one boy to the other. The two seemed about the same age, but where Gover was well-fed and ill-muscled, the stowaway had ribs like an anatomical model's and his muscles were like a man's; and his hands were the battered product of hours of labor. The lad's eyes were dark-ringed. Pallis remembered the imploded foundry and wondered what horrors this young miner had already seen. Now the boy filled his chest defiantly, his hands bunching into fists.

Gover sneered, arms folded. "What do we do, pilot? Throw him to the Boneys?"

Pallis turned on him with a snarl. "Gover, sometimes you disgust me."

Gover flinched. "But—"

"Have you cleaned out the fire bowls yet? No? Then do it. Now!"

With a last, baleful glare at the stowaway, Gover moved clumsily away across the tree.

The stowaway watched him go with some relief; then turned back to Pallis.

The pilot's anger was gone. He raised his hands, palms upwards. "Take it easy. I'm not going to hurt you ... and that idler is nothing to be afraid of. Tell me your name."

The boy's mouth worked but no sound emerged; he licked cracked lips, and managed to say: "Rees."

"All right. I'm Pallis. I'm the tree-pilot. Do you know what that means?"

"I ... Yes."

"By the Bones, you're dry, aren't you? No wonder you stole that water. You did, didn't you? And the food?"

The boy nodded hesitantly. "I'm sorry. I'll pay you back—"

"When? After you return to the Belt?"

The boy shook his head, a glint in his eye. "No. I'm not going back."

Pallis bunched his fists and rested them on his hips. "Listen to me. You'll have to go back. You'll be allowed to stay on the Raft until the next supply tree; but then you'll be shipped back. You'll have to work your passage, I expect. All right?"

Rees shook his head again, his face a mask of determination.

Pallis studied the young miner, an unwelcome sympathy growing inside him. "You're still hungry, aren't you? And thirsty, I'll bet. Come on. I keep my—and Gover's—rations at the trunk."

He led the boy across the tree surface. Surreptitiously he watched as the boy half-walked across the foliated platform, his feet seeking out the points of good purchase and then lodging in the foliage, so allowing him to "stand" on the tree. The contrast with Gover's clumsy stumbling was marked. Pallis found himself wondering what kind of woodsman the lad would make . . .

After a dozen yards they disturbed a spray of skitters; the little creatures whirled up into Rees's face and he stepped back, startled. Pallis laughed. "Don't worry. Skitters are harmless. They are the seeds from which the tree grows . . ."

Rees nodded. "I guessed that."

Pallis arched an eyebrow. "You did?"

"Yes. You can see the shape's the same; it's just a difference of scale."

Pallis listened in surprised silence to the serious, parched voice.

They reached the trunk. Rees stood before the tall cylinder and ran his fingers over the gnarled wood. Pallis hid a smile. "Put your ear against the wood. Go on."

Rees did so with a look of puzzlement—which evolved into an almost comic delight.

"That's the bole turning, inside the trunk. You see, the tree is alive, right to its core."

Rees's eyes were wide.

Now Pallis smiled openly. "But I suspect you

won't be alive much longer if you don't eat and drink. Here ..."

After letting the boy sleep for a quarter-shift Pallis put him to work. Soon Rees was bent over a fire bowl, scraping ash and soot from the iron with shaped blades of wood. Pallis found that his work was fast and complete, supervised or unsupervised. Once again Gover suffered by comparison ... and by the looks he shot at Rees, Pallis suspected Gover knew it.

After half a shift Pallis brought Rees a globe of water. "Here; you deserve a break."

Rees squatted back among the foliage, flexing stiff hands. His face was muddy with sweat and soot and he sucked gratefully at the drink. On an impulse Pallis said, "These bowls hold fire. Maybe you guessed that. Do you understand how they're used?"

Rees shook his head, interest illuminating his tired face.

Pallis described the simple sensorium of the tree. The tree was essentially a huge propeller. The great vegetable reacted to two basic forms of stimuli—gravity fields and light—and in their uncultivated state great forests of trees of all sizes and ages would drift through the clouds of the Nebula, their leaves and branchlets trapping starlight, the nourishment of drifting plants and animals, the moisture of fat rain clouds.

Rees listened, nodding seriously. "So by rotating faster—or slower—the tree pushes at the air and can climb away from gravity wells or towards the light."

"That's right. The art of the pilot is to generate a blanket of smoke to hide the light, and so to guide the flight of the tree."

41

Rees frowned, his eyes distant. "But what I don't understand is how the tree can change its rotation speed."

Once again Pallis was surprised. "You ask good questions," he said slowly. "I'll try to explain. The trunk is a hollow cylinder; it contains another, solid cylinder called the bole, which is suspended in a vacuum chamber. The trunk and the rest of the tree are made of a light, fine-fibred wood; but the bole is a mass of much denser material, and the vacuum chamber is crisscrossed with struts and ribs to keep it from collapsing. And the bole spins in its chamber; muscle-like fibres keep it whirling faster than a skitter.

"Now—when the tree wants to speed its rotation it slows the bole a little, and the spin of the bole is transferred to the tree. And when the tree wants to slow it is as if it pours some of its spin back into the bole." He struggled for phrases to make it clearer; dim, half-understood fragments from Scientists' lectures drifted through his mind: moments of inertia, conservation of angular momentum . . .

He gave up with a shrug. "Well, that's about the best I can explain it. Do you understand?"

Rees nodded. "I think so." He looked oddly pleased with Pallis's answer; it was a look that reminded the pilot of the Scientists he had worked with, a look of pleasure at finding out how things work.

Gover, from the rim of the tree, watched them sullenly.

Pallis stepped slowly back to his station at the trunk. How much education did the average miner get, he wondered. He doubted Rees was even literate. As soon as a child was strong enough he was no doubt forced into the foundry or down to the crushing surface of the iron star, to begin a life of muscle-sapping toil . . .

And he was forced there by the economics of the Nebula, he reminded himself harshly; economics which he—Pallis—helped to keep in place.

He shook his head, troubled. Pallis had never accepted the theory, common on the Raft, that the miners were a species of subhuman, fit only for the toil they endured. What was the life span of the miners? Thirty thousand shifts? Less, maybe? Would Rees live long enough to learn what angular momentum was? What a fine woodsman he would make . . . or, he admitted ruefully, maybe a better Scientist.

A vague plan began to form in his mind.

Rees came to the trunk and collected his shift-end rations. The young miner peered absently around at the empty sky. As the tree climbed up towards the Raft, away from the Core and towards the edge of the Nebula, the air was perceptibly brightening.

A distant sound carried over the sigh of the wind through the branches: a discordant shout, huge and mysterious.

Rees looked questioningly at Pallis. The tree-pilot smiled. "That's the song of a whale." Rees looked about eagerly, but Pallis warned, "I wouldn't bother. The beast could be miles away . . ." The pilot watched Rees thoughtfully. "Rees, something you haven't told me yet. You're a stow-away, right? But you can't have any real idea what the Raft is like. So . . . why did you do it? What were you running from?"

Rees's brow creased as he considered the question. "I wasn't running from anything, pilot. The mine is a tough place, but it was my home. No. I left to find the answer."

"The answer? To what?"

"To why the Nebula is dying."

Pallis studied the serious young miner and felt a chill settle on his spine.

Rees woke from a comfortable sleep in his nest of foliage. Pallis hung over him, silhouetted by a bright sky. "Shift change," the pilot said briskly. "Hard work ahead for all of us: docking and unloading and—"

"Docking?" Rees shook his head clear of sleep. "Then we've arrived?"

Pallis grinned. "Well, isn't that obvious?"

He moved aside. Behind him the Raft hung huge in the sky.

3

Hollerbach lifted his head from the lab report, eyes smarting. He removed his spectacles, set them on the desk top before him, and began methodically to massage the ridge of bone between his eyes. "Oh, do sit down, Mith," he said wearily.

Captain Mith continued to pace around the office. His face was a well of anger under its covering of black beard and his massive belly wobbled before him. Hollerbach noted that Mith's coverall was frayed at the hem, and even the golden Officer's threads at his collar looked dulled. "Sit down? How the hell can I sit down? I suppose you know I've got a Raft to run."

Hollerbach groaned inwardly, "Of course, but—"

Mith took an orrery from a crowded shelf and shook it at Hollerbach. "And while you Scientists swan around in here my people are sick and dying—"

"Oh, by the Bones, Mith, spare me the sanctimony!" Hollerbach thrust out his jaw. "Your father was just the same. All lectures and no damn use."

Mith's mouth was round. "Now, look, Hollerbach—"

"Lab tests take time. The equipment we're work-

45

ing with is hundreds of thousands of shifts old, remember. We're doing our best, and all the bluster in the Nebula isn't going to speed us up. And you can put down that orrery, if you don't mind."

Mith looked at the dusty instrument. "Why the hell should I, you old fart?"

"Because it's the only one in the universe. And nobody knows how to fix it. Old fart yourself."

Mith growled—then barked laughter. "All right, all right." He set the orrery back on its shelf and pulled a hard-backed chair opposite the desk. He sat with legs splayed under his belly and raised troubled eyes to Hollerbach. "Look, Scientist, we shouldn't be scrapping. You have to understand how worried I am, how frightened the crew are."

Hollerbach spread his hands on the desk top; liver-spots stared back at him. "Of course I do, Captain." He turned his ancient spectacles over in his fingers and sighed. "Look, we don't need to wait for the lab results. I know damn well what we're going to find."

Mith spread his hands palm up. "What?"

"We're suffering from protein and vitamin deficiencies. The children particularly are being hit by bone, skin and growth disorders so archaic that the Ship's medical printouts don't even refer to them." He thought of his own grandchild, not four thousand shifts old; when Hollerbach took those slim little legs in his hands he could feel the bones curve ... "Now, we don't think there's anything wrong with the food dispensers."

Mith snorted. "How can you be so sure?"

Hollerbach rubbed his eyes again. "Of course I'm not sure," he said, irritated. "Look, Mith, I'm speculating. You can either accept that or wait for the tests."

Mith sat back and held up his palms. "All right, all right. Go on."

"Very well, then. Of all the Raft's equipment our understanding is, by necessity, greatest of the dispensers. We're overhauling the brutes; but I don't expect anything to be found wrong."

"What, then?"

Hollerbach climbed out of his chair, feeling the familiar twinge in his right hip. He walked to the open door of his office and peered out. "Isn't it obvious? Mith, when I was a kid that sky was blue as a baby's eyes. Now we have children, adults even, who don't know what blue is. The damn Nebula has gone sour. The dispensers are fed by organic compounds in the Nebula atmosphere—and by airborne plants and animals, of course. Mith, it's a case of garbage in, garbage out. The machines can't work miracles. They can't produce decent food out of the sludge out there. And that's the problem."

Behind him Mith was silent for a long time. Then he said, "What can we do?"

"Beats me," said Hollerbach, a little harshly. "You're the Captain."

Mith got out of his chair and lumbered up to Hollerbach; his breath was hot on the old Scientist's neck, and Hollerbach could feel the pull of the Captain's weighty gut. "Damn it, stop patronizing me. What am I supposed to tell the crew?"

Abruptly Hollerbach felt very tired. He reached with one hand for the door frame and wished his chair weren't so far away. "Tell them not to give up hope," he said quietly. "Tell them we're doing all we know how to do. Or tell them nothing. As you see fit."

Mith thought it over. "Of course, not all your results are in." There was a trace of hope in his voice. "And you haven't completed that machine overhaul, have you?"

Hollerbach shook his head, eyes closed. "No, we haven't finished the overhaul."

"So maybe there's something wrong with the machines after all." Mith clapped his shoulder with a plate-sized hand. "All right, Hollerbach. Thanks. Look, keep me informed."

Hollerbach stiffened. "Of course."

Hollerbach watched Mith stride away across the deck, his belly oscillating. Mith wasn't too bright— but he was a good man. Not as good as his father, maybe, but a lot better than some of those who were now calling for his replacement.

Maybe a cheerful buffoon was right for the Raft in its present straits. Someone to keep their spirits up as the air turned to poison—

He laughed at himself. Come on, Hollerbach; you really are turning into an old fart.

He became aware of a prickling over his bald pate; he glared up at the sky. That star overhead was a searing pinpoint, its complex orbit bringing it ever closer to the path of the Raft. Close enough to burn the skin, eh? He couldn't remember a star being allowed to fall so threateningly close before; the Raft should have been shifted long since. He'd have to get on to Navigator Cipse and his boys. He couldn't think what they were playing at.

Now a shadow swept across him, and he made out the silhouette of a tree rotating grandly far above the Raft. That would be Pallis, returning from the Belt. Another good man, Pallis . . . one of the few left.

He dropped his prickling eyes and studied the deck plates beneath his feet. He thought of the human lives that had been expended on keeping this little metal island afloat in the air for so long.

And was it only to come to this, a final few generations of sour sullenness, falling at last to the poisoned air?

Maybe it would be better not to move the Raft out from under that star. Let it all go up in one last blaze of human glory—

"Sir?" Grye, one of his assistants, stood before him; the little round man nervously held out a battered sheaf of paper. "We've finished another test run."

So there was still work to do. "Well, don't stand about like that, man; if you're no use you're certainly no ornament. Bring that in and tell me what it says."

And he turned and led the way into his office.

The Raft had grown in the sky until it blocked out half the Nebula. A star was poised some tens of miles above the Raft, a turbulent ball of yellow fire a mile wide, and the Raft cast a broadening shadow down through miles of dusty air.

Under Pallis's direction Rees and Gover stoked the fire bowls and worked their way across the surface of the tree, waving large, light blankets over the billowing smoke. Pallis studied the canopy of smoke with a critical eye; never satisfied, he snapped and growled at the boys. But, steadily and surely, the tree's rise through the Nebula was moulded into a slow curve towards the Rim of the Raft.

As he worked Rees chanced the wrath of Pallis by drinking in the emergent details of the Raft. From below it showed as a ragged disc a half-mile wide; metal plates scattered highlights from the stars and light leaked through dozens of apertures in the deck. As the tree sailed up to the Rim the Raft foreshortened into a patchwork ellipse; Rees could see the sooty scars of welding around the edges of the nearer plates, and as his eye tracked across the ceiling-like surface the plates crowded into a blur, with the far side of the disc a level horizon.

At last, with a rush of air, the tree rose above the Rim and the upper surface of the Raft began to open out before Rees. Against his will he found himself drawn to the edge of the tree; he buried his hands in the foliage and stared, open-mouthed, as a torrent of color, noise and movement broke over him.

The Raft was an enormous dish that brimmed with life. Points of light were sprinkled over its surface like sugar-sim over a confectionery. The deck was studded with buildings of all shapes and sizes, constructed of wood panels or corrugated metal and jumbled together like toys. All around the Rim machines as tall as two men hulked like silent guardians; and at the heart of the Raft lay a huge silver cylinder, stranded like a trapped whale among the box-like constructions.

A confusion of smells assaulted Rees's senses—sharp ozone from the Rim machines and other workshops and factories, woodsmoke from a thousand chimneys, the hint of exotic cooking scents from the cabins.

And people—more than Rees could count, so many that the Belt population would be easily lost among them—people walked about the Raft in great streams; and knots of running children exploded here and there into bursts of laughter.

He made out sturdy pyramids fixed to the deck, no more than waist high. Rees squinted, scanning the deck; the pyramids stood everywhere. He saw a couple lingering beside one, talking quietly, the man scuffing the metal cone with one foot; and there a group of children chased through a series of the pyramids in a complicated game of catch.

And out of each pyramid a cable soared straight upwards; Rees tilted his face back, following the line of the cables, and he gasped.

To each cable was tethered the trunk of a tree.

To Rees one flying tree had been wonder enough. Now, over the Raft, he was faced with a mighty forest. Every tethering cable was vertical and quite taut, and Rees could almost feel the exertion of the harnessed trees as they strained against the pull of the Core. The light of the Nebula was filtered by its passage through the rotating ranks of trees, so that the deck of the Raft was immersed in a soothing gloom; around the forest dancing skitters softened the light to pastel pink.

Rees's tree rose until it passed the highest layer of the forest. The Raft turned from a landscape back into an island in the air, crowned by a mass of shifting foliage. The sky above Rees seemed darker than usual, so that he felt he was suspended at the very edge of the Nebula, looking down over the mists surrounding the Core; and in all that universe of air the only sign of humanity was the Raft, a scrap of metal suspended in miles of air.

There was a heavy hand on his shoulder. Rees started. Pallis stood over him, the canopy of smoke a backdrop to his stern face. "What's the matter?" he growled. "Never seen a few thousand trees before?"

Rees felt himself flush. "I . . ."

But Pallis was grinning through his scars. "Listen, I understand. Most people take it all for granted. But every time I see it from outside—it gives me a kind of tingle." A hundred questions tumbled through Rees's mind. What would it be like to walk on that surface? What must it have been like to build the Raft, hanging in the void above the Core?

But now wasn't the time; there was work to do. He got to his feet, wrapping his toes in the foliage like a regular woodsman.

"Now, then, miner," Pallis said, "we've got a tree to fly. We have to drop back into that forest. Let's get the bowls brimming; I want a canopy up there so thick I could walk about on it. All right?"

At last Pallis seemed satisfied with the tree's position over the Raft. "All right, lads. Now!"

Gover and Rees ran among the fire bowls, shoving handfuls of damp wood into the flames. Smoke rolled up to the canopy above them. Gover coughed as he worked, swearing; Rees found his eyes streaming, the sooty smoke scouring his throat.

The tree lurched beneath them, almost throwing Rees into the foliage, and began to fall clear of its canopy of smoke. Rees scanned the sky: the falling stars wheeled by noticeably slower than before; he guessed that the tree had lost a good third of its rotation in its attempt to escape smoke's darkness.

Pallis ran to the trunk and uncoiled a length of cable. He thrust his neck and shoulders down through the foliage and began to pay out the cable; Rees could see how he worked the cable to avoid snagging it on other trees.

At last the tree was sliding through the outer layers of the forest. Rees peered across at the trees they passed, each slowly turning and straining with dignity against its tether. Here and there he made out men and women crawling through the foliage; they waved to Pallis and called in distant voices.

As it entered the gloom of the forest Rees sensed the tree's uncertainty. Its leaves turned this way and that as it tried to assess the irregular patterns of light playing over it. At last it came to a slow, grand decision, and its turning accelerated; with a smooth surge it rose by a few yards—

—and came to an abrupt halt. The cable attached to its trunk was taut now; it quivered and bowed through the air as it hauled at the tree. Rees followed the line of the cable; as he had expected its far end had reached the deck of the Raft, and two men were fixing it firmly to one of the waist-high pyramids.

He got to his knees and touched the familiar wood. Sap rushed through the shaped branch, making its surface vibrate like skin; Rees could sense the tree's agitation as it strove to escape this trap, and he felt an odd sympathy pull at his stomach.

Pallis made some final tests of the cable and then walked briskly around the wooden platform, checking that all the glowing bowls had been doused. At last he returned to the trunk and pulled a bundle of paperwork from a cavity in the wood. He crouched down and slipped through the foliage with a quiet rustle—and then popped his head back through. He peered around until he spotted Rees. "Aren't you coming, lad? Not much point staying here, you know. This old girl won't be going anywhere for a good few shifts. Well, come on; don't keep Gover from his food."

Hesitantly Rees made his way to the trunk. Pallis dropped through first. When he'd gone Gover hissed: "You're a long way from home, mine rat. Just remember—nothing here is yours. Nothing." And the apprentice slipped into the screen of leaves.

Heart thumping, Rees followed.

*　　*　　*

Like three water drops they slid down their cable through the scented gloom of the forest.

Rees worked his way hand over hand down the thin cable. At first the going was easy, but gradually a diffuse gravity field began to tug at his feet. Pallis and Gover waited at the base of the cable, peering up at him; he swung through the last few feet, avoiding the sloping sides of the anchor cone, and landed lightly on the deck.

A man walked up bearing a battered clip pad. The man was huge, his black hair and beard barely concealing a mask of scars more livid than Pallis's. A fine black braid was attached to the shoulder of his coverall. He scowled at Rees; the boy flinched at the power of the man's gaze. "You're welcome back, Pallis," the man said, his voice grim. "Although I can see from here you've brought back half your stock."

"Not quite, Decker," said Pallis coolly, handing over his paperwork. The two men moved into a huddle and went through Pallis's lists. Gover scuffed impatiently at the deck, wiping his nose against the back of his hand.

And Rees, wide-eyed, stared.

The deck beneath his feet swept through a network of cables away into a distance he could barely comprehend. He could see buildings and people set out in great swathes of life and activity; his head seemed to spin with the scale of it all, and he almost wished he were back in the comforting confines of the Belt.

He shook his head, trying to dispel his dizziness. He concentrated on immediate things: the easy pull of gravity, the gleaming surface beneath his feet. He tapped experimentally at the deck. It made a small ringing noise.

"Take it easy," Pallis growled. The big tree-pilot

had finished his business and was standing before him. "The plate's only a millimeter thick, on average. Although it's buttressed for strength."

Rees flexed his feet and jumped a few inches into the air, feeling the pull as he settled gently back. "That feels like half a gee."

Pallis nodded. "Closer to forty per cent. We're in the gravity well of the Raft itself. Obviously the Nebula Core is also pulling at us—but that's tiny; and in any event we couldn't feel it because the Raft is in orbit around the Core." He tilted his face up at the flying forest. "Most people think the trees are there to keep the Raft from falling into the Core, you know. But their function is to stabilize the Raft—to keep it from tipping over—and to counteract the effects of winds, and to let us move the Raft when we have to ..." Pallis bent and peered into Rees's face, his scars a crimson net. "Are you OK? You look a little dizzy."

Rees tried to smile. "I'm fine. I suppose I'm just disconcerted at not being in a five-minute orbit."

Pallis laughed. "Well, you'll get used to it." He straightened. "Now then, young man, I have to decide what's to be done with you."

Rees felt a coldness prickle over his scalp as he began to think ahead to the moment when he would be abandoned by the tree-pilot, and scorn for himself ran through his thoughts. Had he boldly left his home only to become dependent on the kindness of a stranger? Where was his courage?

He straightened his back and concentrated on what Pallis was saying.

"... I'll have to find an Officer," the pilot mused, scratching a stubbly chin. "Log you as a stowaway. Get you a temporary Class assignment until the next tree goes out. All that paperwork, damn it ...

"By the Bones, I'm too tired. And hungry, and

dirty. Let's leave it until next shift. Rees, you can stop over at my cabin until it's sorted. You too, Gover, though the prospect is hardly enticing."

The apprentice stared into the distance; he didn't look around at the pilot's words.

"But I don't have supplies for three growing lads like us. Or even one, come to think of it. Gover, get out to the Rim and get a couple of shifts' worth on my number, will you? You too, Rees; why not? You'll enjoy the sightseeing. I'll go scrape a few layers of dust off my cabin."

And so Rees found himself trailing the apprentice through the swarm of cables. Gover stalked ahead, not deigning to wait; in all this murky, tree-shadowed world the apprentice was Rees's only fixed point, and so the miner made sure he didn't lose sight of Gover's unprepossessing back.

They came to a thoroughfare cut through the tangle of cables. It was crowded with people. Gover paused at the edge of the thoroughfare and stood in sullen silence, evidently waiting for something. Rees stood beside him and looked around. The clear, straight path was about ten yards wide: it was like looking along a tree-roofed tunnel. The path was lined with light; Rees made out globes fixed to the cables just like the globes in the depths of the star mine.

There were people everywhere, an even stream that flowed briskly in both directions along the path. Some of them stared at Rees's dishevelled appearance, but most politely looked away. They were all clean and well-groomed—although there were hollow eyes and pale cheeks, as if some sickness were haunting the Raft. Men and women alike wore a kind of coverall of some fine, gray material; some wore gold braid on their shoulders or cuffs, often woven in elaborate designs. Rees glanced down at his own battered tunic—and with a jolt recognized it as an aged descendant of the garments of the Raft population. So miners wore Raft cast-offs?

He wondered what Sheen would say about that . . .

Two small boys were standing before him, gazing with round eyes at his dingy tunic. Rees, horribly embarrassed, hissed to Gover: "What are we waiting for? Can't we move on?"

Gover swivelled his head and fixed Rees with a look of dull contempt.

Rees tried to smile at the boys. They just stared.

Now there was a soft, rushing sound from the center of the Raft. Rees, with some relief, stepped out into the thoroughfare, and he made out the bizarre sight of a row of faces sliding towards him above the crowd. Gover stepped forward and held up a hand. Rees watched him curiously—

—and the rushing grew to a roar. Rees turned to see the blunt prow of a Mole bearing down on him. He stumbled back; the speeding cylinder narrowly missed his chest. The Mole rolled to a halt a few yards from Gover and Rees. A row of simple seats had been fixed to the upper surface of the Mole; people rode in them, watching him incuriously.

Rees found his mouth opening and closing. He had expected some wonderful sights on the Raft, but—this? The little boys' mouths were round with astonishment at his antics. Gover was grinning. "What's the matter, mine rat? Never seen a bus before?" The apprentice walked up to the Mole and, with a practiced swing, stepped up into a vacant seat.

Rees shook his head and hurried after the apprentice. There was a low shelf around the base of the Mole; Rees stepped onto it and turned cautiously, lowering himself into the seat next to

Gover's—and the Mole jolted into motion. Rees tumbled sideways, clinging to chair arms; he had to wriggle around until he was facing outwards, and at last found himself gliding smoothly above the heads of the throng.

The boys ran after the Mole, shouting and waving; Rees did his best to ignore them, and after a few yards they tired and gave up.

Rees stared frankly at the man next to him, a thin, middle-aged individual with a sheaf of gold braid at his cuff. The man studied him with an expression of disdain, then moved almost imperceptibly to the far side of his seat.

He turned to Gover. "You call me a 'mine rat.' What exactly is a 'rat'?"

Gover sneered. "A creature of old Earth. A vermin, the lowest of the low. Have you heard of Earth? It's the place we—" he emphasized the word "—came from."

Rees thought that over; then he studied the machine he was riding. "What did you call this thing?"

Gover looked at him with mock pity. "This is a bus, mine rat. Just a little something we have here in the civilized world."

Rees studied the lines of the cylinder under its burden of furniture and passengers. It was a Mole all right; there were the scorch marks showing where—something—had been cut away. On an impulse he leaned over and thumped the surface of the "bus" with his fist. "Status!"

Gover studiously ignored him. Rees was aware of his thin neighbor regarding him with curious disgust—

—and then the bus reported loudly, "Massive sensor dysfunction."

The voice had sounded from somewhere under

the thin man; he jumped and stared open-mouthed at the seat beneath him.

Gover looked at Rees with a grudging interest. "How did you do that?"

Rees smiled, relishing the moment. "Oh, it was nothing. You see, we have—ah—buses where I come from too. I'll tell you about it some time."

And with a delicious coolness he settled back to enjoy the ride.

The journey lasted only a few minutes. The bus paused frequently, passengers alighting and climbing aboard at each stop.

They passed abruptly out of the mass of cables and slid over a clear expanse of deck. Unimpeded Nebula light dazzled Rees. When he looked back the cables were like a wall of textured metal hundreds of feet tall, topped by discs of foliage.

The nose of the bus began to rise.

At first Rees thought it was his imagination. Then he noticed the passengers shifting in their seats; and still the tilt increased, until it seemed to Rees that he was about to slide back down a metal slope to the cables.

He shook his head tiredly. He had had enough wonders for one shift. If only Gover would give him a few hints about what was going on—

He closed his eyes. Come on, think it through, he told himself. He thought of the Raft as he had seen it from above. Had it looked bowl-shaped? No, it had been flat all the way to the Rim; he was sure of that. Then what?

Fear shot through him. Suppose the Raft was falling! Perhaps the cables on a thousand trees had snapped; perhaps the Raft was tipping over, spilling its human cargo into the pit of air—

He snorted as with a little more thought he saw

it. The bus was climbing out of the Raft's gravity well, which was deepest at the structure's center. If the bus's brakes failed now it would roll back along the plane in from the Rim towards the Raft's heart . . . just as if it were rolling downhill. In reality the Raft was, of course, a flat plate, fixed in space; but its central gravity field made it seem to tilt to anyone standing close to the Rim.

When the slope had risen to one in one the bus shuddered to a halt. A set of steps had been fixed to the deck alongside the bus's path; they led to the very Rim. The passengers jumped down. "You stay there," Gover told Rees; and he set off after the others up the shallow stairs.

Fixed almost at the Rim was the huge, silhouetted form of what must be a supply machine. The passengers formed a small queue before it.

Rees obediently remained in his seat. He longed to examine the device at the Rim. But there would be another shift, time and fresh energy to pursue that.

It would be nice, though, to walk to the edge and peer into the depths of the Nebula . . . Perhaps he might even glimpse the Belt.

One by one the passengers returned to the bus bearing supply packets, like those which Pallis had brought to the Belt. The last passenger thumped the nose of the bus; the battered old machine lurched into motion and set off down the imaginary slope.

Pallis's cabin was a simple cube partitioned into three rooms: there was an eating area, a living room with seats and hammocks, and a cleaning area with a sink, toilet and shower head.

Pallis had changed into a long, heavy robe. The

garment's breast bore a stylized representation of a tree in the green braid which Rees had come to recognize as the badge of Pallis's woodsman Class. He told Rees and Gover to clean themselves up. When it was Rees's turn he approached the gleaming spigots with some awe; he barely recognized the clean, sparkling stuff that emerged as water.

Pallis prepared a meal, a rich meat-sim broth. Rees sat cross-legged on the cabin floor and ate eagerly. Gover sat in a chair wrapped in his customary silence.

Pallis's home was free of decoration save for two items in the living area. One was a cage constructed of woven slats of wood, suspended from the ceiling; within it five or six young trees hovered and fizzed, immature branches whirling. They filled the room with motion and the scent of wood. Rees saw how the skitters, one or two adorned with bright flowers, fizzed towards the cabin lights, bumping in soft frustration against the walls of their cage. "I let them out when they're too big," Pallis told Rees. "They're just—company, I suppose. You know, there are some who bind up these babies with wire to stunt their growth, distort their shapes. I can't envisage doing that. No matter how attractive the result."

The other item of decoration was a photograph, a portrait of a woman. Such things weren't unknown in the Belt—the ancient, fading images were handed down through families like shabby heirlooms—but this portrait was fresh and vivid. With Pallis's permission Rees picked it up—

—and with a jolt he recognized the smiling face.

He turned to Pallis. "It's Sheen."

Pallis shifted uncomfortably in his chair, his scars flaring red. "I should have guessed you'd know her. We—used to be friends."

Rees imagined the pilot and his shift supervisor together. The picture was a little incongruous—but not as immediately painful as some such couplings he had envisaged in the past. Pallis and Sheen was a concept he could live with.

He returned the photo to its frame and resumed his meal, chewing thoughtfully.

At the turn of the shift they settled for sleep.

Rees's hammock was yielding and he relaxed, feeling somehow at home. The next shift would bring more changes, surprises and confusions; but he would face that when it came. For the next few hours he was safe, cupped in the bowl of the Raft as if in the palm of a hand.

A respectful knock jolted Hollerbach out of his trance-like concentration. "Eh? Who the hell is that?" His old eyes took a few seconds to focus—and his mind longer to clear of its whirl of food test results. He reached for his spectacles. Of course the ancient artefact didn't really fit his eyes, but the discs of glass did help a little.

A tall, scarred man loomed into semi-focus, advancing hesitantly into the office. "It's me, Scientist. Pallis."

"Oh, pilot. I saw your tree return, I think. Good trip?"

Pallis smiled tiredly. "I'm afraid not, sir. The miners have had a few troubles—"

"Haven't we all?" Hollerbach grumbled. "I just hope we don't poison the poor buggers with our food pods. Now then, Pallis, what can I do for you—oh, by the Bones, I've remembered. You've brought back that damn boy, haven't you?" He peered beyond Pallis; and there, sure enough, was the skinny, insolent figure of Gover. Hollerbach sighed. "Well, you'd better see Grye and return to your usual duties, lad. And your studies. Maybe we'll make a Scientist of you yet, eh? Or," he muttered as Gover departed, "more likely I'll lob you over the Rim myself. Is that all, Pallis?"

The tree-pilot looked embarrassed; he shifted awkwardly and his scar network flared crimson. "Not quite, sir. Rees!"

Now another boy approached the office. This one was dark and lean and dressed in the ragged remnants of a coverall—and he stopped in surprise at the doorway, eyes fixed to the floor.

"Come on, lad," Pallis said, not unkindly. "It's only carpet; it doesn't bite."

The strange boy stepped cautiously over the carpet until he stood before Hollerbach's desk. He raised his eyes—and again his mouth dropped with obvious shock.

"Good God, Pallis," Hollerbach said, running a hand self-consciously over his bald scalp, "what have you brought me here? Hasn't he ever seen a Scientist before?"

Pallis coughed; he seemed to be trying to hide a laugh. "I don't think it's that, sir. With all respect, I doubt if the lad's ever seen anyone so old."

Hollerbach opened his mouth—then closed it again. He inspected the boy more carefully, noting the heavy muscles, the scarred hands and arms. "Where are you from, lad?"

He spoke up clearly. "The Belt."

"He's a stowaway," Pallis said apologetically. "He travelled back with me and—"

"And he's got to be shipped straight home." Hollerbach sat back and folded his skinny arms. "I'm sorry, Pallis; we're overpopulated as it is."

"I know that, sir, and I'm having the forms processed right now. As soon as a tree is loaded he could be gone."

"Then why bring him here?"

"Because . . ." Pallis hesitated. "Hollerbach, he's a bright lad," he finished in a rush. "He can—he gets status reports from the buses—"

Hollerbach shrugged. "So do a good handful of smart kids every shift." He shook his head, amused. "Good grief, Pallis, you don't change, do you? Do you remember how, as a kid, you'd bring me broken skitters? And I'd have to fix up little paper splints for the things. A damn lot of good it did them, of course, but it made you feel better."

Pallis's scars darkened furiously; he avoided Rees's curious gaze.

"And now you bring home this bright young stowaway and—what?—expect me to take him on as my chief apprentice?"

Pallis shrugged. "I thought, maybe just until the tree was ready . . ."

"You thought wrong. I'm a busy man, tree-pilot."

Pallis turned to the boy. "Tell him why you're here. Tell him what you told me, on the tree."

Rees was staring at Hollerbach. "I left the Belt to find out why the Nebula is dying," he said simply.

The Scientist sat forward, intrigued despite himself. "Oh, yes? We know why it's dying. Hydrogen depletion. That's obvious. What we don't know is what to do about it."

Rees studied him, apparently thinking it over. Then he asked: "What's hydrogen?"

Hollerbach drummed his long fingers on the desk top, on the point of ordering Pallis out of the room . . . But Rees was waiting for an answer, a look of bright inquiry in his eyes.

"Hmm. That would take more than a sentence to explain, lad." Another drum of the fingers. "Well, maybe it wouldn't do any harm—and it might be amusing—"

"Sir?" Pallis asked.

"Are you any good with a broom, lad? The Bones know we could do with someone to back up that useless article Gover. Yes, why not? Pallis, take him to Grye. Get him a few chores to do; and tell Grye from me to start him on a bit of basic education. He may as well be useful while he's eating our damn food. Just until the tree flies, mind."

"Hollerbach, thanks—"

"Oh, get out, Pallis. You've won your battle. Now let me get on with my work. And in future keep your damn lame skitters to yourself!"

4

A handbell shaken somewhere told him that the shift was over. Rees peeled off his protective gloves and with an expert eye surveyed the lab; after his efforts its floor and walls now gleamed in the light of the globes fixed to the ceiling.

He walked slowly out of the lab. The light from the star above made his exposed skin tingle, and he rested for a few seconds, drinking in gulps of antiseptic-free air. His back and thighs ached and the skin of his upper arms itched in a dozen places: trophies of splashes of powerful cleaning agents.

The few dozen shifts before the next tree departure seemed to be flying past. He drank in the exotic sights and scents of the Raft, anticipating a return to a lifetime in a lonely cabin in the Belt; he would pore over these memories as Pallis must treasure his photograph of Sheen.

But what he'd been shown and taught had been precious little, he admitted to himself—despite Hollerbach's vague promises. The Scientists were an unprepossessing collection—mostly middle-aged, overweight and irritable. Brandishing the bits of braid that denoted their rank they moved about their strange tasks and ignored him. Grye, the assistant who'd been assigned the task of educating him, had done little more than provide Rees with a child's picture book to help him read, together with a pile of quite incomprehensible lab reports.

Although he'd certainly learned enough about cleaning, he reflected ruefully.

But occasionally, just occasionally, his skitter-like imagination would be snagged by something. Like that series of bottles, set out like bar stock in one of the labs, filled with tree sap in various stages of hardening—

"You! What's your name? Oh, damn it, you, boy! Yes, you!"

Rees turned to see a pile of dusty volumes staggering towards him. "You, the lad from the mine. Come and give me a hand with this stuff . . ." Over the volumes appeared a round face topped by a bald scalp, and Rees recognized Cipse, the Chief Navigator. Forgetting his aches he hurried towards the puffing Cipse and, with some delicacy, took the top half of the pile.

Cipse panted with relief. "Took your time, didn't you?"

"I'm sorry . . ."

"Well, come on, come on; if we don't get these printouts to the Bridge sharpish those buggers in my team will have cleared off to the bars again, you mark my words, and that'll be another shift lost." Rees hesitated, and after a few paces Cipse turned. "By the Bones, lad, are you deaf as well as stupid?"

Rees felt his mouth working. "I . . . you want me to bring this stuff to the Bridge?"

"No, of course not," Cipse said heavily. "I want you to run to the Rim and dump it over the side, what else . . . ? Oh, for the love of—come on, come on!"

And he set off once more.

Rees stood there for a full half-minute.

The Bridge . . . !

Then he ran after Cipse towards the heart of the Raft.

The city on the Raft had a simple structure. Seen from above—without its covering deck of trees—it would have appeared as a series of concentric circles.

The outermost circle, closest to the Rim, was fairly empty, studded by the imposing bulks of supply machines. Within that was a band of storage and industrial units, a noisy, smoky place. Next came residential areas, clusters of small cabins of wood and metal. Rees had come to understand that the lower-placed citizens occupied the cabins closest to the industrial region. Within the housing area was a small region containing various specialist buildings: a training unit, a crude hospital—and the labs of the Scientist class where Rees was living and working. Finally, the innermost disc of the Raft—into which Rees had not previously been allowed—was the preserve of the Officers.

And at the center, at the hub of the Raft itself, was embedded the gleaming cylinder which Rees had spotted on his first arrival here.

The Bridge . . . And now, perhaps, he might be allowed to enter it.

The Officers' cabins were larger and better finished than those of the ordinary crew; Rees stared with some awe at the carved door frames and curtained windows. Here there were no running children, no perspiring workers; Cipse slowed his bustle to a more stately walk, nodding to the gold-braided men and women they encountered.

Pain lanced through Rees's foot as he stubbed his

toe on a raised deck plate. His load of books tumbled to the surface, yellowed pages opening tiredly to reveal tables of numbers; each page was stamped with the mysterious letters "IBM."

"Oh, by the Bones, you useless mine rat!" Cipse raged. Two young Officer cadets walked by; the braid in their new caps glittered in the starlight and they pointed at Rees, laughing quietly.

"I'm sorry," Rees said, face burning. How had he tripped? The deck was a flat mosaic of welded iron plates . . . or was it? He stared down. The plates here were curved and studded with rivets, and their sheen was silvery, a contrast to the rusty tinge of the iron sheets further out. On one plate, a few feet away, was a blocky, rectangular design; it was tantalizingly incomplete, as if huge letters had once been painted on a curving wall, and the surface cut up and reassembled.

Cipse muttered, "Come on, come on. . . ."

Rees picked up the books and hurried after Cipse. "Scientist," he said nervously, "why is the deck here so different?"

Cipse gave him a glance of exasperation. "Because, lad, the innermost part of the Raft is the oldest. The areas further out were added later, constructed of sheets of star metal; this part was built of hull sections. All right?"

"Hull? The hull of what?"

But Cipse, bustling along, would not reply.

Rees's imagination whirled like a young tree. Hull plates! He imagined the hull of a Mole; if that were cut up and reassembled then that, too, would be an uneven thing of broken curves.

But the shell of a Mole would be much too small to provide all this area. He imagined a huge Mole, its mighty walls curving far above his head . . .

But that wouldn't be a Mole. A Ship, then? Were

the children's tales of the Ship and its Crew true after all?

He felt frustration well up inside him; it was almost like the ache he sometimes felt to reach out to Sheen's cool flesh ... If only someone would tell him what was going on!

At last they passed through the innermost rank of dwellings and came to the Bridge. Rees found his pace slowing despite his will; he felt his heart pump within his chest.

The Bridge was beautiful. It appeared as a half-cylinder twice his height and perhaps a hundred paces long; it lay on its side, embedded neatly in the deck. Rees remembered flying under the Raft and seeing the other half of the cylinder hanging beneath the plates like some vast insect. The pile of books still in his arms, he stepped closer to the curving wall. The surface was of a matt, silvery metal that softened the harsh starlight to a pink-gold glow. An arched door frame had been cut into the wall; its lines were the finest, cleanest work Rees had ever seen. The plates of the disassembled hull lapped around the cylinder, and Rees saw how neatly they had been cut and joined to the wall.

He tried to imagine the men who had done this wonderful work. He had a vague picture of godlike creatures disassembling another, huge cylinder with glowing blades ... And later generations had added their crude accretions around the gleaming heart of the Raft, their grace and power dwindling as thousands of shifts wore away.

"... I said now, mine rat!" The Navigator's face was pink with fury; Rees shook himself out of his daydream and hurried to join Cipse at the doorway.

Another Scientist emerged from the shining interior of the Bridge; he took Rees's load. Cipse gave

Rees one last glance. "Now get back to your work, and be thankful if I don't tell Hollerbach to feed you to the reprocessing plants—" Muttering, the Navigator turned and disappeared into the interior of the Bridge.

Reluctant to leave this magical area Rees reached out and stroked the silver wall with his fingertips—and pulled his hand back, startled; the surface was warm, almost like skin, and impossibly smooth. He pushed his hand flat against the wall and let his palm slide over the surface. It was utterly frictionless, as if slick with some oily fluid—

"What's this? A mine rat nibbling at our Bridge?"

He turned with a start. The two young Officers he had noticed earlier stood before him, hands on hips; they grinned easily. "Well, boy?" the taller of them said. "Do you have any business here?"

"No, I—"

"Because if not, I suggest you clear off back to the Belt where the other rats hide out. Or perhaps we should help you on your way, eh, Jorge?"

"Doav, why not?"

Rees studied the relaxed, handsome young men. Their words were scarcely harsher than Cipse's had been . . . but the youth of these cadets, the way they aped their elders so unthinkingly, made their contempt almost impossible to stomach, and Rees felt a warm anger well up inside him.

But he couldn't afford to make enemies.

Deliberately he turned his face away from the cadets and made to step past them . . . But the taller cadet, Doav, was in his way. "Well, rat?" He extended one finger and poked at Rees's shoulder—

—and, almost against his will, Rees grabbed the finger in one fist; with an easy turn of his wrist he bent the cadet's hand back on itself. The young man's elbow was forced forward to save the finger from snapping, and his knees bent into a half-kneel before Rees. Pain showed in a sheen of sweat on his brow, but he clenched his teeth, refusing to cry out.

Jorge's smile faded; his hands hung at his sides, uncertain.

"My name is Rees," the miner said slowly. "Remember that."

He released the finger. Doav slumped to his knees, nursing his hand; he glared up. "I'll remember you, Rees; have no fear," he hissed.

Already regretting his outburst Rees turned his back and walked away. The cadets didn't follow.

Slowly Rees dusted his way around Hollerbach's office. Of all the areas to which his chores brought him access, this room was the most intriguing. He ran a fingertip along a row of books; their pages were black with age and the gilt on their spines had all but worn away. He traced letters one by one: E ... n ... c ... y ... c ... Who, or what, was an "Encyclopaedia"? He daydreamed briefly about picking up a volume, letting it fall open ...

Again that almost sexual hunger for knowledge swept through him.

Now his eye was caught by a machine, a thing of jewelled cogs and gears about the size of his cupped hands. At its center was set a bright silver sphere; nine painted orbs were suspended on wires around the sphere. It was beautiful, but what the hell was it?

He glanced about. The office was empty. He couldn't resist it.

He picked up the device, relishing the feel of the machined metal base—

"Don't drop it, will you?"

He started. The intricate device juggled through the air, painfully slowly; he grabbed it and returned it to its shelf.

He turned. Silhouetted in the doorway was Jaen, her broad, freckled face creased into a grin. After a few seconds he smiled back. "Thanks a lot," he said.

The apprentice walked toward him. "You should be glad it's only me. Anybody else and you'd be off the Raft by now."

He shrugged, watching her approach with mild pleasure. Jaen was the senior apprentice of Cipse, the Chief Navigator; only a few hundred shifts older than Rees, she was one of the few inhabitants of the labs to show him anything other than contempt. She even seemed to forget he was a mine rat, sometimes . . . Jaen was a broad, stocky girl; her gait was confident but ungainly. Uncomfortably Rees found himself comparing her with Sheen. He was growing fond of Jaen; he believed she could become a good friend.

But her body didn't pull at his with the intensity of the mine girl's.

Jaen stood beside him and ran a casual fingertip over the little device. "Poor old Rees," she mocked. "I bet you don't even know what this is, do you?"

He shrugged. "You know I don't."

"It's called an orrery." She spelt the word for him. "It's a model of the Solar System."

"The what?"

Jaen sighed, then she pointed at the silver orb at the heart of the orrery. "That's a star. And these things are balls of—iron, I suppose, orbiting around it. They're called planets. Mankind—the folk on the Raft, at least—originally came from one of these planets. The fourth, I think. Or maybe the third."

Rees scratched his chin. "Really? There can't have been too many of them."

"Why not?"

"No room. If the planet was any size the gees would be too high. The star kernel back home is only fifty yards wide—and it's mostly air—and it has a surface gravity of five gee."

"Yeah? Well, this planet was a lot bigger. It was—" She extended her hands. "Miles wide. And the gravity wasn't crushing. Things were different."

"How?"

". . . I'm not sure. But the surface gravity was probably only, I don't know, three or four gee."

He thought that over. "In that case, what's a gee? I mean, why is a gee the size it is—no larger and no smaller?"

Jaen had been about to say something else; now she frowned in exasperation. "Rees, I haven't the faintest idea. By the Bones, you ask stupid questions. I'm almost tempted not to tell you the most interesting thing about the orrery."

"What?"

"That the System was huge. The orbit of the planet took about a thousand shifts . . . and the star at the center was a million miles wide!"

He thought that over. "Garbage," he said.

She laughed. "What do you know?"

"A star like that is impossible. It would just implode."

"You know it all." She grinned at him. "I just hope you're as clever at lugging supplies in from the Rim. Come on; Grye has given us a list of stuff to collect."

"OK."

Carrying his cleaning equipment he followed her broad back from Hollerbach's office. He glanced back once at the orrery, sitting gleaming in the shadows of its shelf.

A million miles? Ridiculous, of course.

But what if ... ?

They sat side by side on the bus; the machine's huge tires made the journey soothingly smooth.

Rees surveyed the mottled plates of the Raft, the people hurrying by on tasks and errands of whose nature even now he was uncertain. His fellow passengers sat patiently through the journey, some of them reading. Rees found these casual displays of literacy somehow startling.

He found himself sighing.

"What's the matter with you?"

He grinned ruefully at Jaen. "Sorry. It's just ... I've been here such a short time, and I seem to have learned so little."

She frowned. "I thought you were getting some kind of crammer classes from Cipse and Grye."

"Not really," he admitted. "I guess I can see their point of view. I wouldn't want to waste time on a stowaway who is liable to be dumped back home within a few shifts."

She scratched her nose. "That might be the reason. But the two of them have never been shy of parading their knowledge in front of me. Rees, you ask damn hard questions. I suspect they're a little afraid of you."

"That's crazy—"

"Let's face it, most of those old buggers don't know all that much. Hollerbach does, I think; and one or two others. But the rest just follow the ancient printouts and hope for the best. Look at the way they patch up the ancient instruments with wood and bits of string ... They'd be lost if anything really unexpected happened—or if anyone asked them a question from a strange angle."

Rees thought that over and reflected how far his view of the Scientists had shifted since his arrival here. Now he saw that they were frail humans like himself, struggling to do their best in a world growing shabbier. "Anyway," he said, "it doesn't make a lot of difference. Every time I open my eyes I see questions that don't get answered. For instance, on every page of Cipse's numbers books is written 'IBM.' What does that mean?"

She laughed. "You've got me there. Maybe it's something to do with the way those books were produced. They come from the Ship, you know."

His interest quickened. "The Ship? You know, I've heard so many stories about that I've no idea what's true."

"My understanding is that there really was a Ship. It was broken up to form the basis of the Raft itself."

He pondered that. "And the original Crew printed those books?"

She hesitated, obviously near the limits of her knowledge. "They were produced a few generations later. The first Crew had kept their understanding in some kind of machine."

"What machine?"

". . . I don't know. Maybe a talking machine, like the buses. The thing was more than a recording device, though. It could do calculations and computations."

"How?"

"Rees," she said heavily, "if I knew that I'd build one. OK? Anyway, with the passing of time the machine began to fail, and the crew were afraid they wouldn't be able to continue their computations. So, before it expired, the machine printed out everything it knew. And that includes an ancient type of table called 'logarithms' to help us do calculations. That's what Cipse was lugging in to the Bridge. Maybe you'll learn how to use logarithms, some day."

"Yeah. Maybe."

The bus rolled out of the thicket of cables; Rees found himself squinting in the harsh light of the star poised above the Raft.

Jaen was saying, "You understand Cipse's job, do you?"

"I think so," he said slowly. "Cipse is a Navigator. His job is to work out where the Raft should move to."

Jaen nodded. "And the reason we have to do that is to get out of the path of the stars falling in from the rim of the Nebula." She jerked a thumb at the glowing sphere above. "Like that one. In the Bridge they keep records of approaching stars, so they can move the Raft in plenty of time. I reckon we'll be shifting soon . . . That's a sight to see, Rees; I hope you don't miss it. All the trees tilting in unison, the rush of wind across the deck—and if I get through my appraisal I'll be working on the moving team."

"Good for you," he said sourly.

With a sudden seriousness she patted his arm. "Don't give up hope, miner. You're not off the Raft yet."

He smiled at her, and they spent the rest of the journey in silence.

The bus reached the edge of the Raft's gravity well. The Rim approached like a knife edge against the sky, and the bus strained to a halt beside a broad stairway. Rees and Jaen joined a queue of passengers before a supply dispenser. An attendant sat sullenly beside the machine, silhouetted against the sky; Rees, staring absently, found him vaguely familiar.

The supply machine was an irregular block as tall as two men. Outlets pierced its broad face, surrounding a simple control panel reminiscent to Rees of the Mole's. On the far side a nozzle like a huge mouth strained outwards at the atmosphere of the Nebula; Rees had learned that the machine's raw material was drawn in by that nozzle from the life-rich air, and it wasn't hard to imagine the machine taking huge breaths through those metal lips.

Jaen murmured in his ear: "Powered by a mini black hole, you know."

He jumped. "A what?"

She grinned. "You don't know? I'll tell you later."

"You enjoy this, don't you?" he hissed.

Away from the shelter of the flying forest the starlight from above was intense. Rees found sweat droplets trickling into his eyes; he blinked, and found himself staring at the broad neck of the man in front of him. The flesh was studded with coarse black hair and was glistening damp near the collar. The man raised a wide, pug face to the star. "Damn heat," he grunted. "Don't know why we're still sitting underneath the bloody thing. Mith ought to get off his fat arse and do something about it. Eh?" He glared inquisitively at Rees.

Rees smiled back uncertainly. The man gave him a strange look, then turned away.

After uncomfortable minutes the queue cleared, passengers squeezing past them down the stairs with their packets of food, water and other materials. Watched by the sullen attendant, Rees and Jaen stepped up to the machine; Jaen began to tap into the control panel one of the Scientists' registration numbers, and then a complex sequence detailing their requirements. Rees marveled at the way her fingers flew over the keyboard—yet another skill he might never get the chance to learn . . .

And he became aware that the attendant was grinning at him. The man sat on a tall wooden stool, arms folded; black stripes were stitched into his shabby coverall. "Well, well," he said slowly. "It's the mine rat."

"Hello, Gover," Rees said stiffly.

"Still skivvying for those old farts in Science, eh? I'd have thought they'd chuck you into the nozzles by now. All you mine rats are good for . . ."

Rees found his fists clenching; his biceps bunched almost painfully.

"So you're still the same nasty piece of work, eh, Gover?" Jaen snapped. "Getting thrown out of Science hasn't helped your character development, then."

Gover bared yellow teeth. "I chose to leave. I'm not spending my life with those useless old spacewasters. At least with Infrastructure I'm doing real work. Learning real skills."

Jaen lodged her fists on her hips. "Gover, if it wasn't for the Scientists the Raft would have been destroyed generations ago."

He sniffed, looking bored. "Sure. You keep believing it."

"It's the truth."

"Maybe once. But what about now? Why haven't they moved us out from under that thing in the sky, then?"

Jaen took an angry breath . . . then hesitated, having no easy answer.

Gover didn't seem interested in his small victory. "It doesn't matter. Think what you want. The people who really keep this Raft flying—Infrastructure, the woodsmen, the carpenters and metalworkers—we are going to be heard before long. And that will be the start of the long drop for all the parasites."

Jaen frowned. "What's that supposed to mean?"

But Gover had turned away, smiling cynically; and a man behind them growled, "Come on; move it, you two."

They returned to the bus clutching pallets of supplies. Rees said, "What if he's right, Jaen? What if the Scientists, the Officers are—not allowed to work any more?"

She shivered. "Then it's the end of the Raft. But I know Gover; he's just puffing up his own importance, to make us think he's happy with his move to Infrastructure. He's always been the same."

Rees frowned. Maybe, he thought.

But Gover had sounded very sure.

A few shifts later Hollerbach asked to see Rees.

Rees paused outside the Chief Scientist's office, drawing deep breaths. He felt as if he were poised on the Rim of the Raft; the next few moments might shape the rest of his life.

Pushing his shoulders back he entered the office.

Hollerbach was bent over paperwork by the light of a globe over his desk. He scowled up at Rees's approach. "Eh? Who's that? Oh, yes; the miner lad. Come in, come in." He waved Rees to a chair before the desk; then he rested back in his armchair, bony arms folded behind his head. The light above the desk made the hollows around his eyes seem enormously deep.

"You asked to see me," Rees said.

"I did, didn't I?" Hollerbach stared frankly at Rees. "Now then; I hear you've been making yourself useful around the place. You're a hard worker, and that's something all too rare ... So thank you for what you've done. But," he went on gently, "a supply tree has been loaded and is ready to fly to the Belt. Next shift. What I have to decide is whether you're to be on it or not."

A thrill coursed through Rees; perhaps he still had a chance to earn a place here. Anticipating some kind of test, he hastily reviewed the fragments of knowledge he had acquired.

Hollerbach got out of his chair and began to walk around the office. "You know we're overpopulated here," he said. "And we have ... problems with the supply dispensers, so that's not going to get any easier. On the other hand, now that I've shed that useless article Gover I have a vacancy in the labs. But unless it's really justified I can't make a case for keeping you."

Rees waited.

Hollerbach frowned. "You keep your own counsel, don't you, lad? Very well ... If you were going to ask me one question, now, before you're shipped out of here—and I guaranteed to answer it as fully as I could—what would it be?"

Rees felt his heart pound. Here was the test, the moment of Rim balancing—but it had come in such an unexpected form. One question! What was the one key that might unlock the secrets against which his mind battered like a skitter against a globe lamp?

The seconds ticked away; Hollerbach regarded him steadily, thin hands steepled before his face.

At last, almost on impulse, Rees asked: "What's a gee?"

Hollerbach frowned. "Explain."

Rees bunched his fists. "We live in a universe filled with strong, shifting gravity fields. But we have a standard unit of gravitational acceleration ... a gee. Why should this be so? And why should it have the particular value it does?"

Hollerbach nodded. "And what answer would you anticipate?"

"That the gee relates to the place man came from. It must have had a large area over which gravity was stable, with a value of what we call a gee. So that became the standard. There's nowhere in the universe with such a region—not even the Raft. So maybe some huge Raft in the past, that's now broken up—"

Hollerbach smiled, the skin stretching over his bony jaw. "That's not bad thinking ... Suppose I told you that there has never been anywhere in this universe with such a region?"

Rees thought that over. "Then I'd suggest that men came here from somewhere else."

"Are you sure about that?"

"Of course not," Rees said defensively. "I'd have to check it out ... find more evidence."

The old Scientist shook his head. "Boy, I suspect there's more scientific method in your untrained head than in whole cadres of my so-called assistants."

"But what's the answer?"

Hollerbach laughed. "You are a rare creature, aren't you? More interested in understanding than in your own fate ...

"Well, I'll tell you. Your guess was quite right. Men don't belong in this universe. We came here in a Ship. We passed through something called Bolder's Ring, which was a kind of gateway. Somewhere in the cosmos on the other side of the Ring is the world we came from. It's a planet, incidentally; a sphere, not a Raft, about eight thousand miles wide. And its surface has a gravity of exactly one gee."

Rees frowned. "Then it must be made of some gas."

Hollerbach took the orrery from the shelf and studied the tiny planets. "It's a ball of iron, actually. It couldn't exist . . . here.

"Gravity is the key to the absurd place we're stranded in, you see; gravity here is a billion times as strong as in the universe we came from. Here our home planet would have a surface gravity of a billion gees—if it didn't implode in an instant. And celestial mechanics are a joke. The home world takes more than a thousand shifts to orbit around its star. Here it would take just seventeen minutes!

"Rees, we don't believe the Crew intended to bring the Ship here. It was probably an accident. As soon as the increased gravity hit, large parts of the Ship collapsed. Including whatever they used to propel it through the air. They must have fallen into the Nebula, barely understanding what was happening, frantically seeking a way to stay out of the Core . . ."

Rees thought of the foundry implosion and his imagination began to construct a scene . . .

. . . Crew members hurried through the corridors of their falling Ship; smoke filled the passageways as lurid flames singed the air. The hull was breached; the raw air of the Nebula scoured through the cabins, and through rents in the silver walls the Crew saw flying trees and huge, cloudy whales, all utterly unlike anything in their experience . . .

"The Bones alone know how they survived those first few shifts. But survive they did; they harnessed trees and stayed out of the clutches of the Core; and gradually men spread through the Nebula, to the Belt worlds and beyond—"

"What?" Rees's focus snapped back to the present. "But I thought you were describing how the Raft folk got here . . . I assumed that Belt folk and the others—"

"Came from somewhere else?" Hollerbach smiled, looking tired. "It's rather convenient for us, in comparative comfort here on the Raft, to believe so; but the fact is that all the humans in the Nebula originated on the Ship. Yes, even the Boneys. And in fact this myth of disparate origins is probably damaging the species. We need to cross-breed, to expand the size of our gene pool . . ."

Rees thought that over. In retrospect there were so many obvious points of similarity between life here and in the Belt. But the thought of the obvious differences, of the relentless harshness of Belt life, began to fill him with a cold anger.

Why, for instance, shouldn't the Belt have its own supply machine? If they had a shared origin surely the miners were as entitled as the Raft dwellers . . .

There would be time to think on this later. He tried to concentrate on what Hollerbach was saying. ". . . So I'll be frank with you, young man. We know the Nebula is almost spent. And unless we do something about it we'll be spent too."

"What will happen? Will the air turn unbreathable?"

Hollerbach replaced the orrery tenderly. "Probably. But long before that the stars will go out. It will get cold and dark . . . and the trees will start to fail.

"We'll have nothing to hold us steady any more. We'll fall into the Core, and that will be that. It should be quite a ride . . .

"If we're not to take that death ride, Rees, we need Scientists. Young ones; inquiring ones who might think up a way out of the trap the Nebula is becoming. Rees, the secret of a Scientist is not what he knows. It's what he asks. I think you've got that trick. Maybe, anyway . . ."

A flush warmed Rees's cheeks. "You're saying I can stay?"

Hollerbach sniffed. "It's still probationary, mind; for as long as I think it needs to be. And we'll have to fix up some real education for you. Chase Grye a bit harder, will you?" The old Scientist shuffled back to his desk and lowered himself into his seat. He took his spectacles from a pocket of his robe, perched them on his nose, and bent once more over his papers. He glanced up at Rees. "Anything else?"

Rees found himself grinning. "Can I ask one more question?"

Hollerbach frowned in irritation. "Well, if you must—"

"Tell me about the stars. On the other side of Bolder's Ring. Are they really a million miles across?"

Hollerbach tried to maintain his mask of irritation; but it dissolved into a half-smile. "Yes. And some much bigger! They're far apart, studded around an almost empty sky. And they last, not a thousand shifts like the wretched specimens here, but thousands of billions of shifts!"

Rees tried to imagine such glory. "But . . . how?"

Hollerbach began to tell him.

5

After Rees's interview with Hollerbach Grye took him to a dormitory building. There was room for about fifty people in the long, flat building, and Rees, overwhelmed by self-consciousness, trailed the fussy Scientist down an aisle between two rows of simple pallets. Beside each pallet was a small cupboard and a rack on which clothes could be hung; Rees found himself staring curiously at the few personal possessions scattered on the floor and cupboard tops—combs and razors, small mirrors, simple sewing kits, here and there photographs of families or young women. One young man—another Science apprentice, judging by the crimson strands woven into his coveralls—lounged on a pallet. He raised narrow eyebrows at Rees's unkempt appearance, but he nodded, friendly enough. Rees nodded back, his cheeks burning, and hurried after Grye.

He wondered what this place was. Pallis's cabin—where he had lodged since his arrival—had seemed unimaginably luxurious to his Belt-developed tastes, and this was hardly so grand, but surely still the dwelling of some exalted class. Perhaps Rees was to clean it out; maybe he would be given somewhere to sleep nearby—

They reached a pallet free of sheets or blankets;

87

the cupboard beside it swung open, empty. Grye waved his hand dismissively. "Here will do, I think." And he turned to walk back down the dormitory.

Rees, confused, followed him.

Grye turned on him. "By all the bloody Bones, what's the matter with you, boy? Don't you understand simple speech?"

"I'm sorry—"

"Here." Grye pointed once more at the pallet and spoke slowly and excessively clearly, as if to a simple child. "You will sleep here from now on. Do I need to write it down?"

"No—"

"Put your personal possessions in the cupboard."

"I don't have any—"

"Get yourself blankets from the stores," Grye said. "The others will show you where." And, oblivious to Rees's lost stare at his back, Grye scurried from the building and on to his next chore.

Rees sat on the pallet—it was soft and clean—and ran a finger over the well-worked lines of the little cupboard. His cupboard.

His breath gathered in him and he felt a deep warmth spread through his face. Yes, it was his cupboard, his pallet—this was his place on the Raft.

He really had made it.

He sat on the pallet for some hours, oblivious to the amused stares of the dormitory's other occupants. Just to be still, safe, to be able to anticipate classes tomorrow; that was enough for now.

"I heard how you fooled old Hollerbach."

The words floated through Rees's numbness; looking up, he found himself staring into the fine, cruel face of the Officer cadet he had bested outside the Bridge—he fumbled for the name—Doav?

"As if having to live in these shacks wasn't bad enough. Now we have to share them with the likes of this rat—"

Rees looked within himself and found only calm and acceptance. This wasn't a time for fighting. Deliberately he looked into Doav's eyes, grinned slowly, and winked.

Doav snorted and turned away. With much noise and banging of cupboards he collected his belongings from a pallet a few places from Rees's and moved them to the far end of the hut.

Later, the friendly lad who had acknowledged Rees earlier strolled past his pallet. "Don't worry about Doav. We're not all as bad."

Rees thanked him, appreciating the gesture. But he noticed that the boy did not move his place any nearer to Rees's, and as the shift end neared and more apprentices gathered for sleep it soon became apparent that Rees's pallet was an island surrounded by a little moat of empty places.

He lay down on his unmade bed, tucked his legs, and smiled, not worried one bit.

In theory, Rees learned, the Raft was a classless society. The ranks of Scientists, Officers and the rest were open to anyone regardless of the circumstances of their birth, depending only on merit and opportunity. The "Classes" of the Raft were based on roles of the Crew of the semi-legendary Ship; they denoted function and utility, so he was told, and not power or position. So the Officers were not a ruling class; they were servants of the rest, bearing a heavy responsibility for the day-to-day maintenance of the Raft's social order and infrastructure. In this analysis the Captain was the least of all, weighed down by the heaviest burden.

So he was told.

At first Rees, his experience of human society limited to the harsh environment of the Belt, was prepared to believe what he was taught so solemnly, and he dismissed the snobbish cruelty of Doav and the rest as expressions of immaturity. But as his circle of acquaintances widened, and as his understanding—formally and informally acquired—grew, he formed a rather different picture.

It was certainly possible for a young person from a non-Officer Class to become an Officer. But, oddly enough, it never happened. The other Classes, excluded from power by the hereditary rule of the Officers, reacted by building what power bases they could. So the Infrastructure personnel had turned the Raft's engineering details into an arcane mystery known only to initiates; and without appeasement of their key figures—men like Pallis's acquaintance, Decker—they would exert their power to cut water or food supplies, dam up the sewers built into the deck, or bring the Raft to a halt in any of a hundred ways.

Even the Scientists, whose very reason for being was the pursuit of understanding, were not immune from this rivalry for power.

The Scientists were crucial to the Raft's survival. In such matters as the moving of the Raft, the control of epidemics, the redesign of sections of the Raft itself, their knowledge and structured way of thinking was essential. And without the tradition the Scientists maintained—which explained how the universe worked, how humans could survive in it—the fragile social and engineering web which comprised the Raft would surely disintegrate within a few thousand shifts. It wasn't its orbit around the Core which kept the Raft aloft,

Rees told himself; it was the continuance of human understanding.

So the Scientists had a vital, almost sacred responsibility. But, Rees reflected, it didn't stop them using their precious knowledge for advantage every bit as unscrupulously as any of Decker's workmen blocking up a sewer. The Scientists had a statutory obligation to educate every apprentice of supervisory status regardless of Class, and they did so—to a nominal extent. But only Science apprentices, like Rees, were allowed past the bare facts and actually to see the ancient books and instruments . . .

Knowledge was hoarded. And so only those close to the Scientists had any real understanding of humanity's origins, even of the nature of the Raft, the Nebula. Listening to chatter in refectories and food machine queues Rees came to understand that most people were more concerned about this shift's ration size, or the outcome of spurious sporting contests, than the larger issues of racial survival. It was as if the Nebula was eternal, as if the Raft itself was fixed atop a pillar of steel, securely and for all time!

The mass of people was ignorant, driven by fashions, fads and the tongues of orators . . . even on the Raft. As for the human colonies away from the Raft—the Belt mine and (perhaps) the legendary, lost Boney worlds—there, Rees knew from his own experience, understanding of the human past and the structure of the universe had been reduced to little more than fanciful tales.

Fortunately for the Scientists, most of the other Classes' apprentices were quite happy with this state of affairs. The Officer cadets in particular sat through their lectures with every expression of disdain, clearly eager to abandon this dry stuff for the quick of life, the exercise of power.

So the Scientists went unchallenged, but Rees wasn't sure about the wisdom of their policy. The Raft itself, while still comfortable and well-supplied compared to the Belt, was now riven by shortages. Discontent was widespread, and—since the people did not have the knowledge to understand the (more or less) genuine contribution to their welfare made by the more privileged Classes—those Classes were more often than not the target of unfocused resentment.

It was an unstable mixture.

And the enslaving of knowledge had another adverse effect, Rees realized. Turning facts into precious things made them seem sacred, immutable; and so he saw Scientists pore over old printouts and intone litanies of wisdom brought here by the Ship and its Crew, unwilling—or unable—to entertain the idea that there might be facts beyond the ageing pages, even—breathe it quietly—inaccuracies and mistakes!

Despite all his doubts and questions, Rees found the shifts following his acceptance the happiest of his life. As a fully fledged apprentice he was entitled to more than Grye's grudging picture-book sessions; now he sat in classes with the other apprentices and learned in a structured and consistent way. For hours outside his class time he would pore over his books and photographs—and he would never forget an ageing picture buried in one battered folder, a photograph of the blue rim of the Nebula.

Blue!

The magical color filled his eyes, every bit as clear and cool as he had always imagined.

At first, Rees sat, awkwardly, with apprentices some thousands of shifts younger than himself; but his understanding progressed rapidly, to the grudging admiration of his tutors, and before long he had caught up and was allowed to join the classes of Hollerbach himself.

Hollerbach's style as a teacher was as vivid and captivating as the man himself. Abandoning yellowing texts and ancient photographs the old Scientist would challenge his charges to think for themselves, adorning the concepts he described with words and gestures.

One shift he had each member of the class build a simple pendulum—a dense metal bob attached to a length of string—and time its oscillation against the burning of a candle. Rees set up his pendulum, limiting the oscillations to a few degrees as Hollerbach instructed, and counted the swings carefully. A few benches along he was vaguely aware of Doav languidly going through the motions of the experiment; whenever Hollerbach's fierce eye was averted Doav would poke at the swinging bob before him, elaborately bored.

It didn't take long for the students to establish that the period of the pendulum's swing depended only on the length of the string—and was independent of the mass of the bob.

This simple fact seemed wonderful to Rees (and that he had found it out for himself made it still more so); he stayed in the little student lab for many hours after the end of the class extending the experiment, probing different mass ranges and larger amplitudes of swing.

The next class was a surprise. Hollerbach entered grandly and eyed the students, bade them pick up the retort stands to which their pendulums were still fixed, and beckoned. Then he turned and marched from the lab.

The students nervously followed, clutching their retorts; Doav rolled his eyes at the tedium of it all.

Hollerbach led them on a respectable hike, out along an avenue beneath the canopy of turning trees. The sky was clear of cloud today and starlight dappled the plates of the deck. Despite his age Hollerbach kept up a good pace, and by the time he paused, under open sky a few yards beyond the edge of the flying forest, Rees suspected that his weren't the only young legs that ached a little. He looked around curiously, blinking in the direct starlight; since beginning classes he had scarcely had a chance to come out this way, and the apparent tilt of the riveted deck under his feet felt strange.

Solemnly Hollerbach lowered himself to the deck plates and sat cross-legged, then bade his students do the same. He fixed a series of candles to the plates. "Now, ladies and gentlemen," he boomed, "I would like you to repeat your experiments of our last class. Set up your pendulum."

There were stifled groans around the class, presumably inaudible to Hollerbach. The students began work, and Hollerbach, restless, got up and paced among them. "You are Scientists, remember," he told them. "You are here to observe, not judge; you are here to measure and understand . . ."

Rees's results were . . . odd. As Hollerbach's supply of candles burned through he went over his results carefully, repeating and testing.

At last Hollerbach called them to order. "Conclusions, please? Doav?"

Rees heard the cadet's breathy groan. "No difference," he said languidly. "Same result curve as last time."

Rees frowned. That was wrong; the periods he had measured had been greater than yesterday's—by a small amount, granted, but greater consistently.

The silence gathered. Doav shifted uneasily.

Then Hollerbach let him have it. Rees tried not to grin as the old Scientist tore into the cadet's sloppy methods, his closed mind, his laziness, his lack of fitness to wear the golden braids. By the end of it Doav's cheeks burned crimson.

"Let's have the truth," Hollerbach muttered, breathing hard. "Baert . . . ?"

The next apprentice supplied an answer consistent with Rees's. Hollerbach said, "Then what has happened? How have the conditions of this experiment changed?"

The students speculated, listing the effect of the starlight on the pendulum bobs, the greater inaccuracy of the timing method—Hollerbach's candles flickered far more out here than in the lab—and many other ideas. Hollerbach listened gravely, occasionally nodding.

None of it convinced Rees. He stared at the simple device, willing it to offer up its secrets.

At last the student Baert said hesitantly, "What about gravity?"

Hollerbach raised his eyebrows. "What about it?"

Baert was a slender, tall boy; now he rubbed his thin nose uncertainly. "We're a little further from the Raft's center of gravity here, aren't we? So the pull of gravity on the pendulum bob will be a bit less . . ."

Hollerbach eyed him fiercely, saying nothing. Baert flushed and went on, "It's gravity that makes the bob swing, by pulling at it. So if gravity's less, the period will be longer . . . Does that make sense?"

Hollerbach rocked his head from side to side. "At least that's a little less dubious than some of the other proposals I've heard. But if so, what precisely is the relationship between the strength of gravity and the period?"

"We can't say," Rees blurted. "Not without more data."

"Now that," Hollerbach said, "is the first intelligent thing any of you have said this shift. Well, ladies and gentlemen, I suggest you proceed to gather your facts. Let me know what you find out." He stood, stiffly, and walked away.

The students dispersed to their task with varying degrees of enthusiasm. Rees went at it with a will, and for the next few shifts scoured the deck, armed with his pendulum, notepad and supply of candles. He recorded the period of the pendulum, made careful notes and drew logarithmic scale graphs—and more; carefully he observed how the plane of the pendulum's swing formed various angles with the surface, showing how the local vertical was changing as he moved across the face of the Raft. And he watched the slow, uncertain oscillations of the pendulum at the Rim itself.

At last he took his findings to Hollerbach. "I think I have it," he said hesitantly. "The period of the pendulum is proportional to the square root of its length . . . and also inversely proportional to the square root of the acceleration due to gravity."

Hollerbach said nothing; he steepled liver-spotted fingers before his face and regarded Rees gravely.

At length Rees blurted, "Am I correct?"

Hollerbach looked disappointed. "You must learn, boy, that in this business there are no right answers. There are only good guesses. You have made an empirical prediction; well, fine. Now you must check it against the body of theory you have learned."

Inwardly Rees groaned. But he went away and did so.

Later he showed his findings on the strength and direction of the Raft's gravitational field to Hollerbach. "The way the field varies is quite complex," he said. "At first I thought it might fall off as the inverse square of the distance from the center of the Raft; but you can see that's not true ..."

"The inverse square law holds only for point masses, or for perfectly spherical objects. Not for something shaped like a dinner plate, like the Raft."

"Then what is ... ?"

Hollerbach merely eyed him.

"I know," Rees sighed. "I should go and work it out. Right?"

It took him longer than the pendulum problem. He had to learn to integrate in three dimensions ... and how to use vector forces and equipotential surfaces ... and how to make sensible approximating assumptions.

But he did it. And when he'd done that, there was another problem. And another, and still another ...

It wasn't all work.

One shift Baert, with whom Rees struck up a diffident friendship, offered Rees a spare ticket to something called the Theatre of Light. "I won't pretend you're my first choice companion," Baert grinned. "She was a bit better looking than you ... But I don't want to miss the show, or waste a ticket."

Rees thanked him, turning the strip of cardboard

over in his hands. "The Theatre of Light? What is it? What goes on there?"

"There aren't too many theatres in the Belt, eh? Well, if you haven't heard, wait and see . . ."

The Theatre was situated beyond the tethered forest, about three-quarters of the way to the Rim. There was a bus service from the Raft's central regions but Baert and Rees chose to walk. By the time they had reached the head-high fence which surrounded the Theatre the deck appeared to be sloping quite steeply, and the walk had become a respectable climb. Out here on the exposed deck, far from the cover of the forest canopy, the heat of the star above the Raft was a tangible thing, and both of them arrived with faces slick with sweat.

Baert turned awkwardly, slippered feet gripping at the riveted slope, and grinned down at Rees. "Kind of a hike," he said. "But it'll be worth it. Do you have your ticket?"

Rees fumbled in his pockets until he found the precious piece of cardboard. Bemused, he watched as Baert presented the tickets to a doorkeeper and then followed Baert through a narrow gate.

The Theatre of Light was an oval some fifty yards along its long axis, which ran down the apparent slope of the deck. Benches were fixed across the upper part of the Theatre. Rees and Baert took their places and Rees found himself looking down the slope at a small stage which was fixed on stilts so that it rested at the local horizontal—so at an angle to the "tilted" deck—and beyond the stage, serving as a mighty backdrop to the show, he could see the center of the Raft tip away, a vast metal slope of boxy buildings and whirling, rustling trees.

The Theatre filled up rapidly. Rees estimated there was room for about a hundred people here, and he shivered a little, uncomfortable at the thought of so many people in one place.

"Drinks?"

He turned with a start. A girl, luminously pretty, stood beside his seat with a tray of glasses. He tried to smile back and form an answer, but there was something odd about the way she was standing . . .

Without effort or discomfort she was standing perpendicularly to the deck; she ignored the apparent tilt of the deck and stood as naturally as if it were level. Rees felt his jaw drop, and all his carefully constructed reasoning about the illusory tilt of the deck evaporated. For if she was vertical then he was sitting at an angle with nothing at his back—

With a stifled yell he tumbled backwards.

Baert, laughing, helped him up, and the girl, with an apologetic smile, presented him with a tumbler of some clear, sweet beverage. Rees could feel his cheeks burn like stars. "What was all that about?"

Baert suppressed his laughter. "I'm sorry. It gets them every time. I should have warned you, really . . ."

"But how does she walk like that?"

Baert's thin shoulders moved in a shrug. "If I knew it would spoil the fun. Magnetic soles on her shoes? The funny thing is, it's not the girl that knocks you over . . . It's the collapse of your own perceptions, the failure of your sense of balance."

"Yeah, hilarious." Rees sucked sourly at his drink and watched the girl move through the crowd. Her footsteps seemed easy and natural, and try as he might he failed to see how she kept her balance. Soon, though, there were more spectacular acts to watch. Jugglers, for instance, with clubs that swooped and soared in arcs at quite impossible angles, returning infallibly to their owners' hands.

During applause Rees said to Baert, "It's like magic."

"Not magic," the other said. "Simple physics; that's all there is to it. I guess this is making your miner's eyes pop out, eh?"

Rees frowned. On the Belt there wasn't a lot of time for juggling ... and no doubt the labor of the miners was going to pay for all this, in some indirect fashion. Discreetly he glanced around at the rest of the audience. Plenty of gold and crimson braid, not a lot of black or the other colors. Upper Classes only? He suppressed a stab of resentment and returned his attention to the show.

Soon it was time for the main feature. A trampoline was set up to cover the stage and the crowd grew hushed. Some wind instrument evoked a plaintive melody and a man and a woman dressed in simple leotards took the stage. They bowed once to the audience, climbed onto the trampoline, and together began to soar high into the starlit air. At first they performed simple manoeuvres—slow, graceful somersaults and twists—pleasing to the eye, but hardly spectacular.

Then the couple hit the trampoline together, jumped high, met at the top of their arcs—and, without touching, they twisted around each other, so that each was thrown wide.

Baert gasped. "Now, how did they do that?"

"Gravity," Rees whispered. "Just for a second they orbited around each other's center of mass."

The dance went on. The partners twisted around each other, throwing their lithe bodies into elaborate parabolae, and Rees watched through half-closed eyes, entranced. The physicist in him analyzed the dancers' elaborate movements. Their centers of mass, located somewhere around their waists, traced out hyperbolic orbits in the varying gravity fields of the Raft, the stage and the dancers themselves, so that each time the dancers launched themselves from their trampoline the paths of their centers were more or less determined ... But the dancers adorned the paths with movements of their slim bodies so deceptively that it seemed that the two of them were flying through the air at will, independent of gravity. How paradoxical, Rees thought, that the billion-gee environment of this universe should afford humans such freedom.

Now the dancers launched into a final, elaborate arc, their bodies orbiting, their faces locked together like facing planets. Then it was over; the dancers stood hand-in-hand atop their trampoline, and Rees cheered and stamped with the rest. So there was more to do with billion-strength gravity than measure it and fight it—

A flash, a muffled rush of air, a sudden blossom of smoke. The trampoline, blasted from below, turned briefly into a fluttering, birdlike creature, a dancer itself; the dancers, screaming, were hurled into the air. Then the trampoline collapsed into the splintered ruins of the stage, the dancers falling after it.

The audience, stunned, fell silent. The only sound was a low, broken crying from the wreckage of the stage, and Rees watched, unbelieving, as a red-brown stain spread over the remains of the trampoline.

A burly man bearing orange braids hurried from the wings and stood commandingly before the audience. "Sit down," he ordered. "No one should try to leave." And he stood there as the audience quietly obeyed. Rees, looking around, saw more orange braids at the exits from the Theatre, still more working their way into the ruins of the stage.

Baert's face was pale. "Security," he whispered. "Report directly to the Captain. You don't see them around too often, but they're always there ... undercover as often as not." He sat back and folded his arms. "What a mess. They'll interrogate us all before they let us out of here; it will take hours—"

"Baert, I don't understand any of this. What happened?"

Baert shrugged. "What do you think? A bomb, of course."

Rees felt an echo of the disorientation he had suffered when the drinks girl had walked by. "Someone did this deliberately?"

Baert looked at him sourly and did not reply.

"Why?"

"I don't know. I don't speak for those people." Baert rubbed the side of his nose. "But there's been a few of these attacks, directed against Officers, mostly, or places they're likely to be. Like this.

"Not everyone's happy here, you see, my friend," he went on. "A lot of people think the Officers get more than their share."

"So they're turning to actions like this?" Rees turned away. The red-stained trampoline was being wrapped around the limp bodies of the gravity dancers; he watched with an unshakeable sense of unreality. He remembered his own flash of resentment at Baert, not more than an hour before this disaster. Perhaps he could sympathize with the motives of the people behind this act—why should one group enjoy at leisure the fruits of another's labor?—but to kill for such a reason?

The orange-braided security men began to organize strip searches of the crowd. Resigned, not speaking, Rees and Baert sat back to wait their turn.

Despite isolated incidents like the Theatre attack Rees found his new life fascinating and rewarding, and the shifts wore away unbelievably quickly. All too soon, it seemed, he had finished his Thousand Shifts, the first stage of his graduation process, and it was time for his achievement to be honored.

And so he found himself sitting on a decorated bus and studying the crimson braids of a Scientist (Third Class), freshly stitched to the shoulder of his coverall, and shivering with a sense of unreality. The bus worked its way through the suburbs of the Raft. Its dozen young occupants, Rees's fellow graduate-apprentices, spun out a cloud of laughter and talk.

Jaen was studying him with humorous concern, a slight crease over her broad nose; her hands rested in the lap of her dress uniform. "Something on your mind?"

He shrugged. "I'm fine. You know me. I'm the serious type."

"Damn right. Here." Jaen reached to the boy sitting on the far side from Rees and took a narrow-necked bottle. "Drink. You're graduating. This is your Thousandth Shift and you're entitled to enjoy it."

"Well, it isn't precisely. I was a slow starter, remember. For me it's more like a thousand and a quarter—"

"Oh, you boring bugger, drink some of this stuff before I kick you off the bus."

Rees, laughing, gave in and took a deep draught from the bottle.

He had sampled some tough liquors in the Quartermaster's bar, and plenty of them had been stronger than this fizzing wine-sim; but none of them had quite the same effect. Soon the globe lights lining the avenue of cables seemed to emit a more friendly light; Jaen's gravity pull mingling with his was a source of warmth and stillness; and the brittle conversation of his companions seemed to grow vivid and amusing.

His mood persisted as they emerged from beneath the canopy of flying trees and reached the shadow of the Platform. The great lip of metal jutted inwards from the Rim, forming a black rectangle cut out of the crimson of the sky, its supporting braces like gaunt limbs. The bus wheezed to a halt alongside a set of wide stairs. Rees, Jaen and the rest tumbled from the bus and clambered up the stairs to the Platform.

The Thousandth Shift party was already in full swing, bustling with perhaps a hundred graduates of the various Classes of the Raft. A bar set up on trestle tables was doing healthy business, and a discordant set of musicians was thumping out a rhythmic sound—there were even a few couples tentatively dancing, near the band's low stage. Rees, with Jaen in tolerant tow, set off on a tour of the walls of the Platform.

The Platform was an elegant idea: to fix a hundred-yard-square plate to the Rim at such an angle that it matched the local horizontal, surround it by a wall of glass, and so reveal a universe of spectacular views. At the inward edge was the Raft itself, tilted like some huge toy for Rees's inspection. As at the Theatre the sensation of being on a safe, flat surface gave the proximity of the vast slope a vertiginous thrill.

The space-facing edge of the platform was suspended over the Rim of the Raft, and a section of the floor was inset with sheets of glass. Rees stood over the depths of the Nebula; it felt as if he were floating in the air. He could see hundreds of stars scattered in a vast three-dimensional array, illuminating the air like mile-wide globe lamps; and at the center of the view, towards the hidden Core of the Nebula, the stars were crowded together, so that it was as if he were staring into a vast, star-walled shaft.

"Rees. I congratulate you." Rees turned. Hollerbach, gaunt, unsmiling and utterly out of place in all this gaiety, stood beside him.

"Thank you, sir."

The old Scientist leaned towards him conspiratorially. "Of course, I didn't doubt you'd do well from the first."

Rees laughed. "I can tell you I doubted it sometimes."

"A Thousand Shifts, eh?" Hollerbach scratched his cheek. "Well, I've no doubt you'll go much further . . . And in the meantime here's something for you to think about, boy. The ancients, the first Crew, didn't measure time exclusively in shifts. We know this from their records. They used shifts, yes, but they had other units: a 'day,' which was about three shifts, and a 'year,' which was about a thousand shifts. How old are you now?"

"About seventeen thousand, I believe, sir."

"So you'd be about seventeen 'years' old, eh? Now then—what do you suppose these units, a 'day' and a 'year,' referred to?" But before Rees could answer Hollerbach raised his hand and walked off. "Baert! So they've let you get this far despite my efforts to the contrary—"

Bowls of sweetmeats had been set out around the walls. Jaen nibbled on some fluffy substance and tugged absently at his hand. "Come on. Isn't that enough sightseeing and science?"

Rees looked at her, the combination of wine-sim and stars leaving him quite dazed. "Hm? You know, Jaen, the stories of our home universe notwithstanding, sometimes this seems a very beautiful place." He grinned. "And you don't look too bad yourself."

She punched him in the solar plexus. "And nor do you. Now let's have a dance."

"What?" His euphoria evaporated. He looked past her shoulder at the whirl of dancing couples. "Look, Jaen, I've never danced in my life."

She clicked her tongue. "Don't be such a coward, you mine rat. Those people are just ex-apprentices like you and me, and I can tell you one thing for sure: they won't be watching you."

"Well . . ." he began, but it was too late; with a determined grip on his forearm she led him to the center of the Platform.

His head filled with memories of the unfortunate gravity dancers at the Theatre of Light and their swooping, spectacular ballet. If he lived for fifty thousand shifts he would never be able to match such grace.

Luckily this dance was nothing like that.

Young men eyed girls across a few yards of floor. Those who were dancing were enthusiastic but hardly expert; Rees watched for a few seconds, then began to imitate their rhythmic swaying.

Jaen pulled a face at him. "That's bloody awful. But who cares?"

In the low-gee conditions—gravity here was about half its value near the Labs—the dance had a dreamy slowness. After a while Rees began to relax; and, eventually, he realized he was enjoying himself—

—until his legs whisked out from under him; he clattered to the Platform with a slow bump. Jaen covered her face with one hand, suppressing giggles; a circle of laughter clustered briefly around him. He got to his feet. "I'm sorry—"

There was a tap on his shoulder. "So you should be."

He turned; there, with a broad, glinting grin, stood a tall young man with the braids of a Junior Officer. "Doav," Rees said slowly. "Did you trip me?"

Doav barked laughter.

Rees felt his forearm muscles bunch. "Doav, you've been an irritation to me for the last year . . ."

Doav looked baffled.

". . . I mean, the last thousand shifts." And it was true; Rees could bear the constant sniping, cracks and cruelties of Doav and his like throughout his working day . . . but he would much prefer not to have to. And, since the incident at the Theatre, he had come to see how attitudes like Doav's were the cause of a great deal of pain and suffering on the Raft; and, perhaps, of much more to come.

The wine-sim was like blood now, pounding in his head. "Cadet, if we've something to settle—"

Doav fixed him with a look of contempt. "Not here. But soon. Oh, yes; soon." And he turned his back and walked off through the throng.

Jaen thumped Rees's arm hard enough to make him flinch. "Do you have to turn every incident into an exhibition? Come on; let's get a drink." She stamped her way towards the bar.

"Hello, Rees."

Rees paused, allowing Jaen to slip ahead into the crush around the bar. A thin young man stood before him, hair plastered across his scalp. He wore the black braids of Infrastructure and he regarded Rees with cool appraisal.

Rees groaned. "Gover. I guess this isn't to be the best shift I've ever had."

"What?"

"Never mind. I haven't seen you since not long after my arrival."

"Yeah, but that's not hard to understand." Gover flicked delicately at Rees's braid. "We move in different circles, don't we?"

Rees, already on edge after the incident with Doav, studied Gover as coolly as he could. There were still the same sharp features, the look of petulant anger—but Gover looked more substantial, more sure of himself.

"So you're still skivvying for those old farts in the Labs, eh?"

"I'm not going to respond to that, Gover."

"You're not?" Gover rubbed at his nostrils with the palm of his hand. "Seeing you in this toy uniform made me wonder how you see yourself now. I bet you haven't done a shift's work—real work— since you landed here. I wonder what your fellow rats would think of you now. Eh?"

Rees felt blood surge once more to his cheeks; the wine-sim seemed to be turning sour. There was a seed of confusion inside him. Was his anger at Gover just a way of shielding himself from the truth, that he had betrayed his origins . . . ?

"What do you want, Gover?"

Gover took a step closer to Rees. His stale breath cut through the wine fumes in Rees's nostrils. "Listen, mine rat, believe it or not I want to do you a favor."

"What kind of favor?"

"Things are changing here," Gover said slyly. "Do you understand what I'm saying? Things won't always be as they are now." He eyed Rees, evidently unwilling to go further.

Rees frowned. "What are you talking about? The discontents?"

"That's what some call them. Seekers of justice, others say."

The noise of the revelers seemed to recede from Rees; it was as if Gover and he shared their own Raft somewhere in the air. "Gover, I was in the Theatre of Light, that shift. Was that justice?"

Gover's eyes narrowed. "Rees, you've seen how the elite on this Raft keep the rest of us down—and how their obscene economic system degrades the rest of the Nebula's human population. The time is near when they will have to atone."

Rees stared at him. "You're one of them, aren't you?"

Gover bit his lip. "Maybe. Look, Rees, I'm taking a chance talking to you like this. And if you betray me I'll deny we ever had this conversation."

"What do you want of me?"

"There are good men in the cause. Men like Decker, Pallis—"

Rees guffawed. Decker—the huge Infrastructure worker he had encountered on his first arrival here—he could believe. But Pallis? "Come on, Gover."

Gover was unruffled. "Damn it, Rees, you know what I think of you. You're a mine rat. You don't belong here, among decent people. But where you come from makes you one of us. All I'm asking is that you come along and listen to what they have to say. With your access to the Science buildings you could be . . . useful."

Rees tried to clear his thinking. Gover was a vicious, bitter young man, and his arguments—the contradictory mixture of contempt and appeal to fellow-feeling he directed at Rees, for example—were simple-minded and muddled. But what gave

Gover's words force was their terrible truth. Part of Rees was appalled that such as Gover could so quickly disorient him—but inside him a core of anger flared up in response.

But if some revolution were to occur—if the Labs were smashed, the Officers imprisoned—what then?

"Gover, look up."

Gover raised his face.

"See that star up there? If we don't move the Raft the star will graze us. And then we'll fry. And even if we were to survive that—look further out." He swept an arm around the red-stained sky. "The Nebula's dying and we'll die with it. Gover, only the Scientists, backed by the organization of the Raft, can save us from such dangers."

Gover scowled and spat at the deck. "You seriously believe that? Come on, Rees. I'll tell you something. The Nebula could support us all for a long time yet—if its resources were shared equally. And that's all we want." He paused. "Well?"

Rees closed his eyes. Would sky wolves discuss Gover's case as they descended on the wreck of the Raft and picked clean the bones of his children? "Get lost, Gover," he said tiredly.

Gover sneered. "If that's what you want. I can't say I'm sorry ..." He grinned at Rees with something approaching pure contempt. Then he slid away through the crowd.

The noise seemed to swirl around Rees, not touching him. He pushed his way through the crush to the bar and ordered straight liquor, and downed the hot liquid in one throw.

Jaen joined him and grabbed his arm. "I've been looking for you. Where ... ?" Then she felt the bunched muscles under Rees's jacket; and when he turned to face her, she shrank back from his anger.

6

The Scientist Second Class stood in the doorway of the Bridge. He watched the new Third Class approach and tried to hide a smile. The young man's uniform was so obviously new, he stared with such awe at the Bridge's silver hull, and his pallor was undisputable evidence of his Thousandth Shift celebration, which had finished probably mere hours earlier ... The Second Class felt quite old as he remembered his own Thousandth Shift, his own arrival at the Bridge, a good three thousand shifts ago.

At least this boy had a look of inquiry about him. So many of the apprentices the Second had to deal with were sullen and resentful at best, downright contemptuous at worst; and the rates of absenteeism and dismissal were worsening. He reached out a hand as the young man approached.

"Welcome to the Bridge," said Scientist Second Class Rees.

The boy—blond, with a premature streak of gray—was called Nead. He smiled uncertainly.

A bulky, grim-faced security guard stood just inside the door. He fixed Nead with a threatening stare; Rees saw how the boy quailed. Rees sighed. "It's all right, lad; this is just old Forv; it's his job to remember your face, that's all." It was only recently, Rees realized a little wistfully, that such heavy-handed security measures had come to seem necessary; with the continuing decline in food supplies, the mood on the Raft had worsened, and the severity and frequency of the attacks of the "discontents" were increasing. Sometimes Rees wondered if—

He shook his head to dismiss such thoughts; he had a job to do. He walked the wide-eyed boy slowly through the Bridge's gleaming corridors. "It's enough for now if you get an idea of the layout of the place," he said. "The Bridge is a cylinder a hundred yards long. This corridor runs around its midriff. The interior is divided into three rooms— a large middle chamber and two smaller chambers toward the ends. We think that the latter were once control rooms, perhaps equipment lockers; you see, the Bridge seems to have been a part of the original Ship . . ."

They had reached one of the smaller chambers; it was stacked with books, piles of paper and devices of all shapes and sizes. Two Scientists, bent in concentration, sat cocooned in dust. Nead turned flat, brown eyes on Rees. "What's this room used for now?"

"This is the Library," Rees said quietly. "The Bridge is the most secure place we have, the best protected from weather, accident—so we keep our records here. As much as we can: one copy of everything vital, and some of the stranger artefacts that have come down to us from the past . . ."

They walked on following the corridor to a shallow staircase set into the floor. They began to descend toward a door set in the inner wall, which led to the Bridge's central chamber. Rees thought of warning the boy to watch his step—then decided against it, a slightly malicious humor sparkling within him.

Nead took three or four steps down—then, arms flailing, he tipped face-forward. He didn't fall; instead he bobbed in the stairwell, turning a slow somersault. It was as if he had fallen into some invisible fluid.

Rees grinned broadly.

Nead, panting, reached for the wall. His palms flat against the metal he steadied himself and scrambled back up the steps. "By the Bones," he swore, "what's down there?"

"Don't worry, it's harmless," Rees said. "It caught me the first time too. Nead, you're a Scientist now. Think about it. What happened when you went down those steps?"

The boy looked blank.

Rees sighed. "You passed through the plane of the Raft's deck, didn't you? It's the metal of the deck that provides the Raft's gravity pull. So here—at the center of the Raft, and actually in its plane—there is no pull. You see? You walked into a weightless zone."

Nead opened his mouth—then closed it again, looking puzzled.

"You'll get used to it," Rees snapped. "And maybe, with time, you'll even understand it. Come on."

He led the way through the doorway to the central chamber, and was gratified to hear Nead gasp.

They had entered an airy room some fifty yards wide. Most of its floor area was transparent, a single vast window which afforded a vertiginous view of the depths of the Nebula. Gaunt machines taller than men were fixed around the window. To Nead's untutored eye, Rees reflected, the machines must look like huge, unlikely insects, studded with lenses and antennae and peering into some deep pool of air. The room was filled with a clean smell of ozone and lubricating oil; servomotors hummed softly.

There were perhaps a dozen Scientists working this shift; they moved about the machines making adjustments and jotting copious notes. And because the plane of the Raft passed over the window-floor at about waist height, the Scientists bobbed in the air like boats in an invisible pond, their centers of gravity oscillating above and below the equilibrium line with periods of two or three seconds. Rees, looking at the scene as if through new eyes, found himself hiding another grin. One small, round man had even, quite unselfconsciously, turned upside down to bring his eyes closer to a sensor panel. His trousers rode continually toward the equilibrium plane, so that his short legs protruded, bare.

They stood on a low ledge; Rees took a step down and was soon floating in the air, his feet a few inches from the window-floor. Nead lingered nervously. "Come on, it's easy," Rees said. "Just swim in the air, or bounce up and down until your feet hit the deck."

Nead stepped off the ledge and tumbled forward, slowly bobbing upright. He reminded Rees of a child entering a pool for the first time. After a few seconds a slow smile spread across the young man's face; and soon he was skimming about the room, his feet brushing at the window below.

Rees took him on a tour around the machines.

Nead shook his head. "This is amazing."

Rees smiled. "This equipment is among the best preserved of the Ship's materiel. It's as if it were unloaded only last shift ... We call this place the Observatory. All the heavy-duty sensors are mounted here, and this is where—as a member of my Nebular physics team—you'll be spending most of your time." They stopped beside a tube ten feet long and encrusted with lenses. Rees ran a palm along the instrument's jewelled flank. "This baby's my favorite," he said. "Beautiful, isn't she? It's a Telescope which will work at all wavelengths—including the visual. Using this we can see right down into the heart of the Nebula."

Nead thought that over, then glanced at the ceiling. "Don't we ever need to look outwards?"

Rees nodded approvingly. Good question. "Yes, we do. There are ways of making the roof transparent—in fact, we can opaque the floor, if we want to." He glanced at the instrument's fist-sized status panel. "We're in luck; there are no observations currently running. I'll give you a quick guided tour of the Nebula. You should know most of what I'll tell you from your studies so far, and don't worry about the details for now . . ." Slowly he punched a sequence of commands into the keypad mounted below the sensor. He became aware that the lad was watching him curiously. Maybe he's never seen anyone with such rusty keyboard skills, Rees reflected, here on this Raft of a hundred supply machines—

The stab of old resentment shocked him. Never mind . . .

A disc of ceiling faded to transparency, revealing a red sky. Rees indicated a monitor plate mounted on a slim post close to the Telescope. The plate abruptly filled with darkness punctuated by fuzzy lens shapes; the lenses were all colors, from red through yellow to the purest blue. Once more Nead gasped.

"Let's review a few facts," Rees began. "You know we live in a Nebula, which is an ellipse-shaped cloud of gas about five thousand miles across. Every particle of the Nebula is orbiting the Core. The Raft is in orbit too, embedded in the Nebula like a fly on a spinnng plate; we circle the Core every twelve shifts or so. The Belt mine is further in and only takes about nine shifts to complete its orbit. When the pilots fly between mine and Raft their trees are actually changing orbits ... ! Fortunately the gradients in orbital speeds are so shallow out here that the velocities the trees can reach are enough for them easily to fly from one orbit to another. Of course the pilots must plan their courses carefully, to make sure the Belt mine isn't on the other side of the Core when they arrive at the right orbit ...

"Here we're looking through the Observatory roof and out of the Nebula. Normally the atmosphere shields this view from us, but the Telescope can unscramble the atmospheric scattering and show us what we'd see if the air were stripped away."

Nead peered closer at the picture. "What are those blobs? Are they stars?"

Rees shook his head. "They're other nebulae: some larger than ours, some smaller, some younger—the blue ones—and some older. As far as we can see with this Telescope—and that's hundreds of millons of miles—space is filled with them.

"All right; let's move inwards." With a single keystroke the picture changed to reveal a blue-purple sky; stars glittered, white as diamonds.

"That's beautiful," Nead breathed. "But it can't be in our Nebula—"

"But it is." Rees smiled sadly. "You're looking at the topmost layer, where the lightest gases—hydrogen and helium—separate out. That is where stars form. Turbulence causes clumps of higher density; the clumps implode and new stars burst to life." The stars, balls of fusion fire, formed dense bow waves in the thin atmosphere as they began their long, slow fall into the Nebula. Rees went on, "The stars shine for about a thousand shifts before burning out and dropping, as a cool ball of iron, into the Core . . . Most of them anyway; one or two of the kernels end up in stable orbits around the Core. That's where the star mines come from."

Nead frowned. "And if the path of a falling star intersects the orbit of the Raft—"

"Then we're in trouble, and we must use the trees to change the Raft's orbit. Fortunately star and Raft converge slowly enough for us to track the star on its way toward us . . ."

"If new stars are being formed, why do people say the Nebula is dying?"

"Because there are far fewer than before. When the Nebula was formed it was almost pure hydrogen. The stars have turned a lot of the hydrogen into helium, carbon and other heavy elements. That's how the complex substances which support life here were formed.

"Or rather, it's life for us. But it's a slow, choking death for the Nebula. From its point of view oxygen, carbon and the rest are waste products. Heavier than hydrogen, they settle slowly around the Core; the residual hydrogen gets less and less until—as today—it's reduced to a thin crust around the Nebula."

Nead stared at the sparse young stars. "What will happen in the end?"

Rees shrugged. "Well, we've observed other nebulae. The last stars will fail and die. Deprived of energy the airborne life of the Nebula—the whales, the sky wolves, the trees, and the lesser creatures they feed on—will cease to exist."

"Are there truly such things as whales? I thought they were just stories—"

Rees shrugged. "We never see them out here, but we have plenty of evidence from travellers who've entered the depths of the Nebula."

"What, as far as the Belt mine, you mean?"

Rees suppressed a smile. "No, even further than that. The Nebula is a big place, lad; there is room to hide a lot of mystery. Perhaps there are even lost human colonies; perhaps the Boneys really exist, and all those legends are true . . . of the sub-human whale-singers lost in the sky."

The boy shuddered.

"Of course," Rees mused, "there are puzzles about the native life of the Nebula. For example, how can it exist at all? Our records show that life in the home universe took thousands of billions of shifts to evolve. The Nebula isn't anything like that old—and will be far younger when it dies. So how did life arise?"

"You were telling me what will happen after the stars go out . . ."

"Yes. The atmosphere, darkened, will steadily lose heat, and—less able to resist the gravity of the Core—will collapse. Finally the Nebula will be reduced to a layer a few inches thick around the Core, slowly falling inwards . . ."

The young man, his face pale, nodded slowly.

"All right," Rees said briskly. "Let's look inwards now—past the Raft's level, which is a thousand miles from the edge of the Nebula—and in to the center."

Now the monitor filled up with a familiar ruddy sky. Stars were scattered sparsely through the air. Rees punched a key—

—and stars exploded out of the picture. The

focus plummeted into the Nebula and it was as if they were falling.

Finally the star cloud began to thin and a darker knot of matter emerged at its center.

"What you're seeing here is a layer of detritus in close orbit around the Core," Rees said quietly. "At the heart of this Nebula is a black hole. If you're not sure what that is right now, don't worry . . . The black hole is about a hundredth of an inch wide; the large object we call the Core is a dense mass of material surrounding the hole. We can't see through this cloud of rubble to the Core itself, but we believe it's an ellipsoid about fifty miles across. And somewhere inside the Core will be the black hole itself and an accretion disc around it, a region perhaps a hundred feet wide in which matter is crushed out of existence as it is dragged into the hole . . .

"At the surface of the Core the hole's gravity is down to a mere several hundred gee. At the outer edge of the Nebula—where we are—it's down to about one per cent of a gee; but even though it's so small here the hole's gravity is what binds this Nebula together.

"And if we could travel into the Core itself we would find gravity climbing to thousands, millons of gee. Hollerbach has some theories about what happens near and within the Core, a realm of what he calls 'gravitic chemistry'—"

Nead frowned. "I don't understand."

"I bet you don't." Rees laughed. "But I'll tell you anyway, so you'll know the questions to ask . . .

"You see, in the day-to-day turmoil of things we—even we Scientists—tend to forget the central, astonishing fact of this cosmos—that the gravitational constant is a billon times larger than in the universe from which man arose. Oh, we see the macroscopic effects—for instance, a human body exerts a respectable gravitational field!—but what about the small, the subtle, the microscopic effects?"

In man's original universe, Rees went on, gravity was the only significant force over the interstellar scale. But over short ranges—on the scale of an individual atom—gravity was so tiny as to be negligible. "It is utterly dominated by even the electromagnetic force," Rees said. "And that is why our bodies are shambling cages of electromagnetism; and attractive electrical forces between molecules drive the chemistry that sustains our being.

"But here . . ." He rubbed his nose thoughtfully. "Here, things are different. Here, in certain circumstances, gravity can be as significant on the atomic scale as other forces—even dominant.

"Hollerbach talks of a new kind of 'atom.' Its fundamental particles would be massive—perhaps they would be tiny black holes—and the atom would be bonded by gravity in novel, complex structures. A new type of chemistry—a gravitic chemistry—would be possible; a new realm of nature about whose form even Hollerbach can scarcely begin to speculate."

Nead frowned. "But why haven't we observed this 'gravitic chemistry'?"

Rees nodded approvingly. "Good question. Hollerbach calculates that the right conditions must prevail: the right temperature and pressure, powerful gravitational gradients—"

"In the Core," Nead breathed. "I see. So perhaps—"

There was a soft boom.

The Bridge shifted slightly, as if a wave were passing through its structure. The image in the monitor broke up.

Rees twisted. A sharp smell of burning, of smoke, touched his nostrils. The Scientists were milling in confusion, but the instruments seemed to be intact. Somewhere someone screamed.

Fear creased Nead's brow. "Is that normal?"

"That came from the Library," Rees murmured. "And, no, it's not bloody normal." He took a deep, calming breath; and when he spoke again his voice was steady. "It's all right, Nead. I want you to get out of here as quickly as you can. Wait until ..." His voice tailed away.

Nead looked at him, half-understanding. "Until what?"

"Until I send for you. Now move."

The boy half-swam to the exit and pushed his way through the crowd of Scientists.

Trying to ignore the spreading panic around him Rees ran his fingers over the keyboard of the Telescope, locking the precious instrument into its rest position. Briefly he marveled at his own callous coolness. But in the end, he reflected, he was responding to a harsh, terrible truth. Humans could be replaced. The Telescope couldn't.

When he turned from the keyboard the Observatory was deserted. Paper and small tools lay scattered over the incorruptible floor, or floated in the equilibrium layer. And still that smell of burning hung in the air.

With a sense of lightness he crossed the chamber floor and climbed out into the corridor. Smoke thickened the air, stinging his eyes, and as he approached the Library images of the imploded foundry and of the Theatre of Light confused his thoughts, as if his mind were a Telescope focusing on the buried depths of the past.

Entering the Library was like climbing into an ancient, decayed mouth. Books and papers had been turned to blackened leaves and blasted against the walls; the ruined paper had been soaked through by the efforts of Scientists to save their treasure. There were three men still here, beating at smoldering pages with damp blankets. At Rees's entry one of them turned. Rees was moved to recognize Grye, tears streaking his blackened cheeks.

Rees ran a cautious finger over the shell of ruined books. How much had been lost this shift?—what wisdom that might have saved them all from the Nebula's smoky death?

Something crackled under his feet. There were shards of glass scattered over the floor, and Rees made out the truncated, smoke-stained neck of a wine-sim bottle. Briefly he found himself marveling that such a simple invention as a bottle filled with burning oil could wreak so much damage.

There was nothing he could do here. He touched Grye's shoulder briefly; then he turned and left the Bridge.

There was no sign of security guards at the door. The scene outside was chaotic. Rees had a blurred impression of running men, of flames on the horizon; the Raft was a panorama of fists and angry voices. The harsh starlight from above flattened the scene, making it colorless and gritty.

So it had come. His last hope that this incident might be restricted to just another attack on the Labs evaporated. The fragile web of trust and acceptance that had held the Raft together had finally collapsed . . .

A few hundred yards away he made out a group of youths surrounding a bulky man; Rees thought he recognized Captain Mith. The big man went down under a hail of blows. At first, Rees saw, he tried to defend his head, his crotch; but blood spread rapidly over his face and clothing, and soon fists and feet were pounding into a shapeless, unresisting bulk.

Rees turned his head away.

In the foreground a small group of Scientists sat numbly on the deck, staring into the distance. They surrounded a bundle which looked like a charred row of books—perhaps something recovered from the fire?

But there was the white of bone amid the charring.

He felt his throat constrict; he breathed deeply, drawing on all his experience. This was not a good time to succumb to panic.

He recognized Hollerbach. The old Chief Scientist sat a little apart from the rest, staring at the crumpled remains of his spectacles. He looked up as Rees approached, an almost comical mask of soot surrounding his eyes. "Eh? Oh, it's you, boy. Well, this is a fine thing, isn't it?"

"What's happening, Hollerbach?"

Hollerbach toyed with his glasses. "Look at this. Half a million shifts old, these were, and absolutely irreplaceable. Of course, they never worked—" He looked up vaguely. "Isn't it obvious what's happening?" he snapped with something of his former vigor. "Revolution. The frustration, the hunger, the privations—they're lashing out at what they can reach. And that's us. It's so damn stupid—"

Unexpected anger flared in Rees. "I'll tell you what's stupid. You people keeping the rest of the Raft—and my own people on the Belt—in ignorance and hunger. That's what's stupid . . ."

Hollerbach's eyes in their pools of wrinkles looked enormously tired. "Well, you may be right, lad; but there's nothing I can do about it now, and there never was. My job was to keep the Raft intact. And who's going to do that in the future, eh?"

"Mine rat." The voice behind him was breathless, almost cracked with exhilaration. Rees whirled. Gover's face was flushed, his eyes alive. He had torn the braids from his shoulders and his arms were blood-stained to the elbows. Behind him a dozen or more young men approached; as they studied the Officers' homes their faces were narrow with hunger.

Rees found his fists bunching—and deliberately uncurled them. Keeping his voice level he said, "I should have turned you in while I had the opportunity. What do you want, Gover?"

"Last chance, rat," Gover said softly. "Come with us now, or take what we dish out to these vicious old farts. One chance."

The stares of Gover and Hollerbach were almost palpable pressures: the stink of smoke, the noise, the bloodied corpse on the deck, all seemed to converge in his awareness, and he felt as if he were bearing on his back the weight of the Raft and all its occupants.

Gover waited.

7

The rotation of the tethered tree was peaceful, soothing. Pallis sat by the warm trunk of the tree, chewing slowly on his flight rations.

A head and shoulders thrust their way through the mat of foliage. It was a young man; his hair was filthy and tangled and sweat plastered a straggling beard to his throat. He looked about uncertainly.

Pallis said softly: "I take it you've a good reason for disturbing my tree, lad. What are you doing here?"

The visitor pulled himself through the leaves. Pallis noticed how the boy's coverall bore the scars of recently removed braids. Shame, Pallis reflected, that the coverall itself hadn't been removed—and washed—with equal vigor.

"Regards to you, tree-pilot. My name's Boon, of the Brotherhood of the Infrastructure. The Committee instructed me to find you—"

"I don't care if Boney Joe himself shoved a fibula up your arse to help you on your way," Pallis said evenly. "I'll ask you again. What are you doing in my tree?"

Boon's grin faded. "The Committee want to see you," he said, his voice faint. "Come to the Platform. Now."

Pallis cut a slice of meat-sim. "I don't want anything to do with your damn Committee, boy."

Boon scratched uncertainly at his armpit. "But you have to. The Committee . . . it's an order—"

"All right, lad, you've delivered your message," Pallis snapped. "Now get out of my tree."

"Can I tell them you'll come?"

For reply Pallis ran a fingertip along the blade of his knife. Boon ducked back through the foliage.

Pallis buried the tip of the knife in trunk wood, wiped his hands on a dry leaf and pulled himself to the rim of the tree. He lay facedown among the fragrance of the leaves, allowing the tree's stately rotation to sweep his gaze across the Raft.

Under its canopy of forest the deck had become a darker place: threads of smoke still rose from the ruins of buildings, and Pallis noticed dark stretches in the great cable-walled avenues. That was new; so they were smashing up the globe lamps now. How would it feel to smash the very last one? he wondered. To extinguish the last scrap of ancient light—how would it feel to grow old, knowing that it was your hands that had done such a thing?

At the revolution's violent eruption Pallis had simply retreated to his trees. With a supply of water and food he had hoped to rest here among his beloved branches, distanced from the pain and anger washing across the Raft. He had even considered casting off, simply flying away alone. The Bones knew he owed no loyalty to either side in this absurd battle.

But, he mused, he was still a human. As were the running figures on the Raft—even the self-appointed Committee—and those lost souls in the Belt. And, when all this was over, someone would have to carry food and iron for them once more.

So he had waited above the revolt, hoping it would leave him be . . .

But now his interlude was over.

He sighed. So, Pallis, you can hide from their damn revolution, but it looks as if it isn't going to hide from you.

He had to go, of course. If not they'd come for him with their bottles of burning oil . . .

He took a deep draught of water, tucked his knife in his belt and slid smoothly through the foliage.

He made his way to an avenue and set off toward the Rim.

The avenue was deserted.

Shivering, he found himself listening for echoes of the crowds who had thronged along here not many shifts ago. But the silence of the wide thoroughfare was deep, eerie. The predominant smell was of burnt wood, overlaid with a meat-like stickiness; he turned up his face to the calm canopy of forest, nostrils seeking the soft wood-scented breeze from the branches.

As he had suspected a good fraction of the globe lamps hung in imploded fragments from their cables, dooming the avenue to half-light. The Raft had become a place of moody darkness, the blanket of shadows lifting here and there to reveal glimpses of this fine new world. He saw a small child licking at the remains of a long-empty food pallet. He made out a shape hanging from rope tied to the tree cables; a pool of something brown and thick had dried on the deck beneath it—

Pallis felt the food churn in his stomach. He hurried on.

A group of young men came marching from the direction of the Platform, braids ostentatiously torn from their shoulders. Their eyes were wide with joy; Pallis, despite his muscles, stood aside as they passed.

At length he reached the edge of the cable thicket and—with some relief—emerged to open sky. He made his way up the apparent slope to the Rim and at last climbed the broad, shallow stairs to the Platform. Incongruous memories tugged at him. He hadn't been here since his Thousandth Shift dance. He remembered the glittering costumes, the laughter, the drink, his own big-boned awkwardness . . .

Well, he wouldn't find a party here today.

At the head of the stairs two men blocked the way. They were about Pallis's size but somewhat younger; dim hostility creased their features.

"I'm Pallis," he said. "Woodsman. I'm here to see the Committee"

They studied him suspiciously.

Pallis sighed. "And if you two boneheads will get out of the way I can do what I came for."

The shorter of the two—a square, bald man—took a step up to him. Pallis saw he was carrying a club of wood. "Listen—"

Pallis smiled, letting his muscles bunch under his shirt.

The taller doorman said, "Leave it, Seel. He's expected."

Seel scowled; then he hissed: "Later, funny man."

Pallis let his smile broaden. "My pleasure."

He pushed past the doormen and down to the body of the Platform, wondering at his own actions. Now, what had been the point of antagonizing those two? Was violence, the pounding of fist into bone, so attractive a release?

A fine response to these unstable times, Pallis.

He walked slowly toward the center of the Platform. The place was barely recognizable from former times. Food cartons lay strewn about the deck, no more than half emptied; at the sight of the spoiling stuff Pallis remembered with a flash of anger the starving child not a quarter of a mile from here.

Trestle tables studded the Platform. They bore trophies of various kinds—photographs, uniforms, lengths of gold braid, a device called an orrery Pallis remembered seeing in Hollerbach's office— but also books, charts, listings and heaps of paper. It was clear that such government as still existed on the Raft was based here.

Pallis grinned sourly. It had been a great symbolic gesture, no doubt, to remove control from the corrupt center of the Raft and take it out to this spectacular vantage spot ... But what if it rained on all this paperwork?

However, no one seemed too concerned about such practicalities at the moment, or indeed about the machineries of government in general. Save for a group of subdued, grubby Scientists huddled together at the center of the deck, the Platform's population was clustered in a tight knot at the Nebula-facing wall. Pallis approached slowly. The Raft's new rulers, mostly young men, laughed and passed bottles of liquor from hand to hand, gaping at some attraction close to the wall.

"Hello, tree-pilot." The voice was insolent and unpleasantly familiar. Pallis turned. Gover stood facing him, hands on hips, a grin on his thin face.

"Gover. Well, surprise, surprise. I should have expected you here. You know what they say, eh?"

Gover's smile faded.

"Stir a barrel of shit: what rises to the top?"

Gover's lower lip trembled. "You should watch it, Pallis. Things have changed on this Raft."

Pallis inquired pleasantly: "Are you threatening me, Gover?"

For long seconds the younger man held his gaze; then he dropped his eyes—just a flicker, but enough for Pallis to know he had won.

He let his muscles relax, and the glow of his tiny triumph faded quickly. Two threatened fist-fights in as many minutes? Terrific.

Gover said, "You took long enough to get here."

Pallis allowed his gaze to roam. He murmured, "I'll not speak to the puppet if I know whose hand is working him. Tell Decker I'm here."

Gover flushed with frustration. "Decker's not in charge. We don't work like that—"

"Of course not," Pallis said tiredly. "Just fetch him. All right?" And he turned his full attention on the excited group near the edge.

Gover stalked away.

His height allowed Pallis a view over the milling crowd. They were clustered around a crude breach in the Platform's glass wall. A chill breeze swept over the lip of the deck; Pallis—despite his flying experience—found his stomach tightening at the thought of approaching that endless drop. A metal beam a few yards long had been thrust through the breach and out over the drop. A young man stood on the beam, his uniform torn and begrimed but still bearing Officer's braids. He held his head erect, so bloodied that Pallis failed to recognize him. The crowd taunted the Officer, laughing; fists and clubs poked at his back, forcing him to take one step after another along the beam.

"You wanted to see me, tree-pilot?"

Pallis turned. "Decker. Long time no see."

Decker nodded. His girder-like frame was barely contained by coveralls that were elaborately embroidered with black thread, and his face was a broad, strong mask contoured by old scars.

Pallis pointed to the young Officer on the beam. "Why don't you stop this bloodiness?"

Decker smiled. "I have no power here."

"Balls."

Decker threw his head back and laughed.

Decker was the same age as Pallis; they had grown up boyhood rivals, although Pallis had always considered the other his superior in ability. But their paths as adults had soon parted. Decker had never been able to accept the discipline of any Class, and so had descended, frustrated, into Infrastructure. With time Pallis's face had grown a mask of tree scars, while Decker's had become a map drawn by dozens of fists, boots and knives ...

But he had always given more than he had taken. And slowly he had grown into a position of unofficial power: if you wanted something done fast you went to Decker ... So Pallis knew who would emerge smiling from this revolt, even if Decker himself hadn't instigated it.

"All right, Pallis," Decker said. "Why did you ask to see me?"

"I want to know why you and your band of bloodthirsty apprentices dragged me from my tree."

Decker rubbed his graying beard. "Well, I can only act as a spokesman for the Interim Committee, of course—"

"Of course."

"We have some shipments to be taken to the Belt. We need you to lead the flight."

"Shipments? Of what?"

Decker nodded toward the huddle of Scientists. "That lot for a start. Labor for the mine. Most of them anyway; we'll keep the young, healthy ones."

"Very noble."

"And you're to take a supply machine."

Pallis frowned. "You're giving the Belt one of our machines?"

"If you read your history you'll find they have a right, you know."

"Don't talk to me about history, Decker. What's the angle?"

Decker pursed his lips. "The upswelling of popular affection on this Raft for our brothers on the Belt is, shall we say, not to be opposed at present by the prudent man."

"So you're pleasing the crowd. But if the Raft loses its economic advantage over the Belt you'll lose out too."

Decker smiled. "I'll make that leap when I come to it. It's a long flight to the Belt, Pallis; you know that as well as anybody. And a lot can happen between here and there."

"You'd deliberately lose one of our machines? By the Bones, Decker—"

"I didn't say that, old friend. All I meant was that the transportation of a machine by a tree—or a fleet of trees—is an enormous technical challenge for your woodsmen."

Pallis nodded. Decker was right, of course; you'd have to use a flight of six or seven trees with the machine suspended between them. He'd need his best pilots to hold the formation all the way to the Belt ... names and faces passed through his thoughts ...

And Decker was grinning at him. Pallis frowned, irritated. All a man like Decker had to do was throw him an interesting problem and everything else went out of his head.

Decker turned to watch the activities of his co-revolutionaries.

The young Officer had been pushed a good yard

beyond the glass wall. Tears mingled with the blood caked over his cheeks and, as Pallis watched, the lad's bladder released; a stain gushed around his crotch, causing the crowd to roar.

"Decker—"

"I can't save him," Decker said firmly. "He won't discard his braids."

"Good for him."

"He's a suicidal idiot."

Now a figure broke out of the ranks of cowering Scientists. It was a young, dark man. He cried: "No!" and, scarred fists flailing, he launched himself at the backs of the crowd. The Scientist soon disappeared under a hail of fists and boots; at last he too was thrust, bloodied and torn, onto the beam. And through the fresh bruises, dirt and growth of beard, Pallis realized with a start that he recognized the impetuous young man.

"Rees," he breathed.

Rees faced the baying, upturned faces, head ringing from the blows he had taken. Over the heads of the crowd he could see the little flock of Scientists and Officers; they clung together, unable even to watch his death.

The Officer leaned close and shouted through the noise. "I ought to thank you, mine rat."

"Don't bother, Doav. It seems I'm not ready yet to watch a man die alone. Not even you."

Now fists and clubs came prodding toward them. Rees took a cautious step backwards. Had he traveled so far, learned so much . . . only for it to end like this?

. . . He recalled the time of revolution, the moment he had faced Gover outside the Bridge. As he had sat among the Scientists, signifying where his loyalties lay, Gover spat on the deck and turned his back.

Hollerbach had hissed: "You bloody young idiot. What do you think you are doing? The important thing is to survive . . . If we don't resume our work, a revolution every other shift won't make a damn bit of difference."

Rees shook his head. There was logic in Hollerbach's words—but surely there were some things more important than mere survival. Perhaps when he was Hollerbach's age he would see things differently . . .

As the shifts had worn away he had been deprived of food, water, shelter and sleep, and had been forced to work on basic deck maintenance tasks with the most primitive of tools. He had suffered the successive indignities in silence, waiting for this darkness to clear from the Raft.

But the revolution had not failed. At last his group had been brought here; he suspected that some or all of them were now to be selected for some new trial. He had been prepared to accept his destiny—

—until the sight of the young Officer dying alone had cut through his carefully maintained patience.

Doav seemed calm now, accepting; he returned Rees's gaze with a nod. Rees extended his hand. The Officer gripped it firmly.

The two of them faced their tormentors.

Now a few young men climbed onto the beam, egged on by their companions. Rees fended off their clubs with his forearm, but he was forced to retreat, inch by inch.

Under his bare feet he felt an edge of metal, the coldness of empty air.

But someone was moving through the crowd.

Pallis had followed Decker through the mob, watching the deference the big man was accorded with some amusement. At the wall Decker said, "So now we have two heroes. Eh?"

Laughter rippled.

"Don't you think this is a waste, though?" Decker mused loudly. "You—Rees, is it?—we were going to keep you here. We need good muscles; there's enough work to be done. Now this stupidity of yours is going to leave us short ... I'll tell you what. You. The Officer." Decker beckoned. "Come down and join the rest of the cowards over there." There was a rumble of dissent; Decker let it pass, then said softly: "Of course, this is just my suggestion. Is the will of the Committee opposed?"

Of course not. Pallis smiled.

"Come, lad."

Doav turned uncertainly to Rees. Rees nodded and pushed him gently toward the Platform. The Officer walked gingerly along the beam and stepped down to the deck; he passed through the crowd toward the Scientists, enduring sly punches and kicks.

Rees was left alone.

"As for the mine rat—" An anticipatory roar rose from the crowd. Decker raised his hands for silence. "As for him I can think of a much tougher fate than jumping off that plate. Let's send him back to the Belt! He's going to need all his heroism to face the miners he ran out on—"

His words were drowned by a shout of approval; hands reached out and hauled Rees from the beam.

Pallis murmured, "Decker, if I thought it would mean anything I'd thank you."

Decker ignored his words. "Well, pilot; will you fly your tree as the Committee request?"

Pallis folded his arms. "I'm a pilot, Decker; not a gaoler."

Decker raised his eyebrows; the scars patterned across his cheeks stretched white. "Of course it's your choice; you're a citizen of the Free Raft. But if you don't take this Science rabble I don't know how we'll manage to keep feeding them." He sighed with mock gravity. "At least on the Belt they might have some chance. Here, though—times are hard, you see. The kindest thing might be to throw them over that edge right now." He regarded Pallis with empty, black eyes. "What do you say, pilot? Shall I give my young friends some real sport?"

Pallis found himself trembling. "You're a bastard, Decker."

Decker laughed softly.

It was time for the Scientists to board the tree. Pallis made one last tour of the rim, checking the supply modules lashed to the shaped wood.

Two Committee men pulled themselves unceremoniously through the foliage, dragging a rope behind them. One of them, young, tall and prematurely bald, nodded to him. "Good shift, pilot."

Pallis watched coldly, not deigning to reply.

The two braced their feet on the branches, spat on their hands, and began to haul on the rope. At length a bundle of filthy cloth was dragged through the foliage. The two men dumped the bundle to one side, then removed the rope and passed it back through the foliage.

The bundle uncurled slowly. Pallis walked over to it.

The bundle was a human, a man bound hand and foot: a Scientist, to judge by the remnants of crimson braid stitched to the ragged robes. He struggled to sit up, rocking his bound arms. Pallis reached down, took the man's collar and hauled him upright. The Scientist looked up with dim gratitude; through matted dirt Pallis made out the face of Cipse, once Chief Navigator.

The Committee men were leaning against the trunk of his tree, evidently waiting for their rope to be attached to the next "passenger." Pallis left Cipse and walked across to them. He took the shoulder of the bald man and, with a vicious pressure, forced the Committee man to face him.

The bald man eyed him uncertainly. "What's the problem, pilot?"

Through clenched teeth Pallis said: "I don't give a damn what happens down there, but on my trees what I say goes. And what I say is that these men are going to board my tree with dignity." He dug his fingers into the other's flesh until cartilage popped.

The bald man squirmed away from his grip. "All right, damn it; we're just doing our job. We don't want any trouble."

Pallis turned his back and returned to Cipse. "Navigator, welcome aboard," he said formally. "I'd be honored if you would share my food."

Cipse's eyes closed and his soft body was wracked by shudders.

Slowly the flight of trees descended into the bowels of the Nebula. Before long the Belt hovered in the sky before them; gloomily Rees studied the chain of battered boxes and piping turning around the fleck of rust that was the star core. Here and there insect-like humans crawled between the cabins, and a cloud of yellowish smoke, emitted by the two foundries, hung about the Belt like a stain in the air.

Numbly he worked at the fire bowls. This was a

nightmare: a grim parody of his hope-filled voyage to the Raft, so many shifts ago. During his rest periods he avoided the other Scientists. They clung to each other in a tight circle around Grye and Cipse, barely talking, doing only what they were told.

These were supposed to be men of intelligence and imagination, Rees thought bitterly; but then, he reflected, their future did not exactly encourage the use of the imagination, and he did not have the heart to blame them for turning away from the world.

His only, slight, pleasure was to spend long hours at the trunk of the tree, staring across the air at the formation which hung a few hundred yards above him. Six trees turned at the corners of an invisible hexagon; the trees were in the same plane and were close enough for their leaves to brush, but such was the skill of the pilots that scarcely a twig was disturbed as they descended through miles of air. And suspended beneath the trees, in a net fixed by six thick ropes, was the boxy form of a supply machine. Rees could see the remnants of Raft deck plates still clinging to the base of the machine.

Even now the flight was a sight that lifted his heart. Humans were capable of such beauty, such great feats . . .

The Belt became a chain of homes and factories. Rees saw half-familiar faces turned up toward their approach like tiny buttons.

Pallis joined him at the trunk. "So it ends like this, young miner," he said gruffly. "I'm sorry."

Rees looked at him in some surprise; the pilot's visage was turned toward the approaching Belt, his scars flaring. "Pallis, you've nothing to be sorry about."

"I'd have done you a kindness if I'd thrown you off when you first stowed away. They'll give you a hard time down there, lad."

Rees shrugged. "But it won't be as hard as for the rest of them." He jabbed a thumb toward the Scientists. "And remember I had a choice. I could have joined the revolution and stayed on the Raft."

Pallis scratched his beard. "I'm not sure I understand why you didn't. The Bones know I've no sympathy with the old system; and the way your people had been kept down must have made you burn."

"Of course it did. But . . . I didn't go to the Raft to throw fuel bombs, tree-pilot. I wanted to learn what was wrong with the world." He smiled. "Modest, wasn't I?"

Pallis lifted his face higher. "You were damn right to try, boy. Those problems you saw haven't gone away."

Rees cast a glance around the red-stained sky. "No, they haven't."

"Don't lose hope," Pallis said firmly. "Old Hollerbach's still working."

Rees laughed. "Hollerbach? They won't shift him. They still need someone to run things in there—find them the repair manuals for the supply machines, maybe try to move the Raft from under the falling star—and besides, I think even Decker's afraid of him . . ."

Now they laughed together. They remained by the trunk for long minutes, watching the Belt approach.

"Pallis, do something for me."

"What?"

"Tell Jaen I asked about her."

The tree pilot rested his massive hand on Rees's shoulder. "Aye, lad. She's safe at present—Hol-

lerbach got her a place on his team of assistants—
and I'll do what I can to make sure she stays that
way."

"Thanks. I—"

"And I'll tell her you asked."

A rope uncurled from the trunk of the tree and
brushed against the Belt's rooftops. Rees was the
first to descend. A miner, half his face ruined by a
massive purple burn, watched him curiously. The
Belt's rotation was carrying him away from the
tree; Rees pulled himself after the trailing rope
and assisted a second Scientist to lower himself to
the rooftops.

Soon a gaggle of Scientists were stumbling
around the Belt after the dangling rope. A cluster
of Belt children followed them, eyes wide in thin
faces.

Rees saw Sheen. His former supervisor hung
from a cabin, one brown foot anchored in rope; she
watched the procession with a broad grin.

Rees let the clumsy parade move on. He worked
his way toward Sheen; fixing his feet in the rope
he straightened up and faced her.

"Well, well," she said softly. "We thought you
were dead."

He studied her. The heat-laden pull of her long
limbs still called uncomfortably; but her face was
gaunt, her eyes lost in pools of shadow. "You've
changed, Sheen."

She spat laughter. "So has the Belt, Rees. We've
seen hard times here."

He narrowed his eyes. Her voice was almost bru-
tal, edged with despair. "If you've the brains I once
believed you had," he snapped, "you'll let me help.
Let me tell you some of what I've learned."

She shook her head. "This isn't a time for knowledge, boy. This is a time to survive." She looked him up and down. "And believe me, you and the rest of your flabby colleagues are going to find that quite tough enough."

The absurd, shambling procession, still following the tree rope, had almost completed an orbit of the Belt.

Rees closed his eyes. If only this mess would all go away; if only he were allowed to get back to his work—

"Rees!" It was Cipse's thin voice. "You've got to help us, man; tell these people who we are . . ."

Rees shook off his despair and pulled himself across the rooftops.

8

The winch mechanism impelled the chair toward the star kernel. Rees closed his eyes, relaxed his muscles and tried to blank out his mind.

To get through the next shift: that was his only priority now. Just one shift at a time . . .

If the exile to the Belt had been a descent into hell for Grye, Cipse and the rest, for Rees it had been the meticulous opening of an old wound. Every detail of the Belt—the shabby cabins, the rain hissing over the surface of the kernel—had crowded into his awareness, and it was as if the intervening thousands of shifts on the Raft had never been.

But in truth he had changed forever. At least before he had had some hope . . . Now there was none.

The chair lurched. The dome of rust rocked beneath his feet and already he could sense the tightening pull of the star's gravity field.

The Belt had changed too, he mused . . . and for the worse. The miners seemed coarsened, brutalized, the Belt itself shabbier and less well maintained. He had learned that deliveries from the Raft had grown less and less frequent. As supplies failed to arrive a vicious circle had set in. Increasing illness and malnutrition and, in the longer term, higher mortality were making it ever harder for the miners to meet their quotas, and without iron to trade even less food could be bought from the Raft—which worsened the miners' conditions still further.

In such a situation, surely something had to give. But what? Even his old acquaintances—like Sheen—were reluctant to talk, as if there was some shameful secret they were hiding. Were the miners making some new arrangements, finding some other, darker, way to break out of the food trap? If so, what?

The wheels of his chair impacted the surface of the star and a full five gees descended on his chest, making him gasp. With a heavy hand he released the cable lock and allowed the chair to roll toward the nearest mine entrance.

"Late again, you feckless bastard." The rumbling voice had issued from the gloom of the mine mouth.

"No, I'm not, Roch; and you know it," Rees said calmly. He brought his chair to a halt at the head of the ramp leading down into the mine.

A chair came whirring up from the gloom. Despite the recent privations the miner Roch was still a huge man. His beard merged with the fur and sweat plastered across his chest; a stomach like a sack slumped over his belt. White showed around his eyes, and when he opened his mouth Rees could see stumps of teeth like burnt bones. "Don't talk back, Raft man." Spittle sprayed his chest in tight parabolae. "What's to stop me putting you all on triple shifts? Eh?"

Rees found the breath escaping from him in a slow sigh. He knew Roch of old. Roch, who you always avoided in the Quartermaster's, whether he was drunk or not. Roch, the half-mad troublemaker who had only been allowed to grow past boyhood, Rees suspected, because of the size of his muscles.

Roch. The obvious choice as the Scientists' shift supervisor.

He was still staring at Rees. "Well? Nothing to say? Eh?"

Rees held his tongue, but the other's fury increased regardless.

"What's the matter, Raftshit? Scared of a little work? Eh? I'll show you the meaning of work . . ." Roch gripped the arms of his chair with fingers like lengths of rope; with separate, massive movements, he hauled his feet off their support plates and planted them on the rust.

"Oh, by the Bones, Roch, you've made your point," Rees protested. "You'll kill yourself—"

"Not me, Raftshit." Now Roch's biceps tightened so that Rees could see the structure of the muscles through the sweat-streaked skin. Slowly, grunting, Roch lifted his bulk from the chair, knees and calves shaking under the load. At last he stood, swaying minutely, arms raised for balance. Five gees hauled at his stomach so that it looked like a sack of mercury slung over his belt; Rees almost cringed as he imagined how the belt must be biting into Roch's flesh.

A grin cracked Roch's purpling face. "Well, Raft man?" Now his tongue protruded from his lips. With slow deliberation he raised his left foot a few inches from the surface and shoved it forward; then the right, then the left again; and so, like a huge, grotesque child, Roch walked on the surface of the star.

Rees watched, not trusting himself to speak.

At length Roch was satisfied. He grabbed the chair arms and lowered himself into the seat. He stared at Rees challengingly, his humor apparently restored by his feat. "Well, come on, Raftshit, there's work to do. Eh?"

And he turned his chair and led the way into the interior of the star.

Most of the Scientists' work assignments were inside the star mine. For some imagined misdemeanor Roch had long since put them all on double shift. They were allowed an hour's break between shifts—even Roch had not denied them that yet—and when the break came Rees met Cipse beneath the glow of a globe lamp.

The Scientists sat in companionable silence for a while. They were in one of the porous kernel's larger chambers; lamps were scattered over its roof like trapped stars, casting light over piles of worked metal and the sullen forms of Moles.

The Navigator looked like a pool of fat in his wheelchair, his small features and short, weak limbs mere addenda to his crushed bulk. Rees, with some effort, helped him raise a tube of water to his lips. The Navigator dribbled; the water scattered over the ruin of his coverall and droplets hit the iron floor like bullets. Cipse smiled apologetically. "I'm sorry," he said, wheezing.

Rees shook his head. "Don't worry about it."

"You know," Cipse said at length, "the physical conditions down here are poor enough; but what makes it unendurable is . . . the sheer boredom."

Rees nodded. "There has never been much to do save supervise the Moles. They can make their own decisions, mostly, with occasional human intervention. Frankly, though, one or two experienced miners can run the whole kernel. There's no need for so many of us to be down here. It's just Roch's petty way of hurting us."

"Not so petty." Cipse's breath seemed to be

labored; his words were punctuated by pauses. "I'm quite concerned about the ... health of some of the others, you know. And I suspect ... suspect that we would actually be of more use in some other role."

Rees grimaced. "Of course. But try telling Roch."

"You know I've no wish to appear insulting, Rees, but you clearly have more in ... common with these people than the ... the rest of us." He coughed and clutched his chest. "After all, you are one of them. Can't you ... say something?"

Rees laughed softly. "Cipse, I ran out of here, remember. They hate me more than the rest of you. Look, things will get better, I'm sure of that; the miners aren't barbarians. They're just angry. We must be patient."

Cipse fell silent, his breath shallow.

Rees stared at the Navigator in the dim light. Cipse's round face was white and slick with sweat. "You say you're concerned about the well-being of the others, Navigator, but what about yourself?"

Cipse massaged the flesh of his chest. "I can't admit to feeling wonderful," he wheezed. "Of course, just the fact of our presence down here—in this gravity field—places a terrible strain on our hearts. Human beings weren't designed, it seems, to function in ... such conditions."

"How are you feeling? Do you have any specific pain?"

"Don't fuss, boy," Cipse snapped with the ghost of his old tetchiness. "I'm perfectly all right. And I am the most senior of us, you know. The others ... rely on me ..." His words were lost in a fit of coughing.

"I'm sorry," Rees said carefully. "You're the best judge, of course. But—ah—since your well-being is so vital to our morale, let me help you, for this one shift. Just stay here; I think I can handle the work of both of us. And I can keep Roch occupied. I'm afraid there's no way he'll let you off the star before the end of the shift, but perhaps if you sit still—try to sleep even—"

Cipse thought it over, then said weakly, "Yes. It would feel rather good to sleep." He closed his eyes. "Perhaps that would be for the best. Thank you, Rees . . ."

"No, I don't know what's wrong with him," Rees said. "You're the one with bio training, Grye. He hardly woke up when it came time to return him to the surface. Maybe his heart can't stand up to the gravity down there. But what do I know?"

Cipse lay strapped loosely to a pallet, his face a bowl of perspiration. Grye hovered over the still form of the Navigator, his hands fluttering against each other. "I don't know; I really don't know," he repeated.

The four other Scientists of the group formed an anxious backdrop. The tiny cabin to which they'd all been assigned seemed to Rees a cage of fear and helplessness. "Just think it through," he said, exasperated. "What would Hollerbach do if he were here?"

Grye drew in his stomach pompously and glowered up at Rees. "May I point out that Hollerbach isn't here? And furthermore, on the Raft we had access to dispensers of the finest drugs—as well as the Ship's medical records. Here we have nothing, not even full rations—"

"Nothing except yourselves!" Rees snapped.

A circle of round, grime-streaked faces stared at him, apparently hurt.

Rees sighed. "I'm sorry," he said. "Look, Grye,

there's nothing I can suggest. You must have learned something in all the years you worked with those records. You'll simply have to do what you think best."

Grye frowned, and for long seconds studied Cipse's recumbent form; then he began to loosen the Navigator's clothing.

Rees turned away. With his duty fulfilled claustrophobia swiftly descended on him, and he pushed his way out of the cabin.

He prowled the confines of the Belt. He met few people: it was approaching mid-shift and most Belt folk must be at work or in their cabins. Rees breathed lungfuls of Nebula air and gloomily studied the over-familiar details of the little colony's construction: the battered cabins, walls scarred by generations of passing hands and feet, the gaping nozzles of the roof jets.

A breeze brought him a distant scent of wood, and he looked up. Hanging in the sky in tight formation was the flight of trees which had brought him here from the Raft. The bulk of the supply machine was still slung between them, and Rees made out Pallis's overseer tree hovering in the background. The elegant trees, the faint foliage scent, the figures clambering through the branches: the airy spectacle was quite beautiful, and it brought home to Rees with a sudden, sharp impact the magnitude of what he had lost in returning here.

The rotation of the Belt swept the formation over a horizon of cabins. Rees turned away.

He came to the Quartermaster's. Now the smell of stale alcohol filled his head and on impulse he slid into the bar's gloomy interior. Maybe a couple of shots of something tough would help his mood; relax him enough to get the sleep he needed—

The barman, Jame, was rinsing drink bowls in a bag of grimy water. He scowled through his gray-tinged beard. "I've told you before," he growled. "I don't serve Raft shite in here."

Rees hid his anger under a grin. He glanced around the bar; it was empty save for a small man with a spectacular burn scar covering one complete forearm. "Looks like you don't serve anyone else either," Rees snapped.

Jame grunted. "Don't you know? This shift they're finally going to offload that supply machine from the trees; that's where all the able bodies are. Work to do, see—not like you feckless Raft shite—"

Rees felt his anger uncoil. "Come on, Jame. I was born here. You know that."

"And you chose to leave. Once a Rafter, always a Rafter."

"Jame, it's a small Nebula," Rees snapped. "I've seen enough to teach me that much at least. And we're all humans in it together, Belt and Raft alike—"

But Jame had turned his back.

Rees, irritated, left the bar. It had been—how long? a score of shifts?—since their arrival at the Belt, and the miners had only just worked out how to unship the supply device. And he, Rees, with experience of tree flight and of Belt conditions, hadn't even been told they were doing it . . .

He anchored his toes in the wall of the Quartermaster's and stretched to his full height, peering at the formation of trees beyond the far side of the Belt. Now that he looked more carefully he could see there were many people clinging awkwardly to the branches. Men swarmed over the net containing the supply device, dwarfed by its ragged bulk; they tied ropes around it and threw out lengths that uncoiled toward the Belt.

At last a loose web of rope trailed from the machine. Tiny shouts crossed the air; Rees could see the pilots standing beside the trunks of the great trees, and now billows of smoke bloomed above the canopies. With massive grandeur the trees' rotation slowed and they began to inch toward the Belt. The coordination was skillful; Rees could see how the supply machine barely rocked through the air.

The actual transfer to the Belt would surely be the most difficult part. Perhaps the formation would move to match the Belt's rotation, so that the dangling ropes could be hauled in until the machine settled as a new component of the chain of buildings. Presumably that was how much of the Belt had been constructed—though generations ago ...

One tree dropped a little too fast. The machine rocked. Workers cried out, clinging to the nets. Tree-pilots called and waved their arms. Slowly the smoke over the offending tree thickened and the formation's motion slowed.

Damn it, thought Rees furiously, he should be up there! He was still strong and able despite the poor rations and back-crushing work—

With a distant, slow rip, the net parted.

Rees, wrapped in introspective anger, took a second to perceive the meaning of what he saw. Then all of his being seemed to lock on that small point in the sky.

The pilots worked desperately, but the net became a mist of shreds and tatters; the formation dissolved in slow lurches of wood and smoke. Men wriggled in the air, rapidly drifting apart. The supply machine, freed of its constraints, hovered as if uncertain what to do. One man, Rees saw, was still clinging to the side of the machine itself.

The machine began to fall; soon it was sailing toward the Belt in a slow curve.

Rees dropped to hands and knees and clung tightly to the Belt cables. Where was the damn thing headed? The gravity fields of both star kernel and Nebula Core were hauling at the machine; the Core field was by far the most powerful, but was the machine close enough to the star for the latter to predominate?

The machine could pass through the structure of the Belt like a fist through wet paper.

The immediate loss of life would be enormous, of course; and within minutes the Belt, its integrity gone, would be torn apart by its own spin. A ring-shaped cloud of cabins, trailing pipes, rope fragments and squirming people would disperse until at last each survivor would be alone in the air, facing the ultimate fall into the Core . . .

Or, Rees's insistent imagination demanded, what if the machine missed the Belt but went on to impact the star kernel? He recalled the craters left even by raindrops at the base of a five-gee gravity well; what would the roaring tons of the supply machine do? He imagined a great splash of molten iron which would spray out over the Belt and its occupants. Perhaps the integrity of the star itself would be breached . . .

The tumbling supply machine loomed over him; he stared up, fascinated. He made out details of dispenser nozzles and input keyboards, and he was reminded incongruously of more orderly times, of queuing for supplies at the Rim of the Raft. Now he saw the man who still clung to the machine's ragged wall. He was dark-haired and long-boned and he seemed quite calm. For a moment his eyes locked with Rees's, and then the slow rotation of the machine took him from Rees's view.

The machine grew until it seemed close enough to touch.

Then, with heart-stopping slowness, it slid sideways. The great bulk whooshed by a dozen yards from the closest point of the Belt. As it neared the star kernel its trajectory curved sharply, and then it was hurled away, still tumbling.

Its human occupant a mote on its flank, its path slowly arcing downwards toward the Core, the machine dwindled into infinity.

Above Rees the six scattered trees began to converge. With shouted calls ropes were thrown to workers still stranded in the air.

As fear of a spectacular death faded, Rees began to experience the loss of the machine as an almost physical pain. Yet another fragment of man's tiny heritage lost through stupidity and blundering ... And with every piece gone their chances of surviving the next few generations were surely shrinking even further.

Then he recalled what Pallis had told him of Decker's calculations. The revolution's subtle leader-to-be had hinted darkly that he had no fear of a loss of economic power over the Belt despite the planned gift of a supply machine. Was it possible that this act had been deliberate? Had lives been wasted, an irreplaceable device hurled away, all for some short-term political advantage?

Rees felt as if he were suspended over a void, as if he were one of the unfortunates lost in the catastrophe; but the depths were composed not of air but of the baseness of human nature.

At the start of the next shift Cipse was too weak to be moved; so Rees agreed with Grye and the rest that he should be left undisturbed in the Belt. When Rees reached the surface of the star kernel he told Roch the situation. He kept his words factual, his tone meek and apologetic. Roch glowered, thick eyebrows knotting, but he said nothing, and Rees made his way into the depths of the star.

At mid-shift he rode back to the surface for a break—and was met by the sight of Cipse. The Navigator was wrapped in a grimy blanket and was weakly reaching for the controls of a wheelchair.

Rees rattled painfully over the star's tiny hills to Cipse. He reached out and laid a hand as gently as possible on the Scientist's arm. "Cipse, what the hell's going on? You're ill, damn it; you were supposed to stay in the Belt."

Cipse turned his eyes to Rees; he smiled, his face a bloodless white. "I didn't get a lot of choice, I'm afraid, my young friend."

"Roch . . ."

"Yes." Cipse closed his eyes, still fumbling for the controls of his chair.

"You got something to say about it, Raftshit?"

Rees turned his chair. Roch faced him, his corrupted mouth spread into a grin.

Rees tried to compute a way through this—to search for a lever that might influence this gross man and save his companion—but his rationality dissolved in a tide of rage. "You bastard, Roch," he hissed. "You're murdering us. And yet you're not as guilty as the folk up there who are letting you do it."

Roch assumed an expression of mock surprise. "You're not happy, Raftshit? Well, I'll tell you what—" He hauled himself to his feet. Face purpling, massive fists bunched, he grinned at Rees. "Why don't you do something about it? Come on. Get out of that chair and face me, right now. And if you can put me down—why, then, you can tuck your little friend up again."

Rees closed his eyes. Oh, by the Bones— "Don't listen to him, Rees."

"I'm afraid it's too late, Cipse," he whispered. He gripped the arms of his chair and tensed his back experimentally. "After what I was stupid enough to say he's not going to let me off this star alive. At least this way you have a chance—"

He lifted his left foot from its supporting platform; it felt as if a cage of iron were strapped to his leg. Now the right . . .

And, without giving himself time to think about it, with a single, vein-bursting heave he pushed himself out of his chair.

Pain lapped in great sheets over the muscles of his thighs, calves and back. For a terrible instant he thought he was going to topple forward, to smash face-down into the iron. Then he was stable. His breathing was shallow and he could feel his heart rattle in its cage of bones; it was as if he bore a huge, invisible weight strapped to his back.

He looked up and faced Roch, tried to force a grin onto his swollen face.

"Another attempt at self-sacrifice, Rees?" Cipse said softly. "Godspeed, my friend."

Roch's smile seemed easy, as if the five gees were no more than a heavy garment. Now he lifted one massive leg, forced it through the air and drove his foot into the rust. Another step, and another; at last he was less than a yard from Rees, close enough for Rees to smell the sourness of his breath. Then, grunting with the effort, he lifted one huge fist.

Rees tried to lift his arms over his head, but it was as if they were bound to his sides by massive ropes. He closed his eyes. For some reason a vision of the young, white stars at the fringe of the Nebula came to him; and his fear dissolved.

A shadow crossed his face.

He opened his eyes. He saw red sky—and pain lanced through his skull.

But he was alive, and the loading of the star's five gees had gone. There was a cool surface at his back and neck; he ran his hands over it and felt the gritty surface of an iron plate. The plate juddered beneath him; his stomach tightened and he gagged, dry. His mouth was sour, his tongue like a piece of wood, and he wondered how long he had lain unconscious.

Cautiously he propped himself on one elbow. The plate was about ten feet on a side; over it had been cast a rough net to which he was tethered by a rope around his waist. A pile of roughly cut iron was fixed near the center of the plate. The plate had one other occupant: the barman, Jame, who regarded Rees incuriously as he chewed on a piece of old-looking meat-sim. "You're awake, then," he said. "I thought Roch had bust your skull wide open; you've been out for hours."

Rees stared at him; then the plate gave another shudder. Rees sat up, testing the gravity—it was tiny and wavering—and looked around.

The Belt hung in the air perhaps half a mile away, surrounding its star kernel like a crude bracelet around a child's wrist.

So he was flying. On a metal plate? Vertigo swept through him and he wrapped his fingers in the net.

At length he made his way slowly to the edge of the plate, ducked his head to the underside. He saw four jet nozzles fixed at the corners of the plate, the small drive boxes obviously taken from

Belt rooftops. Occasionally, in response to tugs by Jame on control strings, the nozzles would spout steam and the plate would kick through the air.

So the miners had invented flying machines while he had been gone. Why, he wondered, did they need them all of a sudden?

He straightened up and sat once more facing Jame. Now the barman was sucking water from a globe; at first he acted as if unaware of Rees, but at length, with a hint of pity on his broad, bearded features, he passed Rees the globe.

Rees allowed the water to pour over his tongue, slide down his parched throat. He passed the globe back. "Come on, Jame. Tell me what's going on. What happened to Cipse?"

"Who?"

"The Nav—The Scientist. The ill one."

Jame looked blank. "One of them died down there. Heart packed up, I heard. A fat old guy. Is that who you mean?"

Rees sighed. "Yes, Jame; that's who I mean."

Jame studied him; then he pulled a bottle from his waistband, unstopped it and took a deep draught.

"Jame, why aren't I dead also?"

"You should be. Roch thought he had killed you; that's why he didn't hit you any more. He had you hauled up and brought to the damn Quartermaster's—can you believe it?—and then you started to groan a bit, move around. Roch was all for finishing you off there and then, but I told him, 'Not in my bar, you don't' . . . Then Sheen showed up."

Something like hope spread through Rees. "Sheen?"

"She knew I was due to leave on this ferry so I guess that gave her the idea to get you off the Belt." Jame's eyes slid past Rees. "Sheen is a decent woman. Maybe this was the only way she could think of to save you. But I'll tell you, Roch was happy enough to send you out here. A slower, painful death for you; that's what he thought he was settling for . . ."

"What? Where are you taking me?" Rees, confused, questioned Jame further; but the barman lapsed into silence, nursing his bottle.

Under Jame's direction the little craft descended into the Nebula. The atmosphere became thicker, warmer, harder to breathe; it was like the air in a too-enclosed room. The Nebula grew dark; the enfeebled stars shone brightly against the gloom. Rees spent long hours at the lip of the plate, staring into the abyss below. In the darkness at the very heart of the Nebula Rees fancied he could see all the way to the Core, as if he were back in the Observatory.

There was no way of telling the time; Rees estimated several shifts had passed before Jame said abruptly, "You mustn't judge us, you know."

Rees looked up. "What?"

Jame was nursing a half-finished bottle; he lay awkwardly against the plate, eyes misty with drink. "We all have to survive. Right? And when the shipments of supplies from the Raft dried up, there was only one place to go for food . . ." He thumped his bottle against the plate and fixed Rees with a stare. "I opposed it, I can tell you. I said it was better that we should die than trade with such people. But it was a group decision. And I accept it." He waggled a finger at Rees. "It was the choice of all of us, and I accept my share of the responsibility."

Rees stared, baffled, and Jame seemed to sober a little. Then surprise, even wonder, spread across the barman's face. "You don't know what I'm talking about, do you?"

"Jame, I haven't the faintest idea. Nobody told us exiles a damn thing—"

Jame half-laughed, scratching his head. Then he glanced around the sky, picking out a few of the brighter stars, clearly judging the plate's position. "Well, you'll find out soon enough. We're nearly there. Take a look, Rees. Below us, to my right somewhere—"

Rees turned onto his belly and thrust his face below the plate. At first he could see nothing in the direction Jame had indicated—then, squinting, he made out a small, dark speck of matter.

The hours wore on. Jame carefully adjusted the thrust from the jets. The speck grew to a ball the color of dried blood. At length Rees made out human figures standing on or crawling over all sides of the ball, as if glued there; judging from their size the sphere must have been perhaps thirty yards wide.

Jame joined him. With absent-minded companionship he passed Rees his bottle. "Here. Now, look, boy; what you have to remember if you want to last here more than a half-shift is that these are human beings just like you and me . . ."

They were nearing the surface now. The sphere-world was quite crowded with people, adults and children; they went naked, or wore ragged tunics, and were uniformly short, squat and well-muscled. One man stood under their little craft, watching their approach.

The surface of the worldlet was composed of sheets of something like dried cloth. Hair sprouted from it here and there. In one place the sheets were ripped, exposing the interior structure of the worldlet.

Rees saw the white of bone.

He took a shuddering pull at Jame's bottle.

The man below raised his head; his eyes met Rees's, and the Boney raised his arms as if in welcome.

9

Jame brought the plate to a smooth landing on the crackling surface of the worldlet. Silently he set to work unlashing the batches of iron from the net.

Rees clung to the net and stared wildly around. The cramped horizon was made up of sheets of hairy, brownish material, stirring sluggishly. Again Rees saw the white of bone protruding through breaks in the surface.

He felt his bladder loosen. He closed his eyes and clamped down. Come on, Rees; you've faced greater perils than this, more immediate dangers . . .

But the Boneys were a myth from his childhood, sleep-time monsters to frighten recalcitrant children. Surely, in a universe which contained the calm, machined interior of the Bridge, there was no room for such ugliness?

"Welcome," a high, dry voice said. "So you've yet another guest for us, Jame?" The man Rees had seen from the air was standing over the plate now, accepting an armful of iron from Jame. A few conventional-looking food packages were stacked at the man's feet. Briskly Jame bundled them onto the plate and fixed them to the net.

The Boney was squat and barrel-chested, his

head a wrinkled, hairless globe. He was dressed in a crudely cut sheet of surface material. He grinned and Rees saw that his cavernous mouth was totally without teeth. "What's the matter, boy? Aren't you going to give old Quid a hand?"

Rees found his fingers tightening about the strands of the net. Jame stood over him with a package of iron. "Come on, lad. Take this stuff and get off the plate. You haven't any choice, you know. And if you show you're afraid it will go the worse for you."

Rees felt a whimper rising in his throat; it was as if all the revolting speculation he had ever heard about the Boneys' way of life had returned to unman him.

He clamped his lips together. Damn it, he was a Scientist Second Class. He summoned up the steady, tired gaze of Hollerbach. He would come through this. He had to.

He untwined his fingers from the netting and stood up, forcing the rational half of his mind to work. He felt heavy, sluggish; the gravity was perhaps one and a half gee. So the mass of the little planet must have been—what? Thirty tons?

He took the iron and, without hesitation, stepped off the plate and onto the surface. His feet sank a few inches into the stuff. It was soft, like a coarse cloth, and covered with hair strands which scratched his ankles; and, oh, god, it was warm, like the hide of some huge animal—

Or human.

Now, to his horror, his bladder released; dampness slid down his legs.

Quid opened his toothless mouth and roared with laughter.

Jame, from the security of the plate, said: "There's no shame, lad. Remember that."

162

The strange trade was over, and Jamie worked his controls. With a puff of hot steam the plate lifted, leaving four charred craters in the soft surface. Within a few seconds the plate had dwindled into a fist-sized toy in the air.

Rees dropped his eyes. His urine had formed a pool about his feet and was seeping into the surface.

Quid stepped toward him, his footsteps crunching. "You're a Boney now, lad! Welcome to the arsehole of the Nebula." He gestured to the puddle at Rees's feet. "And I wouldn't worry about that." He grinned and licked his lips. "You'll be glad of it when you're a bit thirstier . . ."

Foul speculations ran through Rees's mind; he shuddered, but kept his gaze steady on Quid. "What do I do now?"

Again Quid laughed. "Well, that's up to you. Stand here and wait for a ride that will never come. Or follow me." He winked and, the iron under his arm, strode away across the yielding surface.

Rees stood there for a few seconds, reluctant to leave even the faint shadow of his link with the world away from this place. But he really had no option; this grotesque character was his only fixed point.

Shifting the weight of iron in his arms he stepped cautiously across the hot, uneven ground.

They walked about halfway round the worldlet's circumference. They passed crude shacks scattered in random patterns over the surface; most of the buildings were simple tents of surface material, barely enough to keep out the rain, but others were more substantial, based, Rees saw, on iron frames.

Quid laughed. "Impressed, miner? We're coming

up in society, aren't we? See, they all used to shun us. The Raft, the miners, everybody. Much too proud to associate with the likes of the Boneys, after the 'crime' we commit to live . . . But now the stars are going out. Eh, miner? Suddenly they're all struggling to survive; and suddenly they're learning the lessons we learned, all those thousands of shifts ago." He leaned closer to Rees and winked again. "It's all trade, you see. For a bit of iron, a few luxuries, we fill the miners' empty food pods. As long as they get a nicely packaged pod they don't have to think too hard about what's in it. Am I right?" And he laughed again, spraying Rees's face with spittle.

Rees shrank away, unable to speak.

A few children emerged from the huts to stare at Rees, their faces dull, their naked bodies squat and filthy. The adults barely registered his passing; they sat in tight circles in their huts, chanting a low, haunting song. Rees could not make out words but the melody was cyclic and compelling.

Quid said, "So sorry if we seem antisocial. There's a whale in the Coreward sky, see; soon we'll be singing him close." Quid's eyes grew dreamy and he licked his lips.

Skirting a particularly shabby hut Rees's foot broke through the surface. He found himself ankle-deep in foul, stinking waste. With a cry he backed away and began rubbing his feet against a cleaner section of surface.

Quid roared with laughter.

From within the hut a voice told him, "Don't worry. You'll get used to it."

Rees glanced up, startled by the voice's familiarity. Forgetting the filth he stepped closer to the gloom of the hut, peered inside. A man sat alone. He was short and blond, and his frame was gaunt and wrapped in the remnants of a tunic. His face was obscured by a tangle of beard—"Gord. Is it you?"

The man who had once been the Belt's chief engineer nodded ruefully. "Hello, Rees. I can't say I expected to see you. I thought you'd stowed away to the Raft."

Rees glanced around; Quid seemed prepared to wait for him, evidently highly amused. Rees squatted down and briefly outlined his story. Gord nodded sympathetically. His eyes were bloodshot and seemed to loom out of the darkness.

"But what are you doing here?"

Gord shrugged. "One foundry implosion too many. One death too many. Finally they decided it was all my fault and sent me down here . . . There are quite a few of us Belters here, you know. At least, quite a few have been brought here . . . Times have worsened since you escaped. A few thousand shifts ago exiling someone down here would have been unthinkable. We barely acknowledged the existence of the place; until we started trading I wasn't even sure the damn Boneys existed." He reached for a globe of some liquid; he raised it to his lips, suppressing a shudder as he drank.

Rees, watching him, became abruptly aware of his own powerful thirst.

Gord lowered the globe and wiped his lips. "But I'll tell you, in a way I was glad when they finally found me guilty." His eyes were red. "I was so sick of it, you see; the deaths, the stink of burning, the struggle to rebuild walls that couldn't even support themselves—" He dropped his eyes. "You see, Rees, those of us who are sent here have earned what's happening to us. It's a judgment."

"I'll never believe that," Rees murmured.

Gord laughed; it was a ghastly, dry sound. "Well,

you'd better." He held out his globe. "Here. Are you thirsty?"

Rees stared at it with longing, imagining the cool trickle of water over his tongue—but then speculations about the origin of the liquid filled him with disgust, and he pushed it away, shaking his head.

Gord, eyes locked on Rees's, took another deep draught. "Let me give you some advice," he said softly. "They're not killers here. They won't harm you. But you have a stark choice. You either accept their ways—eat what they eat, drink what they drink—or you'll finish in the ovens. That's the way it is.

"You see, in some ways it makes sense. Nothing is wasted." He laughed, then fell silent.

An eerie, discordant song floated into the hut. "Quid said something about singing to the whales," Rees said, eyes wide. "Could that be—"

Gord nodded. "The legends are true ... and quite a sight to see. Maybe you'll understand it better than I do. It makes a kind of sense. They need some input of food from outside, don't they? Something to keep this world from devouring itself to skin and bones—although the native life of the Nebula isn't all that nutritious, and there are a few interesting bugs you can catch—I suspect that's the reason the original Boneys weren't allowed to return to the Raft ..."

"Come on, lad," Quid called, shifting the load of iron under his arm.

Rees looked at him, then back to Gord. The temptation to stay with Gord, with at least a reminder of the past, was strong ... Gord dropped his head to his chest, words still dribbling from his mouth. "You'd better go," he mumbled.

If Rees wanted any hope of escaping this place there was only one choice.

Wordlessly he gripped Gord's shoulder. The engineer did not look up. Rees got to his feet and walked out of the hut.

Quid's home was comparatively spacious, constructed around a framework of iron poles. There were no windows, but panels of scraped-thin skin admitted a sickly brown light.

Quid let Rees stay; Rees settled cautiously into one dark corner, his back against the wall. But Quid barely spoke to him and, at length, after a meal of some nameless meat, the Boney threw himself to the floor and settled into a comfortable sleep.

Rees sat for some hours, eyes wide; the eerie keening of the whale-singers washed around him in a tapestry of sound, and he shrank into himself, as if to escape the strangeness of it all. At last fatigue crept over him and he lowered himself to the ground. He rested his face on his folded forearm. The surface was so warm that he had no need for a blanket and he settled into a broken sleep.

Quid, ignoring Rees, came and went on his mysterious errands. He lived alone, but—to judge from the visits he made to his neighbors' tents bearing packets of iron, and from which he would return adjusting his clothing and wiping his mouth—his iron was buying him out of loneliness.

At first Rees suspected Quid was some kind of leader here, but it soon became apparent that there was little in the way of a formal structure. Some of the Boneys had fairly well-defined roles—for example, Quid was the principal interface with the visitors from the mine. But the hideous ecology seemed largely self-sustaining, and there was little need for organized maintenance. Only the whale hunts, it seemed, brought the population together in any sort of cooperation.

Rees stayed in his corner for perhaps two shifts. Then his thirst became an unbearable pain, and with a cracked voice he asked Quid for drink.

The Boney laughed—but, instead of reaching for one of his stock of drink globes, he beckoned to Rees and left the hut.

Rees climbed stiffly to his feet and followed.

They walked around a quarter of the worldlet's circumference and came to a break in the skin surface. It was a ragged hole perhaps a yard wide, looking disturbingly like a dried-out wound. Splinters of bone obtruded from its lip.

Quid squatted by the hole. "So you want a drink, miner?" he demanded, his mouth a downturned slash of darkness. "Well, old Quid's going to show you how you can get as much as you like to eat and drink . . . but the catch is, it's what the rest of us eat and drink. It's either that or starve, laddie; and Quid for one isn't going to mourn the loss of your sneering face from his hut. Right?" And he dropped his feet through the hole and swung himself into the planet's interior.

Fear stirring—but his throat still burning with thirst—Rees approached the hole and peered inside.

The hole was full of bones. A stench like warm meat-sim billowed into his face.

He gagged but held his ground. Shaking his head free of the fumes he sat on the ragged lip of the hole and found purchase for his feet. He stood carefully, holding his breath, and worked his way down into the network of bones.

It was like climbing inside some huge, ancient corpse.

The light, filtering through thick layers of skin, was brown and uncertain. The bright eyes of Quid glittered out of the gloom.

And all around Rees there were bones.

He looked around, his breath still trapped inside his body. He was, he realized, standing on a shelf of bones; his back rested against a small mountain of skulls and gaping, toothless jawbones, and his hands gripped a pillar of fused vertebrae. Starlight slanting through the entrance showed him a cross section of skulls, splintered tibiae and fibulae, ribcages like lightless lanterns; here was a forearm still attached to a child's hand. The bones were mostly bare, their color a weathered-looking brown or yellow; but here and there scraps of skin or hair still clung.

The planet was nothing more than a sparse cage of bones, coated with human skin.

He felt a scream well up from deep within him; he forced it away and expelled his breath in one great sigh, then was forced to draw in the air of this foul place. It was hot, damp and stank of decaying meat.

Quid grinned at him, his gums glistening. "Come on, miner," he whispered, the sound muffled. "We've a little way to go yet." And he began to work his way deeper into the interior.

After some minutes Rees followed.

The gravity grew lighter as they descended and a smaller residuum of corpses lay beneath them; at last Rees was pulling himself through the bone framework in virtual weightlessness. Bone fragments, splinters and knuckles and finger joints, battered at his face until it seemed he was passing through a cloud of decay. As they descended the light grew fainter, lost in the intermeshing layers of bones, but Rees's eyes grew dark-adapted, so that it seemed he could see more and more of the dismal surroundings. The heat, the stench of meat became intolerable. Sweat coated his body, turning his tunic into a sodden mass on his back, and his breath grew shallow and labored; it seemed almost impossible to extract any oxygen from the grimy air.

He tried to remember that the radius of the worldlet was only some fifteen yards. The journey seemed the longest of his life.

At last they reached the heart of the bone world. In the gloom Rees squinted to make out Quid. The Boney waited for him, hands on hips; he was standing on some dark mass. Quid laughed. "Welcome," he hissed. He was running his fingers over the forest of bones around him, evidently looking for something.

Rees pushed his feet through a last layer of ribs to the surface on which Quid stood. It was metal, he realized with a shock; battered and coated with grease, but metal nevertheless. He stood cautiously. There was a respectable gravity pull. This had to be some kind of artefact, buried here at the heart of the Boneys' foul colony.

He dropped to his knees and ran probing fingers across the surface. It was too dark to make out a color but he could tell that the stuff wasn't iron. Could it be Ship hull-metal, like the Raft deck in the region of the Officers' quarters? He closed his eyes and probed at the surface, trying to recall the feel of that faraway deck. Yes, he decided with growing excitement; this had to be an artefact from the Ship.

Pushing his way through the bone framework he paced around the surface. The artefact was a cube some three yards on a side. He stubbed his toe against an extrusion of metal; it turned out to be the remnant of some kind of fin, reminiscent of the stumps he had observed on the Moles of the mine and the Raft's buses. Could this box once have been fitted with jets and flown through the air?

Speculation welled through his head, pushing aside thirst, revulsion, fear ... He imagined the original Ship, huge, dark and crippled, opening like a skitter flower and emitting a shoal of subships. There was the Bridge, its surface slick and fast; there were the buses/Moles, perhaps designed to carry one or two crew or to travel unmanned, to land and roll over uncertain surfaces—and then there was this new type, a box capable of carrying—perhaps—a dozen people. He imagined crewmen setting off in this bulky craft, maybe seeking food, or a way to return to Bolder's Ring ...

But some unknowable accident had hit the box ship. It had been unable to return to the Ship. They had run out of provisions—and to survive, the crew had had to resort to other means.

When at last they had managed to return—or perhaps had been found by a rescue party—they were, in the eyes of their fellows, befouled by their taking of the meat of Nebula creatures—and of their companions.

And so they had been abandoned.

Somehow they had wrestled their wrecked box ship into a stable circular orbit around the Core. And some of them had survived; they had raised children and lived perhaps thousands of shifts before their eyes closed ... And the children, horrified, had found there was no way of ejecting the corpses; in this billion-gee environment the ship's escape velocity was simply too high.

And generations had passed, until the layers of bones covered the original wreck.

Evidently Quid had found what he was looking for. He tugged at Rees's sleeve, and Rees followed him to the far edge of the craft. Quid knelt and pointed downwards; Rees followed suit and peered over the lip of the craft. In the wall below him there was a break, and just enough light seeped in to let Rees make out the contents of the craft.

At first he could make no sense of it. The ship was jammed with cylindrical bundles of some glistening, red substance; some of the bundles were linked to each other by joints, while others were fixed in rough piles to the walls by ropes. Some of the material had been baked to a gray-black crisp. There was a stench of decay, of ageing meat.

Rees stared, bemused. Then, in one "bundle," he saw eyesockets.

Quid's face floated in the gloom, a tormenting mask of wrinkles. "We're not animals, you see, miner," he whispered. "These are the ovens. Where we bake the sickness out of the meat ... Usually it's hot enough down here, what with the decay and all; but sometimes we have to bank fires around the walls ..."

The bodies were all ages and sizes; flayed and butchered, the "bundles" were limbs, torsos, heads and fingers—

He dragged his head back. Quid was grinning. Rees closed his eyes, forcing down the bile that burned the back of his throat. "And there's no waste," Quid whispered with relish. "The dried skin is stitched into the surface, so that we walk on the flesh of our ancestors—"

He felt as if the whole, grotesque worldlet were pulsing around him, so that the forest of bones encroached and receded in huge waves. He took deep breaths, letting the air whistle through his nostrils. "You brought me down here for drink," he said as evenly as he could. "Where is it?"

Quid led Rees to a formation of bone. It was a

set of vertebrae, almost intact; Rees saw that it was part of a branching series of bones which seemed to reach almost to the surface. Quid touched the spine and his finger came away glistening with moisture. Rees looked more closely and realized that a slow trickle of fluid was working its way down the channel of bones.

Quid pressed his face to the vertebrae, extending a long tongue to lap at the liquid. "Runoff from the surface, see," he said. "By the time it's diluted by the odd bit of rain and filtered through all those layers up there, it's fit enough to drink. Almost tasty . . ." He laughed, and with a grotesque flourish invited Rees to take his turn.

Rees stared at the brackish stuff, feeling life and death choices once more weighing on him. He tried to be analytical. Perhaps the Boney was right; perhaps the crude filtering mechanism above his head would remove much of the worst substances . . . After all, the Boney was healthy enough to tell him about it.

He sighed. If he wanted to survive through more than another shift or two he really had no choice.

He stepped forward, extended his tongue until it almost touched the vertebrae, and allowed the liquid to trickle into his mouth. The taste of it was foul and the stuff was almost impossible to swallow; but swallow it he did, and he reached for another mouthful.

Quid laughed. The Boney's angular hand clamped over the back of his neck and Rees's face was forced into the slim pillar of bone; the edges of it scraped at his flesh and the putrid liquid splashed over his hair, his eyes—

With a cry of disgust Rees lashed out with both fists. He felt them connect with perspiring flesh; with a winded grunt the Boney fell away, landing amid a splintering nest of bones. Wiping his face clear Rees jumped into the network of bones and began to clamber up toward the light, his thrusting feet crushing ribs and skeletal fingers. At last he reached the underside of the surface, but he realized with dismay that he had lost his orientation; the surface of skin spread over him like some huge ceiling, unbroken and lightless. With a strangled scream he shoved his hands into the soft material and tore layers of it aside.

At last he broke through to Nebula air.

He dragged himself from the hole and lay exhausted, staring up at the ruddy starlight.

Rees sought out Gord. The former engineer admitted him without a word, and Rees threw himself to the ground and fell into a deep sleep.

Over the ensuing shifts he stayed with Gord, largely in silence. Rees forced himself to drink—even accompanying Gord on a trip into the interior of the worldlet to fill fresh globes—but he could not eat. Gord gloomily studied him in the darkness of the cabin. "Don't think about it," he said. He dropped a fragment of meat into his mouth, chewed the tough stuff and swallowed it. "See? It's just meat. And it's that or die."

Rees let a slice of meat lie in the palm of his hand, visualizing the actions of raising it to his lips, biting into it, swallowing it.

He couldn't do it. He threw the fragment into a corner of the hut and turned away. After a while he heard the slow footsteps of Gord as the engineer crossed the room to collect the scrap of food.

So the shifts passed, and Rees felt his strength subsiding. Brushing a hand over the remnants of his uniform he could feel ribs emerging from their mantle of flesh, and his head seemed to swell.

The Boneys' singing seemed to pulse like blood.

At length Gord laid a hand on his shoulder. Rees sat up, his head floating. "What is it?"

"The whale," Gord said with a hint of excitement. "They're preparing to hunt it. You'll have to come and see, Rees; even in these circumstances it's an incredible sight."

With care Rees stood and followed Gord from the hut.

Peering around groggily he made out the usual groups of adults in their little circles in the huts. They were chanting rhythmically. Even the children seemed spellbound: they sat in attentive groups near the adults, chanting and swaying as best they could.

Gord walked slowly around the worldlet. Rees followed, stumbling; the entire colony seemed to be singing now, so that the skin surface pulsated like a drum.

"What are they doing?"

"Calling to the whale. Somehow the song lures the creature closer."

Rees, befuddled and irritated, said: "I don't see any whale."

Gord squatted patiently on the floor. "Wait a while and you will."

Rees sat beside Gord and closed his eyes. Slowly the singing worked its way into his consciousness until he was swaying with the cyclic rhythms; a mood of calm acceptance, of welcome even, seemed to spread over him.

Was this what the music was supposed to make the whale feel?

"Gord, where do you think the word 'whale' comes from?"

The engineer shrugged. "You were the Scientist.

You tell me. Perhaps there was some great creature on Earth with that name."

Rees scratched the tangle of beard on his jaw. "I wonder what an Earth whale looked like—"

Gord's eyes were widening. "Maybe something like that," he said, pointing.

The whale rose over the horizon of skin like some huge, translucent sun. The bulk of its body was a sphere perhaps fifty yards wide, dwarfing the bone world; within its clear skin organs clustered like immense machines. The leading face of the whale was studded with three spheres about the size of a man. The way they rotated, fixing on the worldlet and the nearby stars, reminded Rees irresistibly of eyes. Attached to the rear of the body were three huge flukes; these semicircles of flesh were as large as the main sphere and they rotated gently, connected to the body by a tube of dense flesh. The whale coasted through the air and the flukes soared no more than twenty yards over Rees's head, washing his laughing face with cool air. "It's fantastic!" he said.

Gord smiled faintly.

The Boneys, still singing, emerged from their huts. Their eyes were fixed on the whale and they carried spears of bone and metal.

Gord leaned close to Rees and said through the song, "Sometimes they just attach ropes to the creatures, have the whales drag the colony a little way out of the Nebula. Adjusting the orbit, you see; otherwise they might have fallen into the Core long ago. This shift, though, it seems they need meat."

Rees was puzzled. "How can you kill a creature like that?"

Gord pointed. "Not difficult. All you have to do is puncture the skin. It loses its structure, you see.

The thing simply crumples into the worldlet's gravity well. Then the trick is to slice the damn thing up fast enough to avoid us all being smothered by flesh . . ."

Now the first spears were flying. The song broke up into shouts of victory. The whale, evidently agitated, began to turn its flukes more quickly. Spears passed clean through the translucent flesh, or embedded themselves in sheets of cartilage—and at last, to a great cry, an organ was hit. The whale lurched toward the surface of the worldlet, its skin crumpling. A mighty ceiling of flesh passed no more than ten feet above Rees's head.

"What about this, miner?" Quid stood beside him, spear in hand. The Boney grinned. "This is the way to live, eh? Better than scratching in the vitals of some dead star—"

More spears hissed through the air; with increasing precision they looped through the compound gravity field of planet and whale and found soft targets within the body of the whale.

"Quid, how can they be so accurate?"

"It's easy. Imagine the planet as a lump below you. And the whale as another small lump somewhere about there—" He pointed. "—Close to its center. That's where all the pull comes from, right? So then you just imagine the path you want your spear to follow and—throw!"

Rees scratched his head, wondering what Hollerbach would have made of this distillation of orbital mechanics. But the need for the Boneys—trapped on their little world—to develop such spear-throwing skills was obvious.

The spears continued to fly until it seemed impossible for the whale to escape. Now its belly was almost brushing the rooftops of the colony. Men and women were producing massive machetes now, and soon the butchery would start. Rees, in his starved, dreamy state, wondered if whale blood would smell different from human—

And suddenly he found himself running, almost without conscious thought. With a light motion he hauled himself to the roof of one of the sturdier huts—could he have moved so cleanly without his recent weight loss?—and stood, staring upwards at the wrinkled, semitransparent roof of flesh that slid over him. It was still just out of his reach— and then a fold a few feet deep came towards him like a descending curtain. He jumped and grabbed with both hands. His fingers passed through flesh that crumbled, dry. He scrabbled for a firm hold, believing for one, panicky second that he would fall again; and then, his arms elbow-deep in pulpy flesh, his fingers bit into a shank of some tougher material and he pulled himself higher onto the whale's body. He managed to swing his feet up and embed them in the fleshy ceiling; and so upside down, he sailed over the Boney colony.

His boarding seemed to galvanize the whale. Its flukes beat the air with renewed vigor and it rose from the surface with wrenches that threatened to tear Rees from his precarious hold.

Angry voices were raised at him, and a spear whistled past his ear and into the soft flesh. Quid and the other Boneys waved furious fists. He saw the pale, upturned face of Gord streaming with tears.

The whale continued to rise and the colony turned from a landscape into a small, brown ball, lost in the sky. The human voices faded to the level of the wind. The warm skin of the whale pulsed with its steady motion; and Rees was alone.

10

Its tormentors far behind, the great beast moved cautiously through the air; the flukes turned with slow strength, and the vast body shuddered. It was as if it were exploring the dull pain of the punctures it had suffered. Through the translucent walls of the body Rees could see triple eyes turn fully backwards, as if the whale were inspecting its own interior.

Then, with a sound like the wind, the flukes' speed of rotation increased. The whale surged forward. Soon it had climbed clear of the bone world's gravity well, and Rees's sensation of clinging to a ceiling was transformed into a sense of being pinned against a soft wall.

With some curiosity he examined the substance before his face. His fingers were still locked in the layer of cartilage beneath the whale's six-inch layer of flesh. The flesh itself had no epidermis and was vaguely pink in color; the stuff had little more consistency than a thick foam and there was no sign of blood, although Rees noticed that his arms and legs had become coated with some sticky substance. He recalled that the Boneys hunted this creature for food, and on impulse he pushed his face into the flesh and tore away a mouthful. The stuff

179

seemed to melt in his mouth, compacting from a fluffy bulk to a small, tough lozenge. The taste was strong and slightly bitter; he chewed and swallowed easily. The stuff even seemed to soothe the dryness of his throat.

Suddenly he was starving, and he buried his face in the whale flesh, tearing chunks away with his teeth.

After some minutes he had cleared perhaps a square foot of the soft flesh, exposing cartilage, and his stomach felt filled. So, then, he could expect the whale to provide for him for some considerable time.

He looked around. Clouds and stars stretched all around him, a vast, sterile array without walls or floor. He was, of course, utterly adrift in the red sky, and surely now beyond hope of seeing another human face again. The thought did not frighten him; rather, he became gently wistful. At least he had escaped the degradation of the Boneys. If he had to die, then let it be like this, with his eyes open to new wonders.

He shifted his position comfortably against the bulk of the whale. It took very little effort to stay in place, and the steady motion, the pumping of the flukes were surprisingly soothing. It might be possible to survive quite some time here, before he weakened and fell away . . .

His arms were beginning to ache. Carefully, one hand at a time, he shifted the position of his fingers; but soon the pain was spreading to his back and shoulders.

Could he be tiring so quickly? The effort to cling on here, in these weightless conditions, was minimal. Wasn't it?

He looked back over his shoulder.

The world was wheeling around him. The stars

and clouds executed vast rotations around the whale; once again he was clinging to a ceiling from which he might fall at any moment . . .

He almost lost his grip. He closed his eyes and dug his fingers tighter into the sheet of cartilage. He should have anticipated this, of course. The whale had rotational symmetry; of course it would spin. It would have to compensate for the turning of its flukes, and spinnng would give it stability as it forged through the air. It all made perfect sense . . .

Wind whipped over Rees's face, pushing back his hair. The rate of spin was increasing; he felt the strain on his fingers mount. If he didn't stop analyzing the damn situation and do something, before many more minutes passed he would be thrown off.

Now his feet lost their tenuous hold. His body swung away from the whale's, so that he was dangling from his hands. The cartilage in his clamped fingers twisted like elastic, and with each swing of his torso pain coursed through his biceps and elbows. The centrifugal force continued to rise, through one, one and a half, two gee . . .

Perhaps he could head for one of the stationary "poles," maybe at the joint between the flukes and the main body. He looked sideways toward the rear of the body; he could see the linking tube of cartilage as a misty blur through the walls of flesh.

It might have been a world away. It was all he could do to cling on here.

The spin increased further. Stars streaked below him and he began to grow groggy; he imagined blood pooling somewhere near his feet, starving his brain. He could hardly feel his arms now, but when he stared up through black-speckled vision he could see that the fingers of his left hand, the weaker, were loosening.

With a cry of panic he forced fresh strength into his hands. His fingers tightened as if in a spasm.

And the cartilage ripped.

It was like a curtain parting along a seam. From the interior of the whale a hot, foul gas billowed out over him, causing him to gasp, his eyes to stream. The ruptured cartilage began to sag. Soon a great fold of it was suspended beneath the belly of the whale; Rees clung on, still swinging painfully.

Now a ripple a foot high came rolling down the whale's belly wall. The whale's nervous system must be slow to react, but surely it could feel the agony of this massive hernia. The wave reached the site of the rupture. The dangling fold of cartilage jerked up and down, once, twice, again; Rees's shoulders felt as if they were being dragged from their sockets and needles thrust into the joints.

Again his fingers loosened.

The rip in the sheet was like a narrow door above him.

Shoulders shaking, Rees hauled himself up until his chin was level with his fists. He released his left hand—

—and almost fell altogether; but his right hand still clutched at the cartilage, and now his left hand was locked over the lip of the wound. He released his right hand; the weaker, numb left slipped over greasy cartilage but—now—he had both hands clamped at the edge of the aperture.

He rested there for a few seconds, the muscles of his arms screaming, his fingers slipping.

Now he worked the muscles of his back and dragged his feet up before his face, shoved them over his head and through the aperture. Then his legs and back slid easily over the inner surface of the cartilage and into the body of the whale, and finally he was able to uncurl his fingers. With the last of his strength he rolled away from the aperture.

Breathing hard he lay on his back, spread-eagled against the whale's inner stomach wall. Below him, obscured by the translucent flesh, were the wheeling stars, and far above, like huge machines in some vast, dimly lit hall, were the organs of the whale.

His lungs rattled; his arms and hands were on fire. Blackness fell over him and the pain dropped away.

He awoke to a raging thirst.

He stared up into the cavernous interior of the whale. The light seemed dimmer: perhaps the whale, for reasons of its own, was flying deeper into the Nebula.

The air was hot, damp, and foul with a stench like sweat; but, though his chest ached slightly, he seemed to be breathing normally. Cautiously he propped himself up on his elbows. The muscles of his arms felt ripped and the fingernails on both hands were torn; but the bones of his fingers seemed intact and in place.

He climbed cautiously to his feet.

Stars still wheeled around the whale, but if he averted his eyes he felt no dizziness. It was as if he were standing in a steady gravity well of about two gees. Looking down he saw that his bare feet had sunk a couple of inches into the resilient cartilage. With some experimentation he found he could walk with little difficulty, provided he avoided slipping on the slick surface.

Again thirst tore at his throat; it felt as if the

back of his mouth were closing up with the dryness.

He made his way to the aperture he had torn in the cartilage sheet. The wound had already closed to a narrow slit barely as wide as his waist. He had no way of telling how long he had been unconscious, but surely it must have taken a shift at least for the healing to progress this far. He knelt down, the cartilage beneath his knees a warm, wet carpet, and pushed his face close to the wound. A breeze bore him welcome fresh air. He could see the dangling flap of cartilage up which he had scrambled to safety: the ripped skin had grown opaque and was covered in a mass of fine creases. Perhaps eventually the dangling fold would be isolated outside the body, atrophy and fall away.

Thanks to Rees's scrambling the area of cartilage around the wound was scraped clear of flesh; only a few clumps clung here and there, like isolated patches of foliage on an old tree. Rees lay on the warm floor, took a fold of cartilage in his left hand, and thrust his head and right arm out through the wound. He swept his arm around the outer wall of the whale's belly, hauling in as much flesh matter as he could reach. As he worked the breeze of the whale's rotation washed steadily over his face and bare arms.

When he was done he withdrew from the wound and hauled away his meager supply. He shoved a fistful into his mouth immediately. Sticky whale juice trickled, soothing, down his parched throat and fluffy flesh clung to his straggling beard; he squatted on the warm floor and, for a few minutes, ate steadily, postponing thoughts of an impossible future.

When he was done, his thirst and hunger at least partially sated, his pile of flesh was reduced by at least half. The damn stuff would last hardly any time at all ... He crammed the rest into the pockets of his filthy coverall.

Now he became aware of another problem, as the pressure in his bladder and lower bowels began to grow painful. He felt oddly reluctant to relieve himself inside the body of another creature; it seemed an obscene violation. But, the muscles of his lower stomach told him, he didn't really have a lot of choice.

At last he loosened his trousers and squatted over the narrowest section of the rent in the stomach wall.

He had a bizarre image of his waste being flung through the air in a cloud of brown and yellow. It was highly unlikely, of course, but perhaps one day the stuff would reach the Belt, or the Raft; would one of his acquaintances look up in horror for the source of this foul rain—and think of him?

He laughed out loud; the sound was absorbed by the soft wall around him. He could think of a few nominations for the recipient of such a message. Gover, Roch, Quid ... Maybe he should take aim.

His needs satisfied, his curiosity began to reassert itself, and he stared around at the mysterious interior of the whale. It was like being inside some great, glass-walled ship. From the leading face a wide tube stretched down the axis of the body, contracting as it neared the rear. Entrails of some kind branched off, looking like fat, pale worms that coiled around the principal esophagus. Sacs which could hold four men were suspended around the axial tube, filled with obscure, unmoving forms. Organs were clustered around the main axial canal; and others, vast and anonymous, were fixed to the inner wall of the skin.

Beyond the body's rear Rees could make out the

joint to the fluke section, and then the great semi-circular flukes themselves, washing through the air with immense assurance and power. The motion of the flukes and the wheeling shadows cast by the starlight through the translucent skin gave the place a superficial impression of motion; but otherwise, apart from a subdued humming, the vast space was still and calm. Rees had read of the great cathedrals of Earth; he remembered staring at the old pictures and wondering what it would be like to stand inside such ancient, huge, still spaces.

Perhaps it would be something like this.

Stepping cautiously over the slippery, yielding surface, he began to make his way toward the whale's leading face.

He neared an organ fixed to the floor. It was an opaque, flattened sphere, twice as tall as he was, and its mass tugged gently at him. He pressed his palm to the tough, lumpy flesh; beneath the surface he could feel hot liquid churn. Perhaps this was the equivalent of a liver or kidney. Crouching, he could see how the organ was attached to the stomach wall by a tight, wrinkled ring of flesh; the ring was clear enough for him to see liquid pulse to and from the dense cartilage.

A Boney spear protruded from the organ, its tip buried an arm's length inside the soft material. Rees took the shaft and carefully slid the spear away from the organ; it emerged damp and sticky. He propped the spear safely within a fold of flesh and walked on.

The floor slanted sharply upwards as he began to climb the slope of the body toward the axis of rotation. At last he was climbing a near-vertical, sheer surface, and he was forced to dig his hands into the cartilage. As he climbed toward the axis the centripetal force lessened, although a Coriolis effect began to make him stagger.

He paused for breath and looked back over the slope he had climbed. The organs fixed to the apparent floor and walls of the chamber were like mysterious engines. The tube of the esophagus stretched away above his head; he noticed now that wrapped around it, close behind the eyes, was a large, spongy mass; filaments like rope connected the sponge to the eyes—optic nerves? Perhaps the convoluted lump was the whale's brain; if so its mass relative to its body must compare favorably with a human's.

Could the whale be intelligent? That seemed absurd . . . but then he remembered the song of the Boney hunters. The whale must have a reasonably sophisticated sensorium to be able to respond to such a lure.

At last he reached a position just below the join of the esophagus to the face. The whale's triple eyes hung over him like vast lamps, staring calmly ahead; it felt as if he were clinging to the inside of some huge mask.

The face rippled, almost casting him free; he clung tighter to the cartilage. Staring up he saw that the center of the face had split, becoming an open mouth which led directly into the huge throat.

Rees looked out through the face. He made out a blur of motion which slowly resolved itself into a shoal of ghost-white plates which whirled in the air before the whale. These plate creatures were no more than three or four feet wide; some of them, perhaps the young, were far smaller. The creatures had upturned rims—no doubt for aerodynamic reasons—and Rees saw how purplish veins crisscrossed the upper surface of the discs.

The creatures scattered in alarm as the whale approached. The whale's three eyes locked on the plate animals, triangulating with hungry precision. Soon the plates were impacting the great, flat face; the cartilage resounded like a drumskin, making Rees flinch. Doomed plate creatures, still spinning feebly, slid into the whale's maw and disappeared into the opaque esophagus, and soon a series of bulges were passing down the great tube. Rees imagined the still living plates hurling themselves against the walls that had closed around them after a lifetime of free air. After some minutes the first bulge reached a branch to the semitransparent entrails. Battered plates emerged into the comparative stillness of the intestines, some still turning feebly. With vast pulses of clear muscle the bodies were worked along the entrails, dissolving as they moved through vats of digestive gases or fluids.

For perhaps thirty minutes the whale cut a path through the cloud of plate creatures . . . and then something fast moved at the rim of Rees's peripheral vision. He twisted, peering.

There was a blur, something red and dense that shot across the sky. Now another, and a third; and now a whole flock of them, raining through the air like missiles. The things descended on the shoal of plate creatures in a great, frenzied blur of motion and blood; when they moved on they left behind a cloud of blood and meat scraps—

—and one of the blurs flew at Rees's face. He cried out and flinched backwards, almost losing his grip on the cartilage mask; then he steadied himself and stared back at the creature.

It had come to a halt mere yards before him. It was little more than a flying mouth. A red stump of a body, limbless, perhaps two yards long, was fronted by a circular maw wider than Rees could reach. Eyes like beads clustered round the mouth, which was ringed by long teeth, needle points turned inwards. Now the mouth closed, the flesh stretching over a rudimentary bone structure, until teeth met in a grind of white flashes.

Rees could almost imagine this sky wolf licking its lips as it studied him.

But the eyes of the whale fixed the wolf with a haughty glare, and after a few seconds the wolf shot away to join its companions amid the easier meat of the plate creatures.

Apparently satiated, the whale surged out of the cloud of plates and into clear air. Looking back, Rees could see the sky wolves continue to feast on the hapless plates.

The sky wolves were creatures of children's tales; Rees had never encountered one before. No doubt, like uncounted other species of Nebula flora and fauna, the plates and wolves were careful to avoid the homes of man. Was he the first human to see such a sight? And would the Nebula die before mankind could explore the marvels this strange universe had to offer?

A heavy depression fell upon Rees, and he pressed his face against the inner face of the whale.

The whale forged ever deeper into the heart of the Nebula; the air outside grew darker.

Rees woke from a dream of falling.

His back was pressed against the inner face of the whale, his hands locked around folds of cartilage; cautiously he uncurled his fingers and worked the stiff joints.

What had woken him? He scanned the cavernous interior of the whale. Shafts of starlight still swept through the body like torch beams—

—but, surely, more slowly than before. Was the whale coming to rest?

He turned to look out of the whale's face . . . and felt a tingle of wonder at the base of his skull. Peering in at him, not a dozen yards from where he stood, were the three eyes of a second whale. Its face was pressed to that of "his" whale, and he saw how the mouths of the two vast creatures worked in sympathetic patterns, almost as if they were speaking to each other.

Now the other whale peeled away, its flukes beating, and the view ahead cleared. Again wonder surged through Rees, causing him to gasp. Beyond the second whale was another, side on, forging through the air—and beyond that another, and another; as far as Rees's eyes could see, above him and below him, there was a great array of whales which swam through the Nebula. The school must have been spread through cubic miles: the more distant of them were like tiny lanterns illuminated by starlight.

Like a great, pinkish river, the whales were all streaming toward the Core.

From behind Rees there was a low grind, as if some great machine were stirring. Turning, he saw that the joint connecting the main body of the whale to its fluke section was swivelling; bones and muscles the size of men hauled at the mass of turning flesh. Soon the whale was banking around a wide arc, its flukes beating purposefully. The whale's rotation increased once more, turning the school of whales into a kaleidoscope of whirling flukes; and at last the whale settled into a place in the vast migration.

For hours the school forged on into increasing darkness. The stars at these depths were older, dimmer, their proximity increasing as the Core neared. Rees made out two stars so close they almost touched: their tired fires were drawn out in great mounds, and they whirled around each other in a pirouette seconds long. Later the whales passed a massive star, miles across; its fusion processes seemed exhausted, but the iron of its surface, compressed by gravity, gave off a dull, somber glow. The surface was a place of constant motion: every few minutes a portion would subside, leaving a crater perhaps yards wide and a spray of molten particles struggling a few feet into the air. Smaller stars circled the giant in orbits of several minutes, and Rees was reminded of Hollerbach's orrery: here was another "solar system" model, made not of metal beads but of stars ...

The school reached another collection of stars bound by gravity; but this time there was no central giant: instead a dozen small stars, some still burning, whirled through a complex, chaotic dance. At one moment it seemed two stars must collide ... but no; they passed no more than yards apart, spun around and hurtled off in new directions. The motion of the star family showed no structure, no periodicity—and Rees, who in his time on the Raft had studied the chaotic aspects of the three-body problem, was not surprised.

Still the gloom deepened. A gathering blackness ahead told Rees they were nearing the Core. He remembered the Telescopic journey into the Nebula he had taken at the time of the revolt with that young Class Three—what was his name? Nead? Little had he dreamt that one day he would repeat the journey in person, and in such a fantastic fashion ...

Again he thought briefly of Hollerbach. What would that old man give to be seeing these wonders? A mood of contentment, perhaps brought on by his memories, settled over Rees.

Now, as on his Telescopic journey, the mists of the Nebula's heart lifted away like veils from a face, and he began to make out the sphere of debris around the Core itself. Through breaks in the shell of rubble a pink light flickered.

Slowly Rees began to realize he was staring at his own death. What would get him first? The hard radiation sleeting from the black hole? Perhaps the tidal effects of the Core's gravitation would tear his head and limbs from his body ... or, as the softer structure of the whale disintegrated, maybe he would find himself tumbling helpless in the air, baked or asphyxiated in the oxygen-starved atmosphere.

But still the odd mood of contentment lingered, and now he felt a slow, soothing music sound within his head. He let his muscles relax and he settled comfortably against the inner face of the whale. If this really were to be his death—well, at least it had been an interesting journey.

And perhaps, after all, death wouldn't be the final end. He recalled some of the simple religious beliefs of the Belt. What if the soul survived the body, somehow? What if his journey were to continue on some other plane? He was struck by a vision of a stream of disembodied souls streaking out into space, their flukes slowly beating—

Flukes? What the hell—?

He shook his head, trying to clear it of the bizarre images and sounds. Damn it, he knew himself well enough to know that he shouldn't be facing death with an elegiac smile and a vision of the afterlife. He should be fighting, looking for a way out ...

But if these thoughts weren't his own, whose were they?

With a shudder he turned and stared at the bulge of brain around the whale's esophagus. Could the beast be semitelepathic? Were the images seeping into his head from that great mound, mere yards from him?

He remembered how the chanting of the Boney hunters had attracted the whales. Perhaps the chanting set up some sort of telepathic lure which baffled and attracted the whales. With a start he realized that the steady music in his head had the same structure, the same compelling rhythm and cyclical melodies, as the Boneys' song. It must be coming from outside him—though whether through his ears or by telepathic means he found it impossible to distinguish. So the Boneys, perhaps by chance, had found a way to make the whales believe they were swimming, not toward a slow death at the hands of tiny, malevolent humans, but toward—

What? Where did these whales, swimming to the Core, think they were going, and why were they so happy to be going there?

There was only one way to find out. He quailed at the thought of opening his mind to further violation; but he fixed his hands tightly around the cartilage, closed his eyes, and tried to welcome the bizarre images.

Again the whales streaked into the air. He tried to observe the scene as if it were a photograph before him. Were these things really whales? Yes; but somehow their bulk had been reduced drastically, so that they became pencil-shaped missiles soaring against minimal air resistance to ... where? He struggled, compressing his eyes with the back of one hand, but it wouldn't come. Well, wherever it was, "his" whale felt nothing but delight at the prospect.

If he couldn't see the destination, what about the source?

Deliberately he lowered his head. The image in his mind panned down, as if he were tracking a Telescope across the sky.

And he saw the source of the whales' flight. It was the Core.

He opened gritty eyes. So the creatures were not plunging to their deaths; somehow they were going to use the Core to gain enormous velocities, enough to send them hurtling out—

—out, he realized with a sudden burst of insight, of the Nebula itself.

The whales knew the Nebula was dying. And, in this fantastic fashion, they were migrating; they would abandon the fading ruin of the Nebula and cross space to a new home. Perhaps they had done this dozens, hundreds of times before; perhaps they had spread among the nebulae in this way for hundreds of thousands of shifts . . .

And what the whales could do, surely man could emulate. A great wave of hope crashed over Rees; he felt the blood burn in his cheeks.

The Core was very near now; shafts of hellish light glared through the shell of debris, illuminating the rubble. Ahead of him he could see whales expelling air through their mouths in great moist plumes; their bodies contracted like slowly collapsing balloons.

The rotation of Rees's whale slowed. Soon it would enter the deepening throat of the Core's gravity well . . . and surely Rees would die. As rapidly as it had grown his bubble of hope disintegrated, wiping away the last traces of his false contentment. He had perhaps minutes to live, and locked in his doomed head was the secret of the survival of his race.

A howl of despair broke from his throat, and his hands clenched convulsively around the cartilage of the face.

The whale shuddered.

Rees stared unbelieving at his hands. Up to now the whale had shown no more awareness of his presence than would he of an individual microbial parasite. But if his physical actions had not disturbed the whale, perhaps his flood of despair had impacted on that vast, slow brain a few yards away . . .

And perhaps there was a way out of this.

He closed his eyes and conjured up faces. Hollerbach, Jaen, Sheen, Pallis tending his forest; he let the agony of their anticipated deaths, his longing to return to and to save his people flood through him and focus into a single, hard point of pain. He physically hauled at the whale's face, as if by brute force he could drag the great creature from its path into the Core.

A monstrous sadness assailed Rees now, a pleading that this human infection should leave the whale be to follow its herd to safety. Rees felt as if he were drowning in sorrow. He fixed on a single image: the wonder on the face of the young Third, Nead, as he had watched the beauty of the Nebula's rim unfold in the Telescope monitor; and the whale shuddered again, more violently.

11

The assault of the mine craft on the Raft had been under way for only thirty minutes, but already the air around the Platform was filled with the cries of wounded.

Pallis crawled through the foliage of his tree, working feverishly at the fire bowls. A glance through the leaves showed him that his blanket of smoke was even and thick. The tree rose smoothly; he felt a warming professional satisfaction—despite the situation.

He raised his head. The dozen trees of his flight were arrayed in a wide, leafy curve which matched the arc of the Raft a hundred yards above: they were just below the Platform, according to his charts of the underside. His trees rose as steadily as if attached by rods of iron; in a few minutes they would sweep over the Raft's horizon.

He could see the nearer pilots as they worked at their fires, their thin faces grim.

"Can't we speed it up?" Nead stood before him, his face stretched with anxiety and tension.

"Keep at your work, lad."

"But can't you hear them?" The young man, blinking away tears, shook a fist toward the thin battle noise drifting down from the Platform.

"Of course I can." Pallis willed the temper to subside from his scarred mask of a face. "But if we go off half-cocked we'll get ourselves killed. Right? On the other hand, if we stick to our formation, our plan, we've a chance of beating the buggers. Think about it, Nead; you used to be a Scientist, didn't you?"

Nead wiped his eyes and nose with the palm of his hand. "Only Third Class."

"Nevertheless, you've been trained to use your brain. So come on, man; there's a job of work to be done here and I'm relying on you to do it. Now then, I think those bowls near the trunk need restocking ..."

Nead returned to work; for a few moments Pallis watched him. Nead's frame was gaunt, his shoulder blades and elbows prominent; his Scientist's coverall had been patched so many times it was barely recognizable as a piece of cloth, let alone a uniform. When his eyes caught Pallis's they were black-ringed.

Nead was barely seventeen thousand shifts old. By the Bones, Pallis thought grimly, what are we doing to our young people?

If only he could believe in his own damn pep talks he might feel better.

The flight swept out of the shadow of the Raft, and leaves blazed golden-brown in the sudden starlight. Pallis could feel the tree's sap churn through its branches; its rotation increased like an eager skitter's and it seemed to leap up at the star which hung in the Raft's sky.

The Rim was mere yards above him now. He felt a growl building in his throat, dark and primeval. He raised a fist above his head; the other pilots waved their arms in silent salute.

... And the line of trees soared over the Platform.

A panorama of blood and flames unfolded before Pallis. People ran everywhere. The deck was crowded with blazing awnings and shelters; where the roofs had been blasted away Pallis could see papers burning in great heaps. The sudden downwash from the trees' branches caused the fires to flicker and belch smoke.

Three mine craft—iron plates fitted with jets— hovered a dozen yards above the Platform. Their jets spat live steam; Pallis saw Raft men squirm, the flesh blistering away from incautious limbs. Miners, two or three to a craft, lay belly down on the plates, dropping bottles which bloomed fire like obscene flowers.

This was the worst assault yet. Previously the miners had targeted the sites of the supply machines—their main objective—and had largely been beaten off, with low casualties on either side. But this time they were striking at the heart of the Raft's government.

There was little sign of organized defense. Even Pallis's flight had been near the end of its patrol of the underside when the miners attacked; if not for a pilot's sharp eyes the Raft might have been unable to mount any real counter-thrust. But at least the Platform's occupants were fighting back. Spears and knives lanced up at the hovering plate craft, forcing the miners to cower behind their flying shields—

—until, as Pallis watched, one spear looped over a craft and made a lucky strike, driving through a miner's shoulder. The man stared at the bloody tip protruding from his muscle, grabbed it with his good hand, and began to scream.

The craft, undirected, tipped.

The other occupants of the craft called out and tried to reach the controls; but within seconds the plate, swaying, had fallen to within a few feet of the deck. Raft men braved live steam to force their way to the craft; a hundred hands grabbed its rim and the steam jets sputtered and died. The miners were hauled, screaming, from the plate, and were submerged by the flailing arms of the Raft men.

Now the tree flight was perhaps a dozen yards above the Rim and was noticed for the first time by the combatants. A ragged cheer spread through the chaotic ranks of the defenders; the miners turned their heads and their faces went slack. Pallis felt a crude pride as he imagined how this awesome dawn of wood and leaves must look to the simple Belt folk.

Pallis turned to Nead. "Almost time," he murmured. "Are you ready?"

Nead stood by the trunk of the tree. He held a bottle of fuel; now he lit the wick with a crude match and held the burning lint before his face. His eyes were deep with hatred. "Oh, I'm ready," he said.

Shame surged through Pallis.

He turned to the battle. "All right, lad," he said briskly. "On my count. Remember, if you can't hit a miner douse your flame; we're not here to bomb our own people." The tree swept over the mêlée; he saw faces turn up to his shadow like scorched skitter flowers. The nearest plate ship was mere yards away. "Three . . . two . . ."

"Pallis!"

Pallis turned sharply. One of the other pilots stood balancing on the trunk of his tree, his hands cupped to his mouth. He turned and pointed skywards. Two more mine craft flew above him, their ragged edges silhouetted against the sky. Squinting,

Pallis could make out miners grinning down at him, the glint of glass in their hands; the miners were obviously trying to get above his trees.

"Shit."

"What do we do, Pallis?"

"We've underestimated them. They've caught us out, ambushed us. Damn it. Come on, lad, don't just stand there. We've got to rise before they get above us. You work on the bowls near the rim, and I'll get to the trunk."

Nead stared at the encroaching forms of the miners as if unable to accept this distraction from the simple verities of the battle below.

"Move!" Pallis snapped, thumping his shoulder. Nead moved.

A floor of smoke spread beneath the trees, spilling over the battlefield. The great wheels lurched up and away from the deck . . . but the mine craft were smaller, faster and far more maneuverable. Effortlessly they moved into position above the flight.

Pallis felt his shoulders sag. He imagined a fire bomb hitting the dry branches of his tree. The foliage would burn like old paper; the structure would disintegrate and send blazing fragments raining over the deck—

Well, he wasn't dead yet. "Scatter!" he yelled to his pilots. "They can't take us all."

The formation broke with what seemed ponderous slowness. The two mine craft split up, each making for a tree . . .

And one of them was Pallis's.

As the plate descended the tree-pilot's eyes met those of the miner above him. Nead came to stand close by the pilot. Pallis reached out, found Nead's shoulder, squeezed hard—

Then a cold breeze shook the tree and a shadow

swept across his face, shocking and unexpected. A huge form sailed across the face of the star above the Raft.

"A whale . . ." Pallis felt his jaw drop. The great beast was no more than a hundred yards above the deck of the Raft; never in his life had he known a whale to come so close.

When the miners attacking Pallis saw the great, translucent ceiling mere yards above them they called out in panic and jerked at their controls. The plate wobbled, spun about, then shot away.

Bewildered, Pallis turned to survey the Platform battle. The whale's cloudy shadow swept across tiny, struggling humans. Men dropped their weapons and fled. The remaining miners' craft squirted into the air and sailed over the lip of the Raft.

Save for the dead and wounded, the Platform was soon deserted. Fires flickered desultorily from a dozen piles of wreckage.

Nead was sobbing. "It's over, isn't it?"

"The invasion? Yes, lad; it's over. For now, at any rate . . . Thanks to that miracle." He stared up at the whale, imagining the confusion it must be causing as people looked up from the Raft's avenues and factories at this monster in the sky. "But the miners will be back. Or maybe," he added grimly, "we'll be forced to go to meet them . . ."

His voice tailed away.

Clinging to the belly of the whale, waving feebly, was a man.

At the outbreak of the miners' attack Gover had joined the mob crowding down the stairway from the Platform, using his fists and elbows to escape the flying glass, the screams, the fire. Now, as suddenly as it had begun, the attack was over. Gover crawled from his shelter under the Platform and climbed cautiously back up the stairs.

Fearfully he scanned the burning shelters, the blackened bodies—until he saw Decker. The big man was stalking through the devastation, bending to assist medical efforts, throwing a kick at the scorched ruin of a bookcase. His motions had the look of a man caged by frustration and anger.

But he was obviously far too busy to have observed that Gover had made himself scarce during the battle. With relief Gover hurried toward Decker, eager to be noticed now; his footsteps crunched over shattered glass.

A shadow swept across the littered deck. Gover quailed, twisted his head and looked up.

A whale! And no more than a hundred yards above the Raft, drifting like a vast, translucent balloon. What the hell was going on? His agile mind bubbled with speculation. He'd heard tales that the whales could be trapped and hunted. Maybe he could have Decker send up some of those damn fool tree-pilots; he had a gratifying vision of standing at the rim of a tree, hurling his fire bombs into a huge, staring eye—

Someone thumped his arm. "Get out of the way, damn you."

Two men were trying to get past him. They half-dragged a woman; her face was ruined by flame, and tears leaked steadily from her remaining eye. Gover, annoyed, prepared to snap at the men—these weren't even Committee members ... but something about the tired tension in their faces made him step aside.

He glanced up once more, noticing without interest that a tree was rising toward the whale ... then he made out a dark, irregular blot on the whale's hide. He squinted against the almost direct starlight.

By the Bones, it was a man. A coarse wonder blossomed in Gover, and for a brief moment his self-centeredness evaporated. How the hell could a man end up riding a whale?

The whale rolled slowly, bringing the man a little closer. There was something naggingly familiar about the whale rider's dimly seen frame—

Gover had no idea what was going on; but maybe he could make something out of this.

His breath hissing through his teeth, Gover worked his way through the wounded and battle-weary, searching for Decker.

In the hours after he had "persuaded" the whale to leave its school, Rees had often wished he could die.

The whale climbed steadily out of the Nebula's depths, convulsed with loneliness and regret at leaving its companions. It drowned Rees in a huge pain, burnt him with the fierce, enormous agony of it all. He had been unable to eat, sleep; he had lain against the stomach wall, barely able to move, even his breathing constricted; at times, barely conscious, he had found himself squirming across the belly floor's warm slime.

But he kept his concentration. Like match flames in a wind he held before his mind's eye images of Hollerbach, Pallis and the rest; and with the Raft fixed in his thoughts, he crooned the whales' song, over and over.

Shifts had passed as Rees lay there, dreading sleep. Then, quite abruptly, he sensed a change; a breeze of confusion had been added to the whale's mental storm, and the beast seemed to be sweeping through tight curves in the air. He rolled onto his belly and peered through the murky cartilage.

At first he could not recognize what he saw. A vast, rust-brown disc which dwarfed even the whale, a sparse forest of trees turning slowly over unlit avenues of metal . . .

It was the Raft.

With sudden strength he had torn at the cartilage before his face, forcing his fingers through the dense, fibrous material.

The tree rose steadily toward the rolling bulk of the whale.

"Come on, boy," Pallis snapped. "Whoever's up there saved our skins. And now we're going to save him."

Reluctantly Nead worked at his fire bowls. "Surely you don't think he brought the whale here intentionally?"

Pallis shrugged. "What other explanation is there? How many times have you seen a whale come so close to the Raft? Never, that's how many. And how often do you see a man riding a whale?

"Two impossible events in one shift? Nead, the law of the simplest hypothesis tells you that it's all got to be connected." Nead glanced at him curiously. "You see," Pallis grinned, "even Scientists Third Class don't have the monopoly on knowledge. Now work those bloody bowls!"

The tree rose from its blanket of smoke. Soon the whale filled the sky; it was a monstrous, rolling ceiling, with the passenger carried around and around like a child on a roundabout.

As the tree closed, its rotation slowed jerkily, despite all Nead's efforts. At last it came to rest altogether perhaps twenty yards beneath the belly of the whale.

The whale's three eyes rolled downwards toward the succulent foliage.

"There's nothing I can do," Nead called. "The damn smoke's thick enough to walk on, but she just won't budge."

"Nead, a tree has about the same affection for a whale as a plate of meat-sim has for you. She's doing her best; just hold her steady." He cupped his hands and bellowed across the air. "Hey, you! On the whale!"

He was answered by a tentative wave.

"Listen, we can't get any closer. You'll have to jump! Do you understand?"

A long pause, then another wave.

"I'll try to help you," Pallis called. "The whale's spin should throw you across; all you have to do is let go at the right time."

The man buried his face in the flesh of the whale, as if utterly weary. "Nead, the guy doesn't look too healthy," Pallis murmured. "When he comes this way he might not do a good job of grabbing hold. Forget the fire bowls for a minute, and stand ready to run where he hits."

Nead nodded and straightened up, toes locked in the foliage.

"You up there . . . we'll do this on the next turn. All right?"

Another wave.

Pallis visualized the man parting from the whale. He would leave the spinning body tangentially, travel in a more or less straight line to the tree. There should really be no problem—provided the whale didn't take it into its head to fly off at the last second—

"Now! Let go!"

The man raised his head—and, with agonizing slowness, curved his legs beneath him.

"That's too slow!" Pallis cried. "Hold on or you'll . . ."

The man kicked away, sailing along a path that was anything but tangential to the whale's spin.

". . . Or you'll miss us," Pallis whispered.

"By the Bones, Pallis, it's going to be close."

"Shut up and stand ready."

The seconds passed infinitely slowly. The man seemed limp, his limbs dangling like lengths of rope. Thanks to the man's release the whale's spin had thrown him to Pallis's right—but, on the other hand, his kick had taken him to the left—

—and the two effects together were bringing him down Pallis's throat; suddenly the man became an explosion of arms and legs that plummeted out of the sky. The man's bulk crumpled against Pallis's chest, knocking him backwards into the foliage.

The whale, with a huge, relieved shudder, soared into the sky.

Nead lifted the man off Pallis and laid him on his back. Under a tangle of filthy beard the man's skin was stretched tight over his cheek bones. His eyes were closed, and the battered remnants of a coverall clung to his frame.

Nead scratched his head. "I know this guy . . . I think."

Pallis laughed, rubbing his bruised chest. "Rees. I should have bloody known it would be you."

Rees half-opened his eyes; when he spoke his voice was dry as dust. "Hello, tree-pilot. I've had a hell of a trip."

Pallis was embarrassed to find his eyes misting up. "I bet you did. You nearly missed, you damn idiot. It would have been easy if you hadn't decided to turn somersaults on the way."

"I had every . . . confidence in you, my friend." Rees struggled to sit up. "Pallis, listen," he said.

Pallis frowned. "What?"

A smile twisted Rees's broken lips. "It's kind of difficult to explain. You have to take me to Hollerbach. I think I know how to save the world . . ."

"You know what?"

Rees looked troubled. "He's still alive, isn't he?"

Pallis laughed. "Who, Hollerbach? They could no more get rid of that old bugger than they can get rid of you, it seems. Now lie back and I'll take you home."

With a sigh, Rees settled among the leaves.

By the time the tree had docked Rees seemed stronger. He emptied one of Pallis's flasks of water and made inroads into a slab of meat-sim. "The whale flesh kept me alive in the short term, but who knows what vitamin and protein deficiencies I suffered . . ."

Pallis eyed his remaining food warily. "Just make sure you relieve your protein deficiencies before you start on my foliage."

With Pallis's support Rees slid down the tree's tether cable to the deck. At the base Pallis said, "Now, come back to my cabin and rest before—"

"There's no time," Rees said. "I have to get to Hollerbach. There's so much to do . . . we have to get started before we become too weak to act . . ." His eyes flickered anxiously around the cable thicket. ". . . It's dark," he said slowly.

"That's a good word for it," Pallis said grimly. "Look, Rees, things haven't got any better here. Decker's in charge, and he's neither a fool nor a monster; but the fact is that things are steadily falling apart. Maybe it's already too late—"

Rees met his eyes with a look of clear determination. "Pilot, take me to Hollerbach," he said gently.

Pallis, surprised, felt invigorated by Rees's

answer. Under his physical weakness Rees had changed, become confident—almost inspiring. But then, given all his fantastic experiences, perhaps it would have been stranger if he hadn't changed—

"We don't want any trouble, pilot."

The voice came from the gloom of the cable thicket. Pallis stepped forward, hands on hips. "Who's that?"

Two men stepped forward, one tall, both looming as wide as supply machines. They wore the ostentatiously ripped tunics that were the uniform of Committee functionaries.

"Seel and Plath," Pallis groaned. "Remember these two clowns, Rees? Decker's tame muscles . . . What do you boneheads want?"

Seel, short, square and bald, stepped forward, finger stabbing at Pallis's chest. "Now, look, Pallis, we've come for the miner, not you. I know we've locked fists before . . ."

Pallis lifted his arms, letting the muscles bunch under his shirt. "We have, haven't we?" he said easily. "I'll tell you what. Why don't we finish it off? Eh?"

Seel took a pace forward.

Rees stepped between them. "Forget it, tree-pilot," he said sadly. "I'd have to face this crap sometime; let's get it over . . ."

Plath took Rees's arm, none too gently, and they began to make their way through the cable thicket. Rees's footsteps were airy and unsteady.

Pallis shook his head angrily. "The poor bastard's just hitched a ride on a whale, for God's sake; can't you let him be? Eh? Hasn't he suffered enough?"

But—with only a last, longing stare from Seel—the little party walked away.

Pallis growled with frustration. "Finish up the work here," he spat at Nead.

Nead straightened from his work at the cable anchor. "Where are you going?"

"After them, of course. Where else?" And the tree-pilot stalked away through the cables.

By the time they'd reached the Platform Rees felt his gait become watery, wavering; his two captors weren't so much restraining him, he thought wryly, as holding him up. After they climbed the shallow staircase to the deck of the Platform he murmured, "Thanks . . ."

Then he raised a heavy head and found himself staring at a battlefield. "By the Bones."

"Welcome to the Raft's seat of government, Rees," Pallis said grimly.

Something crackled under Rees's tread; he bent and picked up a smashed bottle, its glass scorched and half-melted. "More fire bombs? What's happened here, pilot? Another revolt?"

Pallis shook his head. "Miners, Rees. We've been at this futile war since we lost the supply machine we sent to the Belt. It's a stupid, bloody affair . . . I'm sorry you have to see this, lad."

"Well. What have we here?" A vast belly quivered, close enough for Rees to feel its gross gravity field; it made him feel weak, insubstantial. He looked up into a broad, scarred face.

"Decker . . ."

"But you walked the beam. Didn't you?" Decker sounded vaguely puzzled, as if pondering a child's riddle. "Or are you one of those I sent to the mine?"

Rees didn't answer. He studied the Raft's leader; Decker's face was marked by deep creases and his eyes were hollow and restless. "You've changed," Rees said.

Decker's eyes narrowed. "We've all bloody changed, lad."

"Mine rat. I thought I recognized you, clinging to that whale." The words were almost a hiss. Gover's thin face was a mask of pure hatred, focused on Rees.

Rees suddenly felt enormously tired. "Gover. I never imagined I'd see you again." He looked into Gover's eyes, recalling the last time he had seen the apprentice. It had been at the time of the revolt, he supposed, when Rees had silently joined the group of Scientists outside the Bridge. Rees remembered his contempt for the other man—and recalled how Gover had recognized that contempt, and how his thin cheeks had burned in response—

"He's an exile." Gover sidled up to Decker, his small fists clenching and unclenching. "I saw him approaching on the whale and had him brought to you. You threw him off the Raft. Now he's back. And he's a miner . . ."

"So?" Decker demanded.

"Make the bastard walk the beam."

Stray emotions chased like shadows across Decker's complex, worn face. The man was tired, Rees realized suddenly; tired of the unexpected complexity of his role, tired of the blood, the endless privations, the suffering . . .

Tired. And looking for a few minutes' diversion.

"So you'd have him over the side, eh?"

Gover nodded, eyes still fixed on Rees.

Decker murmured, "Shame you weren't so brave while the miners were in the sky." Gover flinched. A cruel smile surfaced through Decker's tiredness. "All right, Gover. I agree with your judgment. But with one proviso."

"What?"

"No beam. There's been enough cowardly killing

this shift. No. Let him die the way a man is meant to. Hand to hand." Gover's eyes widened, shocked. Decker stepped back, leaving Rees and Gover facing each other. A small crowd gathered around them, a ring of bloodstained faces eager for diversion.

"More bloody games, Decker?"

"Shut up, Pallis."

From the corner of his eye Rees saw the two heavies—Plath and Seel—clamp the tree-pilot's arms tight.

Rees looked into Gover's twisted, frightened face. "Decker, I've come a long way," he said. "And I've something to tell you ... something more important than you can dream."

Decker raised his eyebrows. "Really? I'll be fascinated to hear about it ... later. First, you fight."

Gover crouched, hands spread like claws.

It seemed he had no choice. Rees raised his arms, tried to think himself into the fight. Once he could have taken Gover with one arm behind his back. But—after so many shifts with the Boneys and riding the whale—now he wasn't sure ...

Gover seemed to sense his doubt; his fear seemed to evaporate, and his posture adjusted subtly, became more aggressive. "Come on, mine rat." He stepped toward Rees.

Rees groaned inwardly. He didn't have time for this. Come on, think; hadn't he learned anything on his journey? How would a Boney handle this? He remembered the whale-spears lancing through the air with deadly accuracy—

"Watch it, Gover," someone called. "He's got a weapon."

Rees found the half-bottle still in his hand ... and an idea blossomed. "What, this? All right, Gover—hand to hand. Just you and me." He closed his eyes, felt the pull of the Raft and Platform play on the gravitational sense embedded in his stomach—then he hurled the glass as hard as he could, not quite vertically. It sparkled through the starlit air.

Gover showed his teeth; they were even and brown.

Rees stepped forward. Time seemed to slow, and the world around him froze; the only motion was the twinkling of the glass in the air above him. Everything became bright and vivid, as if illuminated by some powerful lantern within his eyes. Detail overwhelmed him, sharp and gritty: he counted the beads of sweat on Gover's brow, saw how the apprentice's nostrils flared white as he breathed. Rees's throat tightened and he felt the blood pump in his neck; and all the while the half-bottle, small and graceful, was orbiting perfectly through the complex gravitational field . . .

Until, at last, it dipped back toward the deck. And slammed into Gover's back.

Gover went down howling. For some seconds he writhed on the deck, the blood pooling over the metal around him. Then, at last, he was still, and the blood ceased to flow.

For long moments nobody moved, Decker, Pallis and the rest forming a shocked tableau.

Rees knelt. Gover's back had been transformed into a mash of blood and torn cloth. Rees forced his hands into the wound and dug out the glass, then he stood holding aloft the grisly trophy, Gover's blood trickling down his arm.

Decker scratched his head. "By the Bones . . ." He half-laughed.

Rees felt a cold, hard anger course through him. "I know what you're thinking," he told Decker quietly. "You don't expect the likes of me to fight dirty. I cheated; I didn't follow the rules. Right?"

Decker nodded uncertainly.

"Well, this isn't a bloody game!" Rees screamed, spraying Decker's face with spittle. "I wasn't going to let this fool kill me, not before I make you hear what I've got to say.

"Decker, you'll destroy me if you want to. But if you want any chance of saving your people you'll hear me out." He brandished the glass in Decker's face. "Has this earned me the right to be heard? Has it?"

Decker's mask of scars was impassive. He said quietly, "You'd better take this one home, tree-pilot. Get him cleaned up." With one last, narrow glare, he turned away.

Rees dropped the glass. Abruptly his fatigue crashed down. The deck seemed to quiver, and now it was rising to meet his face—

Arms around his shoulders and waist. He raised his head blearily. "Pallis. Thanks ... I had to do it, you see. You understand that, don't you?"

The tree-pilot would not meet his eyes; he stared at Rees's bloody hands and shuddered.

12

The Belt was a shabby toy hanging in the air above Pallis. Two plate craft hovered between Pallis's tree and the Belt; every few minutes they emitted puffs of steam and spurted a few yards through the clouds. Miners glared down from the craft across the intervening yards at the tree.

The craft were motes of iron in a vast pit of red-lit air. But, Pallis reflected with a sigh, they marked a wall as solid as any of wood or metal. He stood by the trunk of his tree and stared up at the sentries, rubbing his chin thoughtfully. "Well, it's no use hanging about here," he said. "We'll have to go in."

Jaen's broad face was smudged with soot from the fire bowls. "Pallis, you're crazy. They're obviously not going to let us past." She waved a muscular arm at the miners. "The Raft and the Belt are at war, for goodness' sake!"

"The trouble with having you Science rejects as apprentice woodsmen is that you argue at every damn thing. Why the hell can't you just do as you're told?"

Jaen's broad face split into a grin. "Would you rather have Gover back, pilot? You shouldn't complain if the revolution's brought you such a high caliber of staff."

Pallis straightened up and dusted off his hands. "All right, high caliber; we need to work. Let's get these bowls stoked."

She frowned. "You're serious? We're going on?"

"You heard what Rees said . . . What we have to tell these miners is possibly the most important news since the Ship arrived in the Nebula in the first place. And we're going to make those damn miners listen whether they like it or not. If that means we let them blast us out of the sky, then we accept it. And another tree will come, and that will be destroyed too; and then another, and another, until finally these damn fool mine rats work out that we really do want to talk to them."

Throughout his awkward speech Jaen had kept her head down, fiddling with the kindling in a fire bowl; now she looked up. "I suppose you're right." She bit her lip. "I just wish—"

"What?"

"I just wish it wasn't Rees who had come back from the dead to save the human race. That little mine rat was pompous enough as he was . . ."

Pallis laughed. "Fill your bowl, apprentice."

Jaen set to work. Pallis took a silent pleasure in working with her. She was a good woodsman, fast and efficient; somehow she knew what to do without being told, and without getting in his damn way . . .

The blanket of smoke gathered beneath the platform of foliage. The tree rotated faster and surged up at the Belt, the air rushing through its foliage evoking sharp, homely scents in Pallis's nostrils. The sentry craft were immobile shadows against the red sky. Pallis braced his legs against the trunk of his tree, the strength of the wood a comforting base below him, and cupped his hands to his mouth. "Miners!"

Faces scowled over the rim of each craft. Pallis, squinting, could make out weapons held ready: spears, knives, clubs.

He held his hands wide. "We come in peace! You can see that, for the love of the Bones. What do you think I've got, an armada tucked under my branches?"

Now a miner called down. "Piss off home, woodsman, before you get yourself killed."

He felt a slow anger suffuse his scars. "My name is Pallis, and I'm not about to piss off anywhere. I've got news that will affect every man, woman and child on the Belt. And you're going to let me deliver it!"

The miner scratched his head suspiciously. "What news?"

"Let us through and I'll tell you. It comes from one of your own. Rees—"

The miners conferred with each other; then the spokesman turned back to Pallis. "You're lying. Rees is dead."

Pallis laughed. "No, he isn't; and his story is what my news is all about—"

With shocking suddenness a spear arced over the rim of the plate. He called a sharp warning to Jaen; the spear slid through the foliage and dwindled into the depths of the Nebula.

Pallis stood, hands on hips, and glared up at the miners. "You're lousy listeners, aren't you?"

"Woodsman, we're starving here because of Raft greed. And good men are dying trying to put that right—"

"Let them die! No one asked them to attack the Raft!" Jaen roared.

"Shut up, Jaen," Pallis hissed.

She snorted. "Look, pilot, those bastards are armed and we aren't. They're obviously not listening to a damn word we say. If we try to get any closer they'll probably just torch the tree with their jets. There's no point in suicide, is there? We'll just have to find another way."

He rubbed his beard. "But there is no other way. We have to talk to them." And, without letting himself think about it, he reached out with one foot and kicked over the nearest fire bowl. The kindling spilled out, smoking, and soon tiny flames were licking at the foliage.

Jaen stared, motionless, for perhaps five seconds; then she broke into a flurry of motion. "Pallis, what the hell—I'll get the blankets—"

He wrapped her forearm in one massive hand. "No, Jaen. Let it burn."

She stared into his face, her expression blank and uncomprehending.

The flames spread like living things. Above them the miners stared down, evidently baffled.

Pallis found he had to lick his lips before he could speak. "The foliage is very dry, you see. It's a consequence of the failing of the Nebula. The air is too arid; and the spectrum of starlight now isn't suitable for photosynthesis in the leaves ..."

"Pallis," Jaen said firmly, "stop babbling."

"... Yes. I'm gambling they'll pick us up. It's the only choice." He forced himself to study the blackened and twisting wood, the scorched leaves blowing in the air.

Jaen touched his scarred cheek; her fingertips came away damp. "This is really hurting you, isn't it?"

He laughed painfully. "Jaen, it's taking all my willpower to keep from the blankets." Suddenly anger coursed through his grief. "You know, of all the lousy, terrible things human beings do in this universe, this is the worst. People can do what they like to each other and I'll turn away; but now I'm forced to destroy one of my own trees . . ."

"You can let go of my arm."

"What?" Surprised, he glanced down to find he still gripped her forearm. He released it. "I'm sorry."

She rubbed her flesh ruefully. "I understand, tree-pilot; I won't try to stop you." She held out her hand. With gratitude he took it, gently this time.

The platform lurched, making them both stumble. The flames at the heart of the blaze now stood taller than Pallis. "It's happening fast," he murmured.

"Yes. Do you think we should grab hold of some supply pods?"

The thought made him laugh out loud. "What, so we can take light snacks on our way down to the Core?"

"OK, stupid idea. Not as stupid as setting fire to the bloody tree, though."

"Maybe you've a point."

A complete section of the rim gave way now, disappearing in a shower of burning embers; truncated branches burned like fat candles. "I think it's time," Pallis said.

Jaen peered about. "I guess the best strategy is to run to the rim and jump for it. Get as much speed as we can, and hope that that plus the rotation of the tree will take us far enough from all this debris."

"OK."

They looked into each other's eyes—and Pallis's feet were pumping over the crisp foliage; the rim approached and he fought the instincts of a lifetime to stop and then the rim was under his feet and—

—and he was sailing through the empty, bottomless air, his hand still locked to Jaen's.

It was almost exhilarating.

They tumbled, their flight slowing rapidly in the smoky air, and Pallis found himself hanging in the sky, feet toward the Belt, Jaen to his right, the tree before him.

The tree rim was a girdle of fire. Smoke billowed from the mass of foliage packed into the platform. With cracks like explosions the shaped branches failed and whole sectors of the disc, soaked in flame, came away with great rustles of sparks. Soon only the trunk remained, a gnarled remnant ringed by the stumps of its branches.

At last the disintegrated tree fell away into the sky, and Pallis and Jaen were left, hands still locked, hanging in a void.

The miners were nowhere to be seen.

Pallis looked at Jaen, oddly embarrassed. What, he wondered, should they talk about? "You know, Raft children grow up with a fear of falling," he said. "I guess the flat, steady surface beneath their feet gets taken for granted. They forget that the Raft is no more than a leaf hovering in the air . . . nothing like as substantial as those huge, impossible planets in that other universe you Scientists tell us about.

"But Belt children grow up on a tatty string of boxes circling a shrunken star. They have no safe plane to stand on. And their fear now wouldn't be of falling, but of having nothing to hang on to . . ."

Jaen pushed her hair back from her broad face. "Pallis, are you frightened?"

He thought it over. "No. I don't suppose I am. I

was more frightened before I kicked the bloody fire bowl over."

She shrugged, a mid-air gesture that made her body rock. "I don't seem to be either. I only regret your gamble didn't pay off—"

"Well, it was worth a try."

"—And I'd love to know how it all works out in the end . . ."

"How long do you think we'll last?"

"Maybe days. We should have brought food pallets. But at least we'll get to see some sights—Pallis!" Her eyes widened with shock; she let go of Pallis's hand and began to make scrambling, swimming motions, as if trying to crawl up through the air.

Pallis, startled, looked down.

The hard surface of a mine sentry craft was flying up toward him; two miners clung to a net cast over the metal. The iron rushed at him like a wall—

There was a taste of blood in his mouth.

Pallis opened his eyes. He was on his back, evidently on the mine craft; he could feel the knots of the netting through his shirt. He tried to sit up—and wasn't totally surprised to find his wrists and ankles bound to the net. He relaxed, trying to present no threat.

A broad, bearded face loomed over him. "This one's all right, Jame; he landed on his head."

"Thanks a lot," Pallis snapped. "Where's Jaen?"

"I'm here," she called, out of his sight.

"Are you OK?"

"I would be if these morons would let me sit up."

Pallis laughed—and winced as pain lanced through his mouth and cheeks. Evidently he would have a few new scars to add to his collection. Now a second face appeared, upside down from Pallis's point of view. Palis squinted. "I remember you. I thought I recognized the name. Jame, from the Quartermaster's."

"Hello, Pallis," the barman said gloomily.

"Still watering your ale, barman?"

Jame scowled. "You took a hell of a chance, tree-pilot. We should have let you drop . . ."

"But you didn't." Pallis smiled and relaxed.

During the short journey with the miners to the Belt Pallis remembered his wonder on hearing Rees's tale for the first time. In his role as a friend of the returned exile, he had sat with Rees, Decker and Hollerbach in the old Scientist's office, eyes transfixed by the simple hand movements Rees used to emphasize aspects of his adventures.

It was so fantastic, the stuff of legends: the Boneys, the hollow world, the whale, the song . . . but Rees's tone was dry, factual and utterly convincing, and he had responded to all Hollerbach's questions with poise.

At last Rees reached his description of the whales' great migration. "But of course," Hollerbach breathed. "Hah! It's so obvious." And he banged his old fist into his desk top.

Decker jumped, startled out of his enthrallment. "You silly old fart," he growled. "What's obvious?"

"So many pieces fit into place. Internebular migrations . . . ! Of course; we should have deduced it." Hollerbach got out of his chair and began to pace the room, thumping a bony fist into the palm of his hand.

"Enough histrionics, Scientist," Decker said. "Explain yourself."

"First of all, the whales' songs: these old speculations which our hero has now confirmed. Tell me this: why should the whales have such sizeable brains, such significant intelligence, such sophisticated communication? If you think it through they're basically just grazing creatures, and—by virtue of their sheer size—they are reasonably immune from the attentions of predators, as Rees testifies. Surely they need do little more than cruise through the atmosphere, munching airborne titbits, needing barely more sense than, say, a tree—avoid this shadow, swim around that gravity well . . ."

Pallis rubbed the bridge of his nose. "But a tree would never fly into the Core—not by choice anyway. Is that what you're saying?"

"Exactly, tree-pilot. To submit oneself to such a regime of tidal stress and hazardous radiation clearly calls for a higher brain function, a farsighted imperative to override the more elemental instincts, a high degree of communication—telepathic, perhaps—so that the correct behavior may be instilled in each generation."

Rees smiled. "Also a whale needs to select its trajectory around the Core quite precisely."

"Of course, of course."

Decker's face was a cloud of baffled anger. "Wait . . . Let's take it one step at a time." He scratched his beard. "What advantage do the whales gain by diving into the Core? Don't they just get trapped down there?"

"Not if they get the trajectory right," said Hollerbach, a little impatiently. "That's the whole point . . . Do you see? It's a gravitational slingshot." He held up a gaunt fist, mimed rotation by twisting it. "Here's the Core, spinning away. And—" The other hand was held flat; it swooped in toward the Core. "Here comes a whale." The model whale swooped past the Core, not quite touching, its hyperbolic path twisting in the same direction as the Core's rotation. "For a brief interval whale and Core are coupled by gravity. The whale picks up a little of the Core's angular momentum . . . It actually gains some energy from its encounter with the Core."

Pallis shook his head. "I'm glad I don't have to do that every time I fly a tree."

"It's quite elementary. After all, the whales manage it . . . And the reason they go through all this is to pick up enough energy to reach the Nebula's escape velocity."

Decker thumped a fist onto the desk top. "Enough of your babbling. What is the relevance of all this?"

Hollerbach sighed; his fingers reached for the bridge of his nose, searching for long-vanished spectacles. "The relevance is this. By reaching escape velocity the whales can leave the Nebula."

"They migrate," Rees said eagerly. "They travel to another nebula . . . A new one, with plenty of fresh stars, and a blue sky."

"We're talking about a grand transmission of life among the nebulae," Hollerbach said. "No doubt the whales aren't the only species which swim between the clouds . . . but even if they were they would probably carry across enough spores and seedlings in their digestive systems to allow life to gain a new foothold."

"It's all very exciting." Rees seemed almost intoxicated. "You see, the fact of migration solves another long-standing puzzle: the origin of life here. The Nebula is only a few million shifts old. There simply hasn't been time for life to evolve here in anything like the fashion we understand it did so on Earth."

"And the answer to this puzzle," Hollerbach

said, "turns out to be that it probably didn't evolve here after all."

"It migrated to the Nebula from somewhere else?"

"That's right, tree-pilot; from some other, exhausted cloud. And now this Nebula is finished; the whales know it is time to move on. There may have been other nebulae before the predecessor of our Nebula: a whole chain of migrations, reaching back in time as far as we can see."

"It's a marvellous picture," Rees said dreamily. "Once life was established somewhere in this universe it must have radiated out rapidly; perhaps all the nebulae are already populated in some way, with unimaginable species endlessly crossing empty space—"

Decker stared from one Scientist to the other. He said quietly, "Rees, if you don't come to the point—in simple words, and right now—so help me I'll throw you over the bloody Rim with my own bare hands. And the old fart. Got that?"

Rees spread his hands flat on the desk top, and again Pallis saw in his face that new, peculiar certainty. "Decker, the point is—just as the whales can escape the death of the Nebula, so can we."

Decker's frown deepened. "Explain."

"We have two choices." Rees chopped the edge of his hand into the table. "One. We stay here, watch the stars go out, squabble over the remaining scraps of food. Or—" Another chop. "Two. We emulate the whales. We fall around the Core, use the slingshot effect. We migrate to a new nebula."

"And how, precisely, do we do that?"

"I don't, precisely, know," Rees said acidly. "Maybe we cut away the trees, let the Raft fall into the Core."

Pallis tried to imagine that. "How would you keep the crew from being blown off?"

Rees laughed. "I don't know, Pallis. That's just a sketch; I'm sure there are better ways."

Decker sat back, his scarred face a mask of intense concentration.

Hollerbach held up a crooked finger. "Of course you almost made the trip involuntarily, Rees. If you hadn't found a way to deflect that whale, even now you'd be travelling among the star clouds with it."

"Maybe that's the way to do it," Pallis said. "Cut our way into the whales, carry in food and water, and let them take us to our new home."

Rees shook his head. "I don't think that would work, pilot. The interior of a whale isn't designed to support human life."

Once more Pallis struggled with the strange ideas. "So we'll have to take the Raft ... but the Raft will lose all its air, won't it, outside the Nebula? So we'll have to build some sort of shell to keep in the atmosphere ..."

Hollerbach nodded, evidently pleased. "That's good thinking, Pallis. Maybe we'll make a Scientist of you yet."

"Patronizing old bugger," Pallis murmured affectionately.

Again the fire burned in Rees. He turned his intense gaze on Decker. "Decker, somewhere buried in all this bullshit is a way for the race to survive. That's what's at stake here. We can do it; have no doubt about that. But we need your support." Rees fell silent.

Pallis held his breath. He sensed that he was at a momentous event, a turning point in the history of his species, and somehow it all hinged on Rees. Pallis studied the young Scientist closely, thought he observed a slight tremble of his cheeks; but Rees's determination showed in his eyes.

At length Decker said quietly, "How do we start?"

Pallis let his breath out slowly; he saw Hollerbach smile, and a kind of victory shone in Rees's eyes; but wisely neither of them exulted in their triumph. Rees said: "First we contact the miners."

Decker exploded: "What?"

"They're humans too, you know," Hollerbach said gently. "They have a right to life."

"And we need them," said Rees. "We're likely to need iron. Lots of it . . ."

And so Pallis and Jaen had destroyed a tree, and now sat on a Belt rooftop. The star kernel hung above them, a blot in the sky; a cloud of rain drizzled around them, plastering Pallis's hair and beard to his face. Sheen sat facing them, slowly chewing on a slab of meat-sim. Jame was behind her, arms folded. Sheen said slowly, "I'm still not sure why I shouldn't simply kill you."

Pallis grunted, exasperated. "For all your faults, Sheen, I never took you for a fool. Don't you understand the significance of what I've traveled here to tell you?"

Jame smirked. "How are we supposed to know it isn't some kind of trick? Pilot, you forget we're at war."

"A trick? You explain how Rees survived his exile from the Belt—and how he came to ride home on a whale. My god, his tale comes close to the simplest hypothesis when you think about it."

Jame scratched his dirt-crusted scalp. "The what?"

Jaen smiled. Pallis said, "I'll explain sometime . . . Damn it, I'm telling you the time for war is gone, barman. Its justification is gone. Rees has shown us a way out of this gas prison we're in . . . but we have to work together. Sheen, can't we get out of this bloody rain?"

The rain trickled down her tired face. "You're not welcome here. I told you. You're here on sufferance. You're not entitled to shelter . . ."

Her words were much as they had been since Pallis had begun describing his mission here—but was her tone a little more uncertain? "Look, Sheen, I'm not asking for a one-way deal. We need your iron, your metal-working skills—but you need food, water, medical supplies. Don't you? And for better or worse the Raft still has a monopoly on the supply machines. Now I can tell you, with the full backing of Decker, the Committee, and whoever bloody else you want me to produce, that we're willing to share. If you like we'll allocate you a sector of the Raft with its own set of machines. And in the longer term . . . we offer the miners life for their children."

Jame leant forward and spat into the rain. "You're full of crap, tree-pilot."

Beside Pallis Jaen bunched a fist. "You bloody clod—"

"Oh, shut up, both of you." Sheen pushed wet hair from her eyes. "Look, Pallis; even if I said 'yes' that's not the end of it. We don't have a 'Committee,' or a boss, or any of that. We talk things out among us."

Pallis nodded, hope bursting in his heart. "I understand that." He stared directly into Sheen's brown eyes; he tried to pour his whole being, all their shared memories, into his words. "Sheen, you know me. You know I'm no fool, whatever else I'm

228

RAFT

guilty of ... I'm asking you to trust me. Think it through. Would I have stranded myself here if I wasn't sure of my case? Would I have lost something so precious as—"

Jame sneered. "As what, your worthless life?"

With genuine surprise Pallis turned to the barman. "Jame, I meant my tree."

A complex expression crossed Sheen's face. "Pallis, I don't know. I need time."

Pallis held up his palms. "I understand. Take all the time you want; speak to whoever you want. In the meantime ... will you let us stay?"

"You're not stopping at the Quartermaster's, that's for sure."

Pallis smiled serenely. "Barman, if I never sup your dilute piss again it will be too soon."

Sheen shook her head. "You don't change, do you, pilot ... ? You know, even if—if—your story is true, your madcap scheme is full of holes." She pointed to the star kernel. "After working on that thing maybe we have a better feel for gravity than you people. I can tell you, that gravitational slingshot maneuver is going to be bloody tricky. You'll have to get it just right ..."

"I know. And even as we sit here we're getting some advice on that."

"Advice? Who from?"

Pallis smiled.

Gord woke to a sound of shouting.

He pushed himself upright from his pallet. He wondered vaguely how long he had slept ... Here, of course, there was no cycle of shifts, no Belt turning like a clock—nothing to mark the time but sour sleep, dull, undemanding work, foul expeditions to the ovens. Still, the former engineer's stomach told him that at least a few hours had elapsed. He

229

looked to the diminishing pile of food stacked in the corner of his hut—and found himself shuddering. A little more time and perhaps he'd be hungry enough to eat more of the stuff.

The shouting grew in volume and a slow curiosity gathered in him. The world of the Boneys was seamless and incident-free. What could be causing such a disturbance? A whale? But the lookouts usually spotted the great beasts many shifts before their arrival, and no song had been initiated.

Almost reluctantly he got to his feet and made his way to the door.

A crowd of a dozen or so Boneys, adults and children alike, stood on the leather surface of the world with faces upturned. One small child pointed skywards. Puzzled, Gord stepped out to join them.

Air washed down over him, carrying with it a scent of wood and leaves that briefly dispersed the taint of corruption in his nostrils. He looked up and gasped.

A tree rotated in the sky. It was grand and serene, its trunk no more than fifty yards above him.

Gord hadn't seen a tree since his exile from the Belt. Perhaps some of these Boneys had never seen one in their lives.

A man dangled upside down from the trunk, dark, slim and oddly familiar. He was waving. "Gord? Is that you . . . ?"

"Rees? It can't be . . . You're dead. Aren't you?"

Rees laughed. "They keep telling me I ought to be."

"You survived your jump to the whale?"

"More than that . . . I made it back to the Raft."

"You're not serious."

"It's a long story. I've travelled from the Raft to see you."

Gord shook his head and spread his hands to indicate the sack of bones that was his world. "If that's true, you're crazy. Why come back?"

Rees called, "Because I need your help . . ."

13

On clouds of steam the plate ship swam toward the Belt. Sheen and Grye stood at the entrance to the Quartermaster's and watched it approach with its cargo of Boneys. Sheen felt dread build up in her, and she shuddered.

She turned to Grye. When the Scientist had first been exiled here by the Raft he had been quite portly, Sheen remembered; now the skin hung from his bones in folds, as if emptied of substance. He caught her studying him. He shifted his drink bowl from hand to hand and dropped his eyes.

Sheen laughed. "I believe you're blushing."

"I'm sorry."

"Look, you've got to lighten up. You're one of us now, remember. Here we are, all humans together, the past behind us. It's a new world. Right?"

He flinched. "I'm sorry . . ."

"Stop saying that."

"It's just that it's hard to forget the hundreds of shifts we have had to endure since coming here." His voice was mild, but somewhere buried in there was a spark of true bitterness. "Ask Roch if the past is behind us. Ask Cipse." Now Sheen felt her own face redden. Reluctantly she recalled her own hatred for the exiles, how she had willingly al-

233

lowed their cruel treatment to continue. A hot shame coursed through her. Now that Rees had changed the perspective—given the whole race, it seemed, a new goal—such actions seemed worse than contemptible.

With an effort she forced herself to speak. "If it means anything, I'm sorry."

He didn't reply.

For some moments they stood in awkward silence. Grye's posture softened a little, as if he felt a little more comfortable in her company.

"Well," Sheen said briskly, "at least Jame isn't barring you from the Quartermaster's any more."

"We should be grateful for small mercies." He took a sip from his bowl and sighed. "Not so small, maybe . . ." He indicated the approaching plate. "You miners do seem to have accepted us a lot more easily since the first Boneys arrived."

"I can understand that. Perhaps the presence of the Boneys shows the rest of us how much we have in common."

"Yes."

The Belt's rotation carried the Quartermaster's beneath the approaching plate once again. Sheen could see that the little craft carried three Boneys, two men and a woman. They were all squat and broad, and they wore battered tunics provided by the Belt folk. Sheen had heard legends of what they chose to wear on their home worldlet . . . She found herself shuddering again.

The Belt was being used as a way station between the Bone world and the Raft; Boneys traveling to the Raft would stay here for a few shifts before departing on a supply tree. At any one time there was, Sheen reminded herself, only a handful of Boneys scattered around the Belt . . . but most miners felt that handful was too many.

The Boneys stared down at her, thick jaws gaping. One of the men caught Sheen's eye. He winked at her and rolled his hips suggestively. She found her food rising to her throat; but she held his stare until the plate had passed over the Belt's narrow horizon. "I wish I could believe we need those people," she muttered.

Grye shrugged. "They are human beings. And, according to Rees, they didn't choose the way they live. They have just tried to survive, as we all must do . . . Anyway, we might not need them. Our work with the Moles on the star kernel is proceeding well."

"Really?"

Grye leaned closer, more confident now that the conversation had moved onto a topic he knew about. "You understand what we're trying to do down there?"

"Vaguely . . ."

"You see, if Rees's gravitational slingshot idea is going to work we will have to drop the Raft onto a precise trajectory around the Core. The asymptotic direction is highly sensitive to the initial conditions—"

She held up her hands. "You'd better stick to words of one syllable. Or less."

"I'm sorry. We're going into a tight orbit, very close to the Core. The closer we pass, the more our path will be twisted around the Core. But the differences for a small deviation are dramatic. You have to imagine a pencil of neighboring trajectories approaching the Core. As they round the singularity they fan out, like unraveling fibers; and so a small error could give the Raft a final direction very different from the one we want."

"I understand . . . I think. But it doesn't make

much difference, surely? You're aiming at a whole nebula, a target thousands of miles wide."

"Yes, but it's a long way away. It's quite a precise piece of marksmanship. And if we miss, by even a few miles, we could end up sailing into empty, airless space, on without end . . ."

"So how is the Mole helping?"

"What we need to do is work out all the trajectories in that pencil, so we can figure out how to approach the Core. It takes us hours to work the results by hand—work which, apparently, was performed by slavelike machines for the original Crew. It was Rees who had the idea of using the Mole brains."

Sheen pulled a face. "It would be."

"He argued that the Moles must once have been flying machines. And if you look closely you can see where the rockets, fins and so on must have fitted. So, argued Rees, the Moles must understand orbital dynamics, to some extent. We tried putting our problems to a Mole. It took hours of question-and-answer down there on the kernel surface . . . but at last we started getting usable results. Now the Mole provides concise answers, and we're proceeding quickly."

She nodded, juggling her drink. "Impressive. And you're sure of the quality of the results?"

He seemed to bridle a little. "As sure as we can be. We've checked samples against hand calculations. But none of us are experts in this particular field." His voice hardened again. "Our Chief Navigator was Cipse, you see."

She could think of no reply. She drained the last of her globe. "Well, look, Grye, I think it's time I—"

"Now, then, where can old Quid take a drink around here?"

The voice was low and sly. She turned, startled, and found herself looking down at a wide, wrinkled face; a grin revealed rotten stumps of teeth, and black eyes traveled over her body. She couldn't help but shrink away from the Boney. Vaguely she was aware of Grye quailing beside her. "What ... do you want?"

The Boney stroked a finely carved spear of bone. His eyes widened in mock surprise. "Why, darling, I've only just arrived, and what kind of welcome is that? Eh? Now that we're all friends together ..." He took a step closer. "You'll like old Quid when you get to know him—"

She stood her ground and let her disgust show in her face. "You come any nearer to me and I'll break your bloody arm."

He laughed evenly. "I'd be interested to see you try, darling. Remember I grew to my fine stature in high-gee ... not this baby-soft micro gravity you have here. You're muscled very attractively; but I bet your bones are as brittle as dead leaves." He looked at her acutely. "Surprised to find old Quid using phrases like 'micro gravity,' girl? I may be a Boney, but I'm not a monster; nor am I stupid." He reached out and grabbed her forearm. His grip was like iron. "It's a lesson you evidently need to learn—"

She thrust at the wall of the Quartermaster's with both legs and performed a fast back flip, shaking free his hand. When she landed she had a knife in her fist.

He held up his hands with an admiring grin. "All right, all right ..." Now Quid turned his gaze on Grye; the Scientist clutched his drink globe to his chest, trembling. "I heard what you were saying," Quid said. "All that stuff about orbits and trajectories ... But you won't make it, you know."

Grye's cheeks quivered and stretched. "What do you mean?"

"What are you going to do when you're riding your bit of iron, down there by the Core himself—and you find you're on a path that isn't in your tables of numbers? At the critical moment—at closest approach—you'll have maybe minutes to react. What will you do? Turn back and draw some more curves on paper? Eh?"

Sheen snorted. "You're an expert, are you?"

He smiled. "At last you're recognizing my worth, darling." He tapped his head. "Listen to me. There's more on orbits locked in here than on all the bits of paper in the Nebula."

"Rubbish," she spat.

"Yes? Your little friend Rees doesn't think so, does he?" He hefted his spear in his right hand; Sheen kept her eyes on the spear's bone tip. "But then," Quid went on, "Rees has seen what we can do with these things—"

Abruptly he twisted so that he faced the star kernel; with surprising grace he hurled the spear. The weapon accelerated into the five-gee gravity well of the kernel. Moving so fast that it streaked in Sheen's vision, it missed the iron horizon by mere yards and twisted behind the star—

—and now it emerged from the other side of the kernel, exploding at her like a fist. She ducked, grabbing for Grye; but the spear passed a few yards above her head and sailed away into the air.

Quid sighed. "Not quite true. Old Quid needs to get his eye in. Still—" He winked. "Not bad for a first try, eh?" He prodded Grye's sagging paunch. "Now, that's what I call orbital dynamics. And all in old Quid's head. Astonishing, isn't it? And that's why you need the Boneys. Now then, Quid needs his drink. See you later, darling . . ."

And he brushed past them and entered the Quartermaster's.

Gord shoved his thinning blond hair from his eyes and thumped the table. "It can't be done. I know what I'm talking about, damn it."

Jaen towered over the little engineer. "And I'm telling you you're wrong."

"Child, I've more experience than you will ever—"

"Experience?" She laughed. "Your experience with the Boneys has softened your brains."

Now Gord stood. "Why, you—"

"Stop, stop." Tiredly Hollerbach placed his age-spotted hands on the table top.

Jaen simmered. "But he won't listen."

"Jaen. Shut up."

"But—ah, damn it." She subsided.

Hollerbach let his eyes roam around the cool, perfect lines of the Bridge's Observation Room. The floor was covered with tables and spread-out diagrams: Scientists and others pored over sketches of orbital paths, models of grandiose protective shells to be built around the Raft, tables showing rates of food consumption and oxygen exhaustion under various regimes of rationing. The air was filled with feverish, urgent conversation. Wistfully Hollerbach recalled the studied calm of the place when he had first joined the great Class of Scientists; in those days there had still been some blue in the sky, and there had seemed all the time in the world for him to study . . .

At least, he reflected, all this urgent effort was in the right direction, and seemed to be producing the results they needed to carry through this scheme. The tables and dry graphs told a slowly emerging tale of a modified Raft hurtling on a courageous trajectory around the Core; these sober Scientists and their assistants were together engaged on man's most ambitious project since the building of the Raft itself.

But now Gord had walked in with his scraps of paper and his pencil jottings ... and his devastating news. Hollerbach forced his attention back to Gord and Jaen, who still confronted each other—and he found his eyes meeting Decker's. The Raft's leader stood impassively before the table, his scarred face clouded by a scowl of concentration.

Hollerbach sighed inwardly. Trust Decker, with his instinct for the vital, to arrive at the point of crisis. "Let's go through it again, please, engineer," he said to Gord. "And this time, Jaen, try to be rational. Yes? Insults help nobody."

Jaen glowered, her broad face crimson.

"Scientist, I am—was—the Belt's chief engineer," Gord began. "I know more than I care to remember about the behavior of metals under extreme conditions. I've seen it flow like plastic, turn brittle as old wood ..."

"No one is questioning your credentials, Gord," Hollerbach said, unable to contain his irritation. "Get to the point."

Gord tapped his papers with his fingertips. "I've studied the tidal stresses the Raft will undergo at closest approach. And I've considered the speeds it must attain after the slingshot, if it's to escape the Nebula. And I can tell you, Hollerbach, you haven't a hope in hell. It's all here; you can check it out—"

Hollerbach waved his hand. "We will, we will. Just tell us,"

"First of all, the tides. Scientist, the stresses will rip this Raft to pieces, long before you get to closest approach. And the fancy structures your bright

240

kids are planning to erect over the deck will simply blow apart like a pile of twigs."

"Gord, I don't accept that," Jaen burst out. "If we reconfigure the Raft, perhaps buttress some sections, make sure our attitude is correct at closest approach—"

Gord returned her gaze and said nothing.

"Check his figures later, Jaen," Hollerbach said. "Go on, engineer."

"Also, what about air resistance? At the speeds required, down there in the thickest air of the whole Nebula, whatever shoal of fragments emerges from closest approach is simply going to burn up like so many meteors. You'll achieve a spectacular fireworks display and little more. Look, I'm sorry this is so disappointing, but your scheme simply cannot work. The laws of physics are telling you that, not me . . ."

Decker leaned forward. "Miner," he said softly, "if what you say is true then we may after all be doomed to a slow death in this stinking place. Now, maybe I'm a poor judge of people, but you don't seem too distressed by the prospect. Do you have an alternative suggestion?"

A slow smile spread over Gord's face. "Well, as it happens . . ."

Hollerbach sat back, letting his jaw drop. "Why the hell didn't you tell us in the first place?"

Gord's grin widened. "If you'd troubled to ask—"

Decker laid a massive hand on the table. "No more word games," he said quietly. "Miner, get on with it."

Gord's grin evaporated; shadows of fear chased across his face, reminding Hollerbach uncomfortably of how much this blameless little man had endured. "Nobody's threatening you," he said. "Just show us."

Looking more comfortable, Gord stood and led them out of the Bridge. Soon the four of them—Gord, Hollerbach, Decker and Jaen—stood beside the dull glow of the Bridge's hull; the starlight beat down, causing beads of perspiration to erupt over Hollerbach's bald scalp. Gord stroked the hull with his palm. "When was the last time you touched this stuff? Perhaps you walk past it every day, taking it for granted; but when you come at it fresh, it's quite a revelation."

Hollerbach pressed his hand to the silver surface, feeling his skin glide smoothly over it . . . "It's frictionless. Yes. Of course."

"You tell me this was once a vessel in its own right, before it was incorporated into the deck of the Raft," Gord went on. "I agree with you. And furthermore, I think this little ship was designed to travel through the air."

"Frictionless," Hollerbach breathed again, still rubbing his palm over the strange metal. "Of course. How could we all have been so stupid? You see," he told Decker, "this surface is so smooth the air will simply slide over it, no matter what speed it travels. And it won't heat up as would ordinary metal . . .

"And no doubt this structure would be strong enough to survive the tidal stresses close to the Core; far better, at least, than our ramshackle covered Raft. Decker, obviously we'll have to go through Gord's calculations, but I think we'll find he's correct. Do you see what this means?" Something like wonder coursed through Hollerbach's old brain. "We'll have no need to build an iron bell to keep our air in place. We can simply close the Bridge port. We will ride a ship as our ancestors rode . . . Why, we can even use our instruments to study the Core as we pass. Decker, a door has closed; but another has opened. Do you understand?"

Decker's face was a dark mask. "Oh, I understand, Hollerbach. But there's another point you might have missed."

"What?"

"The Raft is half a mile wide. This Bridge is merely a hundred yards long."

Hollerbach frowned; then the implications began to hit him.

"Find Rees," Decker snapped. "I'll meet you both in your office in a quarter of an hour." With a curt nod, he turned and walked away.

Rees found the atmosphere in Hollerbach's office electric.

"Close the door," Decker growled.

Rees sat before Hollerbach's desk. Hollerbach sat opposite, long fingers pulling at the papery skin of his hands. Decker sucked breath through his wide nostrils; eyes downcast, he paced around the small office.

Rees frowned. "Why the funereal atmosphere? What's happened?"

Hollerbach leaned forward. "We have a ... complication." He sketched out Gord's reservations. "We have to check his figures, of course. But—"

"But he's right," Rees said. "You know he is, don't you?"

Hollerbach sighed, the air scraping over his throat. "Of course he's right. And if the rest of us hadn't got carried away with glamorous speculations about gravitational slingshots and a mile-wide dome, we'd have asked the same questions. And come to the same conclusions."

Rees nodded. "But if we use the Bridge we're facing problems we didn't anticipate. We thought we could save everybody." His eyes flicked to Decker. "Now we have to choose."

Decker's face was dark with anger. "And so you turn to me."

Rees rubbed the space between his eyes. "Decker, provided we manage the departure cleanly those left behind will survive for hundreds, thousands of shifts—"

"I hope those abandoned by your shining ship will take it so philosophically." Decker spat. "Scientists. Answer me this. Will this adventure work? Could the passengers of the Bridge actually survive a passage around the Core, and then through space to the new nebula? We're looking at a very different set-up from Rees's original idea."

Rees nodded slowly. "We'll need supply machines, whatever compressed air we can carry in the confines of the Bridge, perhaps plants to convert stale air to—"

"Spare me the trivia," Decker snapped. "This absurd project will entail backbreaking labor, injury, death. And no doubt the departing Bridge will siphon off many of mankind's best brains, worsening the lot of those left behind still further.

"If this mission does not have a reasonable chance of success then I won't back it. It's as simple as that. I won't shorten the lives of the bulk of those I'm responsible for, solely to give a few heroes a pleasure ride."

"You know," Hollerbach said thoughtfully, "I doubt that when you—ah, acquired—power on this Raft you imagined having to face decisions like this."

Decker scowled. "Are you mocking me, Scientist?"

Hollerbach closed his eyes. "No."

"Let's think it through," Rees said. "Hollerbach,

we need to transport a genetic pool large enough to sustain the race. How many people?"

Hollerbach shrugged. "Four or five hundred?"

"Can we accommodate so many?"

Hollerbach paused before answering. "Yes," he said slowly. "But it will take careful management. Strict planning, rationing . . . It will be no pleasure ride."

Decker growled, "Genetic pool? Your five hundred will arrive like babies in the new world, without resources. Before they breed they will have to find a way of not falling into the Core of the new nebula."

Rees nodded. "Yes. But so did the Crew of the original Ship. Our migrants will be worse off materially . . . but at least they will know what to expect."

Decker drove his fist into his thigh. "So you're telling me that the mission can succeed, that a new colony could survive? Hollerbach, you agree?"

"Yes," Hollerbach said quietly. "We have to work out the details. But—yes. You have my assurance."

Decker closed his eyes and his great shoulders slumped. "All right. We must continue with your scheme. And this time, try to foresee the problems."

Rees felt a vast relief. If Decker had decided otherwise—if the great goal had been taken away—how would he, Rees, have whiled away the rest of his life?

He shuddered. It was unimaginable.

"Now we face further actions," Hollerbach said. He held up his skeletal hand and counted points on his fingers. "Obviously we must continue our studies on the mission itself—the equipage, separation, guidance of the Bridge. For those left behind, we have to think about moving the Raft."

Decker looked surprised.

"Decker, that star up there isn't going to go away. We'd have shifted out from under it long ago, in normal times. Now that the Raft is fated to stay in this Nebula, we must move it. And finally ..." Hollerbach's voice tailed away.

"And finally," Decker said bitterly, "we have to think about how to select those who travel on the Bridge. And those who stay behind."

Rees said, "Perhaps some kind of ballot would be fair ..."

Decker shook his head. "No. This jaunt will only succeed if you have the right people."

Hollerbach nodded. "You're right, of course."

Rees frowned. "... I guess so. But—who selects the 'right' crew?"

Decker glared at him, the scars on his face deepening into a mask of pain. "Who do you think?"

Rees cradled his drink globe. "So that's it," he told Pallis. "Now Decker faces the decision of his life."

Pallis stood before his cage of young trees, poked at the wooden bars. Some of the trees were almost old enough to release, he reflected absently. "Power brings responsibility, it seems. I'm not certain Decker understood that when he emerged on top from that joke Committee. But he sure understands it now ... Decker will make the right decision; let's hope the rest of us do the same."

"What do you mean, the rest of us?"

Pallis lifted the cage from its stand; it was light, if bulky, and he held it out to Rees. The young Scientist put down his drink globe and took the cage uncertainly, staring at the agitated young trees. "This should go on the journey," Pallis said. "Maybe you should take more. Release them into the new nebula, let them breed—and, in a few hundred shifts, whole new forests will begin to form. If the new place doesn't have its own already ..."

"Why are you giving this to me? I don't understand, tree-pilot."

"But I do," Sheen said.

Pallis whirled. Rees gasped, juggling the cage in his shock.

She stood just inside the doorway, diffuse starlight catching the fine hairs on her bare arms.

Pallis, with hot shame, felt himself blush; seeing her standing there, in his own cabin, made him feel like a clumsy adolescent. "I wasn't expecting you," he said lamely.

She laughed. "I can see that. Well, am I not to be invited in? Can't I have a drink?"

"Of course ..."

Sheen settled comfortably to the floor, crossing her legs under her. She nodded to Rees.

Rees looked from Pallis to Sheen and back, his color deepening. Pallis was surprised. Did Rees have some feeling for his former supervisor ... even after his treatment during his return exile on the Belt? Rees stood up, awkwardly fumbling with the cage. "I'll talk to you again, Pallis—"

"You don't have to go," Pallis said quickly.

Sheen's eyes sparkled with amusement.

Again Rees looked from one to the other. "I guess it would be for the best," he said. With mumbled farewells, he left.

Pallis handed Sheen a drink globe. "So he's carrying a torch for you."

"Adolescent lust," she said starkly.

Pallis grinned. "I can understand that. But Rees is no adolescent."

"I know that. He's become determined, and he's driving us all ahead of him. He's the savior of the world. But he's also a bloody idiot when he wants to be."

"I think he's jealous . . ."

"Is there something for him to be jealous of, tree-pilot?"

Pallis dropped his eyes without reply.

"So," she said briskly, "you're not travelling on the Bridge. That was the meaning of your gift to Rees, wasn't it?"

He nodded, turning to the space the cage had occupied.

"There's not much of my life left," he said slowly. "My place on that Bridge would be better to go to some youngster."

She reached forward and touched his knee; the feeling of her flesh was electric. "They'll only invite you to go if they think they need you."

He snorted. "Sheen, by the time those caged skitters have grown, my stiffening corpse will long since have been hurled over the Rim. And what use will I be without a tree to fly?" He pointed to the flying forest hidden by the cabin's roof. "My life is the forest up there. After the Bridge goes, the Raft will still be here, for a long time to come. And they're going to need their trees."

She nodded. "Well, I understand, even if I don't agree." She fixed him with her clear eyes. "I guess we can debate it after the Bridge has gone."

He gasped; then he reached out and took her hand. "What are you talking about? Surely you're not planning to stay too? Sheen, you're crazy—"

"Tree-pilot," she snapped, "I did not insult you on the quality of your decision." She let her hand rest in his. "As you said, the Raft is going to be here for a long time to come. And so is the Belt. It's going to be grim after the Bridge departs, taking away—all our hope. But someone will have to keep things turning. Someone will have to call the shift changes. And, like you, I find I don't want to leave behind my life."

He nodded. "Well, I won't say I agree—"

She said warningly, "Tree-pilot—"

"But I respect your decision. And—" He felt the heat rise to his face again. "And I'm glad you'll still be here."

She smiled and moved her face closer to his. "What are you trying to say, tree-pilot?"

"Maybe we can keep each other company."

She reached up, took a curl of his beard, and tugged it gently. "Yes. Maybe we can."

14

A cage of scaffolding obscured the Bridge's clean lines. Crew members crawled over the scaffolding fixing steam jets to the Bridge's hull. Rees, with Hollerbach and Grye, walked around the perimeter of the work area. Rees eyed the project with a critical eye. "We're too slow, damn it."

Grye twisted his hands together. "Rees, I'm forced to say that your detailed understanding of this project is woefully lacking. Come—" He beckoned. "Let me show you how much progress we have made." He slapped a plump hand against the wooden cage surrounding the Bridge; it was a rectangular box securely fastened to the deck, and it supported three broad hoops which wrapped around the Bridge itself. "We can't take chances with this," Grye said. "The last stage in the launch process will be the cutting away of the Bridge from the deck. When that is done, all that will support the Bridge will be this scaffolding. A mistake made here could cause catastrophic—"

"I know, I know," Rees said, irritated. "But the fact is we're running out of time . . ."

They came to the Bridge's open port. Under the supervision of Jaen and another Scientist, two burly workmen were manhandling an instrument

251

out of the Observatory. The instrument—a mass spectrometer, Rees recognized—was dented and scratched, and its power lead terminated in a melted stump. The spectrometer was placed with several others in an eerie group some yards from the Bridge; the discarded instruments turned blinded sensors to the sky.

Hollerbach shuddered. "And this is something I certainly hesitate over," he said, his voice strained. "We face an awful dilemma. Every instrument we vandalize and throw out gives us floor space and air for another four or five people. But can we afford to leave behind this telescope, that spectrometer? Is this device a mere luxury—or, in the unknown environs of our destination, will we leave ourselves blind in some key spectrum?"

Rees suppressed a sigh. Hesitation, delays, obfuscations, more delays ... Obviously the Scientists could not metamorphose into men of action in mere hours—and he sympathized with the dilemmas they were trying to resolve—but he wished they could learn to establish and stick to priorities.

Now they came to a group of Scientists probing cautiously at a food machine. The huge device loomed over them, its outlets like stilled mouths. Rees knew that the machine was too large to carry into the Bridge's interior, and so it—and a second companion machine—would, rather absurdly, have to be lodged close to the port in the Bridge's outer corridor.

Grye and Hollerbach both made to speak, but Rees held up his hands. "No," he said acidly. "Let me go into the reasons why we can't possibly rush this particular process. We've calculated that if strict rationing is imposed during the flight two machines should satisfy our needs. This one even has an air filtration and oxygenation unit built into it, we've discovered . . ."

"Yes," Grye said eagerly, "but that calculation depends on a key assumption: that the machines will work at full efficiency inside the Bridge. And we don't know enough about their power supply to be sure. We know this machine's power source is built into it somehow—unlike the Bridge instruments, which shared a single unit by way of cables—and we even suspect, from the old manuals, that it's based on a microscopic black hole—but we're not sure. What if it requires starlight as a source of replenishment? What if it produces volumes of some noxious gas which, in the confines of the Bridge, will suffocate us all?"

Rees said, "We have to test and be sure, I accept that. If the efficiency of the machine goes down by just ten per cent—then that's fifty more people we have to leave behind."

Grye nodded. "Then you see—"

"I see that these decisions take time. But time is what we just don't have, damn it . . ." Pressure built inside him: a pressure which, he knew, would not be relieved until, for better or worse, the Bridge was launched.

Walking on, they met Gord. The mine engineer and Nead, who was working as his assistant, were carrying a steam jet unit to the Bridge. Gord nodded briskly. "Gentlemen."

Rees studied the little mine engineer, his worries momentarily lifting. Gord had returned to his old efficient, bustling, slightly prickly self; he was barely recognizable as the shadow Rees had found on the Boneys' worldlet. "You're doing well, Gord."

Gord scratched his bald pate. "We're progessing," he said lightly. "I'll say no more than that; but, yes, we're progressing."

Hollerbach leaned forward, hands folded behind his back. "What about this control system problem?"

Gord nodded cautiously. "Rees, are you up to date on this one? To direct the Bridge's fall—to change its orbit—we need some way to control the steam jets we'll have fixed to the hull; but we don't want to make any breaches in the hull through which to pass our control lines. We don't even know if we can make breaches, come to that.

"Now it looks as if we can use components from the cannibalized Moles. Some of their motor units operate on an action-at-a-distance principle. I'm just a simple engineer; maybe you Scientists understand the ins and outs of it. But what it boils down to is that we may be able to operate the jets from inside the Bridge with a series of switches which won't need any physical connection to the jets at all. We're about to run tests on the extent to which the hull material blocks the signals."

Hollerbach smiled. "I'm impressed. Was this your idea?"

"Ah . . ." Gord scratched his cheek. "We did get a little guidance from a Mole brain. Once you ask the right questions—and get past its complaints about 'massive sensor dysfunction'—it's surprising how . . ." His voice tailed away and his eyes widened.

"Rees." The vast voice came from behind Rees; the Scientist stiffened. "I thought I'd find you hanging around here."

Rees turned and lifted his face up to Roch's. The huge miner's eyes were, as ever, red-rimmed with inchoate anger; his fists opened and closed like pistons. Grye whimpered softly and edged behind

Hollerbach. "I have work to do, Roch," Rees said calmly. "So must you; I suggest you return to it."

"Work?" Roch's filth-rimmed nostrils flared and he waved a fist at the Bridge. "Like hell will I work so you and your pox-ridden friends can fly off in this fancy thing."

Hollerbach said sternly, "Sir, the lists of passengers have not yet been published; and until they are it is up to all of us—"

"They don't need to be published. We all know who'll be on that trip ... and it won't be the likes of me. Rees, I should have sucked your brains out of your skull while I had the chance down on the kernel." Roch held up a rope-like finger. "I'll be back," he growled. "And when I find I'm not on that list I'm going to make damn sure you're not either." He stabbed the finger at Grye. "And the same goes for you!"

Grye turned ash white and trembled convulsively.

Roch stalked off. Gord hefted his jet and said wryly, "Good to know that in this time of upheaval some things have stayed exactly the same. Come on, Nead; let's get this thing mounted."

Rees faced Hollerbach and Grye. He jabbed a thumb over his shoulder toward the departed Roch. "That's why we are running out of time," he said. "The political situation on this Raft—no, damn it, the human situation—is deteriorating fast. The whole thing is unstable. Everyone knows that a 'list' is being drawn up ... and most people have a good idea who'll be on it. How long can we expect people to work toward a goal most of them cannot share? A second uprising would be catastrophic. We would descend into anarchy—"

Hollerbach emitted a sigh; suddenly he seemed

to stagger. Grye took his arm. "Chief Scientist—are you all right?"

Hollerbach fixed rheumy eyes on Rees. "I'm tired, you see ... terribly tired. You're right, of course, Rees, but what can any of us do, other than give our best efforts to this goal?"

Rees realized suddenly that he had been unloading his own doubts onto the weakening shoulders of Hollerbach, as if he were still a child and the old man some kind of impregnable adult. "I'm sorry," he said. "I shouldn't burden you—"

Hollerbach waved a shaky hand. "No, no; you're quite right. In a way it helps clarify my own thinking." His eyes twinkled with a faint amusement. "Even your friend Roch helps, in a way. Look at the comparison between us. Roch is young, powerful; I'm too old to stand up—let alone to pass on my frailties to a new generation. Which of us should go on the mission?"

Rees was appalled. "Hollerbach, we need your understanding. You're not suggesting ..."

"Rees, I suspect a grave flaw in the way we live our lives here has been our refusal to accept our place in the universe. We inhabit a world which places a premium on physical strength and endurance—as your friend Roch so ably demonstrates—and on agility, reflex and adaptabilty—for example, the Boneys—rather than 'understanding.' We are little more than clumsy animals lost in this bottomless sky. But our inheritance of ageing gadgetry from the Ship, the supply machines and the rest, has let us maintain the illusion that we are masters of this universe, as perhaps we were masters of the world man came from.

"Now, this enforced migration is going to force us to abandon most of our cherished toys—and with them our illusions." He looked vaguely into the distance. "Perhaps, looking far into man's future, our big brains will atrophy, useless; perhaps we will become one with the whales and sky wolves, surviving as best we can among the flying trees—"

Rees snorted. "Hollerbach, you're turning into a maundering bugger in your old age."

Hollerbach raised his eyebrows. "Boy, I was cultivating old age while you were still chewing iron ore on the kernel of a star."

"Well, I don't know about the far future, and there's not a damn thing I can do about it. All I can do is solve the problems of the present. And frankly, Hollerbach, I don't believe we've a hope of surviving this trip without your guidance.

"Gentlemen, we've a lot to do. I suggest we get on with it."

The plate hung over the Raft. Pallis crept to its edge and peered out over the battered deckscape.

Smoke was spreading across the deck like a mask over a familiar face.

Suddenly the plate jerked through the air, bowling Pallis onto his back. With a growl he reached out and grabbed handfuls of the netting that swathed the fragile craft. "By the Bones, innkeeper, can't you control this bloody thing?"

Jame snorted. "This is a real ship. You're not dangling from one of your wooden toys now, treepilot."

"Don't push your luck, mine rat." Pallis thumped a fist into the rough iron of the plate. "It's just that this way of flying is—unnatural."

"Unnatural?" Jame laughed. "Maybe you're right. And maybe you people spent too much time lying around in your leafy bowers, while the miners came along to piss all over you."

"The war is over, Jame," Pallis said easily. He let his shoulders hang loose, rolled his hands into half fists. "But perhaps there are one or two loose ends to be tied up."

The barman's broad face twisted into a grin of anticipation. "I'd like nothing better, tree swinger. Name the time and place, and choice of weapons."

"Oh, no weapons."

"That will suit me fine—"

"By the Bones, will you two shut up?" Nead, the plate's third occupant, glared over the charts and instruments spread over his lap. "We have work to do, if you recall."

Jame and Pallis exchanged one last stare, then Jame returned his attention to the controls of the craft. Pallis shifted across the little deck until he sat beside Nead. "Sorry," he said gruffly. "How's it going?"

Nead held a battered sextant to his eye, then tried to compare the reading to entries in a handwritten table. "Damn it," he said, clearly frustrated. "I can't tell. I just don't have the expertise, Pallis. Cipse would know. If only—"

"If only he weren't long dead, then everything would be fine," Pallis said. "I know. Just do your best, lad. What do you think?"

Again Nead ran his fingers over the tables. "I think it's taking too long. I'm trying to measure the sideways speed of the Raft against the background stars, and I don't think it's moving fast enough."

Pallis frowned. He lay on his belly and once more surveyed the Raft. The mighty old craft lay spread out below him like a tray of fantastic toys. Suspended over the deck and marked by the occasional plume of steam he could see other plate craft, more observers of this huge dislocation. A wall of smoke climbed up from one side of the Rim—the port side, as he looked down—and, additionally, each of the trees in the central tethered forest had its own smoke cloak. The smoke was having the desired effect—he could see how the trees' cables leaned consistently to his right as the flying plants sought to escape the shadow of the smoke—and he imagined he could hear the strain of the cables as the Raft was hauled aside. Cable shadows were beginning to lengthen over the deck; the Raft was indeed moving out from under the star which hung poised over it. It was an inspiring sight, one which Pallis in his long life had seen only twice previously; and for such cooperation to be achieved after the turmoil of revolution and war—and at a time when so many of the Raft's best were occupied with the Bridge project—was, he decided, something to be admired.

In fact, perhaps the need to move the Raft had provided the glue which had held society together this far. Here was a project which would clearly benefit all.

Yes, it was all admirable—but if it was too slow it wouldn't mean a damn thing. The falling star was still miles overhead, and there was no immediate danger of impact, but if pressure was maintained on the trees for too long the great plants would tire. Not only would they prove unable to drag the Raft anywhere—it was even conceivable that some might fail altogether, threatening the Raft's security in the air.

Damn it. He hung his head over the lip of the plate, trying to judge where the problem lay. The Rim wall of smoke looked solid enough; the distant stars cast a long shadow over the masked workers who labored at the base of the cliff of smoke.

Then the problem must be with the tethered trees themselves. There was a pilot, plus assistants, in each tree, and each of them was trying to maintain his own fence of smoke. Those small barriers were probably the most significant factor in influencing the movement of the individual trees. And, even from up here, Pallis could see how ragged and insubstantial some of those barriers were.

He thumped his fist into the deck of the craft. Damn it; the purges of the revolution, and the fevers and starvation that had followed, had left his corps of pilots as depleted of skilled people as most other sectors of Raft society. He remembered Raft translations of the past: the endless calculations, the shift-long briefings, the motion of the trees like components of a fine machine . . .

There had been time for none of that. Some of the newer pilots barely had the skill to keep from falling out of their trees. And building a lateral wall was one of the most difficult of a pilot's arts; it was like sculpting with smoke . . .

He spotted a group of trees whose barriers were particularly ragged. He pointed them out to Jame.

The barman grinned and yanked at his control cables.

Pallis tried to ignore the gale in his face, the stink of steam; he put aside his nostalgia for the stately grandeur of the trees. Beside him he heard Nead curse as his papers were blown like leaves. The plate swooped among the trees like some huge, unlikely skitter; Pallis couldn't help but flinch as branches shot past, mere feet from his face. At last the craft came to rest. From here those smoke barriers looked even more tenuous; Pallis watched, despairing, as raw pilots waved blankets at wisps of smoke.

He cupped his hands to his mouth. "You!"

Small faces turned up to him. One pilot tumbled backwards.

"Build up your bowls!" Pallis called angrily. "Get a decent amount of smoke. All you're doing with those damn blankets is blowing around two fifths of five per cent of bugger all . . ."

The pilots inched their way to their bowls and began feeding fresh kindling to the tiny flames.

Nead tugged at Pallis's sleeve. "Pilot. Should that be happening?"

Pallis looked. Two trees, wrapped in distorted blankets of smoke, were inclining blindly towards one another, their amateur pilots evidently absorbed in the minutiae of blankets and bowls.

"No, it bloody shouldn't be happening." Pallis spat. "Barman! Get us down there, and fast—"

The trees' first touch was almost tender: a rustle of foliage, a gentle kiss of snapping twigs. Then the first snag occurred, and the two platforms locked and shuddered. The crews of the trees gaped with sudden horror at each other.

The trees kept turning; now sections of rim were torn away and wooden shards rained through the air. A branch caught and with a scream like some animal's was torn away by the root. Now the trees began to roll into each other, in a vast, slow, noisy collision. The smooth platforms of foliage shattered. Fist-sized splinters sailed past the plate craft; Nead howled and covered his head.

Pallis glared down at the crews of the dying trees. "Get off there! The damn trees are finished. Get down your cables and save yourselves."

They stared up at him, frightened and confused. Pallis shouted on until at last he saw them slide down rippling cables to the deck.

The trees were now locked in a doomed embrace, their angular momenta mingling, their trunks orbiting in a whirl of foliage and branch stumps. Wall-sized sections of wood splintered away and the air was filled with the creak of rending timber; Pallis saw fire bowls go sailing through the air, and he prayed that the crews had had the foresight to douse their flames.

Soon little was left but the trunks, locked together by a tangle of twisted branches; now the trees' anchoring cables were torn loose like shoulders from sockets, and the freed trunks pirouetted with a strange grace, half tumbling.

At last the trunks crashed to the deck, exploding in a storm of fragments. Pallis saw men running for their lives from the rain of wood. For some minutes splinters fell, like a hail of ragged daggers; then, slowly, men began to creep back to the crash site, stepping over tree cables which lay like the limbs of a corpse among the ruins.

Silently Pallis motioned to Jame. "There's nothing we can do here; let's get on." The plate craft lifted and returned to its patrols.

For several more hours Pallis's plate skimmed about the flying forest. At the end of it Jame was muttering angrily, his face blackened by the rising smoke, and Pallis's throat was raw with shouting. At last Nead placed his sextant in his lap and sat back with a smile. "That's it," he said. "I think, anyway . . ."

"What's what?" Jame growled. "Is the Raft out from under the bloody star now?"

"No, not yet. But it's got enough momentum without further impulse from the trees. In a few hours it will drift to a halt far enough from the path of the star to be safe."

Pallis lay back in the netting of the plate and took a draught from a drink globe. "So we've made it."

Nead said dreamily, "It's not quite over for the Raft yet. When the star passes through the plane in which the Raft lies there will be a few interesting tidal effects."

Pallis shrugged. "Nothing the Raft hasn't endured before."

"It must be a fantastic sight, Pallis."

"Yes, it is," the pilot mused. He remembered watching cable shadows lengthen across the deck; at last the circumference of the star disc would touch the horizon, sending light flaring across the deck. And when the main disc had dropped below the Rim there would be an afterglow, what the Scientists call a corona . . .

Jame squinted into the sky. "How often does this happen, then? How often does the Raft get in the way of a falling star?"

Pallis shrugged. "Not often. Once or twice a generation. Often enough for us to have built up skills to deal with it."

"But you need the Scientists—the likes of this one—" Jame jerked a thumb at Nead "—to work out what to do."

"Well, of course." Nead sounded amused. "You can't do these things by sticking a wet finger into the wind."

"But a lot of the Scientists are going to bugger off, on this Bridge thing."

"That's true."

"So what's going to happen when the next star comes down? How will they move the Raft then?"

Nead sipped a drink easily. "Well, our observations show that the next star—a long way up there—" he pointed upwards "—is many thousands of shifts away from endangering the Raft."

Pallis frowned. "That doesn't answer Jame's question."

"Yes, it does." Nead's blank young face bore a look of puzzlement. "You see, by that time we don't expect the Nebula to be sustaining life anyway. So the problem's rather academic, isn't it?"

Pallis and Jame exchanged glances; then Pallis turned to the rotating forest under his craft and tried to lose himself in contemplation of its steady serenity.

Rees hardly slept during his last rest period before the Bridge's departure.

A bell tolled somewhere.

At last it was time. Rees rose from his pallet, washed quickly, and emerged from his temporary shelter, feeling only a vast relief that the time had come.

The Bridge in its box of scaffolding was the center of frantic activity. It lay at the heart of a fenced-off area two hundred yards wide which had become a miniature city; former Officers' quarters had been commandeered to give hopeful migrants temporary accommodation. Now small knots of people walked uncertainly toward the Bridge. Rees recognized representatives of all the Nebula's cultures: the Raft itself, the Belt, and even a few Boneys. Each refugee carried the few pounds of personal belongings allowed. A queue was forming at the open port of the Bridge, behind a human chain which passed into the interior a few final supplies, books, small environmental monitoring instruments. There was an air of purposefulness about the scene and Rees slowly began to believe that this thing was actually going to happen . . .

Whatever the future held he could only be glad that this period of waiting, with all its divisiveness and bitterness, was over. After the moving of the Raft, society had disintegrated rapidly. It had been a race to complete their preparations before things fell apart completely; and as time had passed—and more delays and problems had been encountered—Rees had felt the pressure build until it seemed he could hardly bear it.

The amount of personal animosity he had encountered had astonished him. He longed to explain to people that it was not he who was causing the Nebula to fail; that it was not he who decreed the physical laws which constrained the number of evacuees.

... And it had not been he—alone—who had drawn up the list.

The preparation of that list had been agonizing. The idea of a ballot had been rejected quickly; the composition of this colony could not be left to chance. But how to select humans—families, chains of descendants—for life or extinction? They had tried to be scientific, and so had applied criteria like physical fitness, intelligence, adaptabilty, breeding age ... And Rees, embarrassed and disgusted by the whole process, had found himself on most of the candidate lists.

But he had stayed with it; not, he prayed, merely in order to ensure his own survival, but to do the best job he could. The selection process had left him feeling soiled and shabby, unsure even of his own motivations.

In the end a final list had emerged, an amalgam of dozens of others drawn together by Decker's harsh arbitration. Rees was on it. Roch wasn't. And so, Rees reflected with a fresh burst of self-loathing, he had finished by neatly fulfilling the worst expectations of Roch and his like.

He walked to the perimeter fence. Perhaps he would see Pallis, get a last chance to say goodbye. Burly guards patrolled, hefting clubs uncertainly. Rees felt depressed as he stared along the length of the fence. Yet more resources diverted from the main objective . . . but there had been riots already; who was to say what might have happened if not for the protection of the fence and its guards? A guard caught his eye and nodded, his broad face impassive; Rees wondered how easy it would be for this man to fight off his own people in order to save a privileged few . . .

An explosion somewhere on the other side of the Bridge, like a massive heel stamping into the deck. A pall of smoke rose over the scaffolding.

The guards near Rees turned to stare. Rees hurried around the Bridge.

Distant shouts, a scream . . . and the fence was down and burning along ten feet of its length. Guards ran to the breach, but the mob beyond seemed overwhelming, both in numbers and in ferocity; Rees saw a wall of faces, old and young, male and female, united by a desperate, vicious anger. Now fire bombs rained toward the Bridge, splashing over the deck.

"What the hell are you doing here?" It was Decker; the big man took Rees's arm and pulled him back toward the Bridge.

"Decker, can't they understand? They can't be saved; there simply isn't room. If they attack now the mission will fail and nobody will—"

"Lad." Decker took his shoulders and shook him, hard. "The time for talk is over. We can't hold off that lot for long . . . You have to get in there and launch. Right now."

Rees shook his head. "That's impossible."

"I'll show you what's bloody impossible." A small fire burned amid the ruins of a fire bomb; Decker bent, lit a chunk of scrap wood, and hurled it into the scaffolding surrounding the Bridge. Soon flames were licking at the dry wood.

Rees stared. "Decker—"

"No more discussion, damn you!" Decker roared into his face, spittle spraying. "Take what you can and get out of here—"

Rees turned to run.

He looked back once. Decker was already lost in the mêlée at the breach.

Rees reached the port. The orderly queue of a few minutes earlier had disintegrated; people were trying to force their way through the doorway, screaming and holding their absurd packages of luggage above their heads. Rees used his fists and elbows to fight his way through to the interior. The Observatory was a cage of noisy chaos, with equipment and people jumbled and crushed together; the single remaining large instrument—the Telescope—loomed over the crowd like some aloof robot.

Rees rammed his way through the crowd until he found Gord and Nead. He pulled them close. "We launch in five minutes!"

"Rees, that's impossible," Gord said. "You can see the state of things. We'd cause injury, death even, to the passengers and those outside—"

Rees pointed to the transparent hull. "Look out there. See that smoke? Decker has fired the damn scaffolding. So your precious explosive bolts are going to blow in five minutes anyway. Right?"

Gord paled.

Suddenly the noise outside grew to a roar; Rees saw that more sections of the fence were failing. The few guards still fighting were being overwhelmed by a wave of humanity.

"When they reach us we're finished," Rees said. "We have to launch. Not in five minutes. Now."

Nead shook his head. "Rees, there are still people—"

"Close the damn door!" Rees grabbed the young

267

man's shoulder and shoved him toward a wall-mounted control panel. "Gord, fire those bolts. Just do it—"

His eyes narrow, his cheeks trembling with fear, the little engineer disappeared into the crush.

Rees forced his way to the Telescope. He clambered up the old instrument's mount until he was looking down over a confused sea of people. "Listen to me!" he bellowed. "You can see what's happening outside. We have to launch. Lie down if you can. Help your neighbors; watch the children—"

Now fists were battering against the hull, desperate faces pressing to the clear wall—

—and, with a synchronized crackle, the scaffolding's explosive bolts ignited. The fragile wooden frame disintegrated rapidly; now nothing held the Bridge to the Raft.

The floor dipped. Screams rose like flames; the passengers clung to each other. Beyond the clear hull the Raft deck rose around the Bridge like a liquid, and the Raft's gravitational field hauled the passengers into the air, bumping them almost comically against the roof.

A crescendo of cries came from the doorway. Nead had failed to close the port in time; stragglers were leaping across the widening chasm between Bridge and deck. A last man clattered through the closing door; his ankle was trapped in the jamb and Rees heard the shin snap with sickening suddenness. Now a whole family tumbled off the Raft deck and impacted against the hull, sliding into infinity with looks of surprise . . .

Rees closed his eyes and clung to the Telescope.

At last it was over. The Raft turned into a ceiling above them, distant and abstract; the thin rain of humans against the hull ceased, and four hundred people had suddenly entered free fall for the first time in their lives.

There was a yell, as if from very far away. Rees looked up. Roch, burning club in hand, had leapt through the hole in the heart of the Raft. He fell through the intervening yards spreadeagled; he stared, eyes bulging, in through the glass at horrified passengers.

The huge miner smashed face-down into the clear roof of the Observatory. He dropped his club and scrabbled for a handhold against the slick wall; but helplessly he slid over the surface, leaving a trail of blood from his crushed nose and mouth. Finally he tumbled over the side—then, at the last second, he grabbed at the rough protrusion of a steam jet.

Rees climbed down from the Telescope and found Gord. "Damn it, we have to do something. He'll pull that jet free."

Gord scratched his chin and studied the dangling miner, who glared in at the bemused passengers. "We could fire the jet. The steam would miss him, of course, since he's hanging beneath the orifice itself—but his hands would burn—yes; that would shake him loose . . ."

"Or," Rees said, "we could save him."

"What? Rees, that joker tried to kill you."

"I know." Rees stared out at Roch's crimson face, his straining muscles. "Find a length of rope. I'm going to open the door."

"You're not serious . . ."

But Rees was already heading for the port.

When at last the huge miner lay exhausted on the deck, Rees bent over him. "Listen to me," he said steadily. "I could have let you die."

Roch licked blood from his ruined mouth.

"I saved you for one reason," Rees said. "You're

a survivor. That's what drove you to risk your life in that crazy leap. And where we're going we need survivors. Do you understand? But if I ever—even once—think that you're endangering this mission with your damn stupidity I'll open that door and let you finish your fall."

He held the miner's eyes for long minutes; at last, Roch nodded.

"Good." Rees stood. "Now then," he said to Gord, "what first?"

There was a stink of vomit in the air.

Gord raised his eyebrows. "Weightlessness education, I think," he said. "And a lot of work with mops and buckets . . ."

His hands around his assailant's throat and weapon arm, Decker turned to see the Bridge scaffolding collapse into its flimsy components. The great cylinder hung in the air, just for a second; then the steam jets spurted white clouds and the Bridge fell away, leaving a pit in the deck into which people tumbled helplessly.

So it was over; and Decker was stranded. He turned his attention back to his opponent and began to squeeze away the man's life.

On the abandoned Raft the killing went on for many hours.

15

The crowded ship's first few hours after the fall were nearly unbearable. The air stank of vomit and urine, and people of all ages swarmed about the chamber, scrambling, shrieking and fighting.

Rees suspected that the problem was not merely weightlessness, but also the abrupt reality of the fall itself. Suddenly to face the truth that the world wasn't an infinite disc after all—to know that the Raft really had been no more than a mote of patched iron floating in the air—seemed to have driven some of the passengers to the brink of their sanity.

Maybe it would have been an idea to keep the windows opaqued during the launch.

Rees spent long hours supervising the construction of a webbing of ropes and cables crisscrossing the Observatory. "We'll fill the interior with this isotropic structure," Hollerbach had advised gravely. "Make it look the same in every direction. Then it won't be quite so disconcerting when we reach the Core and the whole bloody universe turns upside down . . ."

Soon the passengers were draping blankets over the ropes, fencing off small volumes for privacy. The high-technology interior of the Bridge began to take on a homely aspect as the makeshift shanty town spread; human smells, of food and children, filled the air.

Taking a break, Rees made his way out of the crushed interior to what had formerly been the roof of the Observatory. The hull was still transparent. Rees pressed his face to the warm material and peered out, irresistibly reminded of how he had once peered out of the belly of a whale.

After the fall from the Raft the Bridge had rapidly picked up speed and reoriented itself so that its stubby nose was pointing at the heart of the Nebula. Now it hurtled down through the air, and the Nebula had turned into a vast, three-dimensional demonstration of perspective motion. Nearby clouds shot past, middle distance stars glided toward space—and even at the limits of vision, many hundreds of miles away, pale stars slowly drifted upwards.

The Raft had long since become a mote lost in the pink infinity above.

The hull shuddered briefly. A soundless plume of steam erupted a few yards above Rees's head and was instantly whipped away, a sign that Gord's ramshackle attitude control system was doing its job.

The hull felt warmer than usual against his face. The wind speed out there must be phenomenal, but the virtually frictionless material of the Bridge was allowing the air to slide harmlessly past with barely a rise in temperature. Rees's tired mind ambled down speculative alleyways. If you measured the temperature rise, he reasoned, you could probably get some kind of estimate of the hull's coefficient of friction. But, of course, you would also need some data on the material's heat conduction properties—

"It's astonishing, isn't it?"

Nead was at his side. The younger man cradled a sextant in his arms. Rees smiled. "What are you doing here?"

"I'm supposed to be measuring our velocity."

"And?"

"We're at terminal velocity for the strength of gravity out here. I estimate we will reach the Core in about ten shifts . . ."

Nead delivered his words dreamily, his attention taken up by the view; but they had an electric effect on Rees. Ten shifts . . . in just ten shifts he would stare at the face of the Core, and the destiny of the race would be made or lost.

He pulled himself back to the present. "We never did get to finish your training, did we, Nead?"

"Other events were more pressing," Nead said drily.

"Let's find a home where we will always have time to train people properly . . . time, even, to stare out of the window—"

Jaen started talking even before she reached them. ". . . And if you don't tell this insufferable old buffoon that he's left his sense of priorities back on the Raft, then I won't be responsible for my actions, Rees!"

Rees groaned inwardly. Evidently his break was over. He turned; Jaen bore down on him with Hollerbach following, hauling himself cautiously through the network of ropes. The old Scientist muttered, "I don't believe I've been spoken to like that by a mere Second Class since—since—"

Rees held his hands up. "Slow down, you two. Start from the top, Jaen. What's the problem?"

"The problem," Jaen spat, jerking her thumb, "is this silly old fart, who—"

"Why, you impudent—"

"Shut up!" Rees snapped.

Jaen, simmering, made a visible effort to calm down. "Rees. Am I or am I not in charge of the Telescope?"

"That's my understanding."

"And my brief is to make sure that the Navigators—and their Boney so-called assistants—get all the data they need to guide our trajectory around the Core. And that has to be our number one priority. Right?"

Rees rubbed his nose doubtfully. "I can't argue with that ..."

"Then tell Hollerbach to keep his damn hands off my equipment!"

Rees turned to Hollerbach, suppressing a smile. "What are you up to, Chief Scientist?"

"Rees ..." The old man wrapped his long fingers together, pulling at the loose flesh. "We have left ourselves with only one significant scientific instrument. Now, I've no wish to revisit the arguments behind the loading of this ship. Of course the size of the gene pool must come first ..." He thumped one fist into his palm. "Nevertheless it is at precisely this moment of blindness that we are approaching the greatest scientific mystery of this cosmos: the Core itself—"

"He wants to turn the Telescope on the Core," Jaen said. "Can you believe it?"

"The understanding to be acquired by even a superficial study is incalculable."

"Hollerbach, if we don't use that damn telescope to navigate with we might get a closer look at the Core than any of us have bargained for!" Jaen glared at Rees. "Well?"

"Well what?"

Hollerbach looked sadly at Rees. "Alas, lad, I suspect this little local difficulty is only the first impossible arbitration you will be called on to make."

Rees felt confused, isolated. "But why me?"

Jaen snapped, "Because Decker is still on the Raft. And who else is there?"

"Who indeed?" Hollerbach murmured. "I'm sorry, Rees; I don't think you have very much choice . . ."

"Anyway, what about this bloody Telescope?"

Rees tried to focus. "All right. Look, Hollerbach, I have to agree that Jaen's work is a priority right now—"

Jaen whooped and punched the air.

"So your studies must fit in around that work. All right? But," he went on rapidly, "when we get close enough to the Core the steam jets will become ineffectual anyway. So navigation will become a waste of time . . . and the Telescope can be released, and Hollerbach can do his work. Maybe Jaen will even help." He puffed out his cheeks. "How's that for a compromise?"

Jaen grinned and punched him on the shoulder. "We'll make a Committee member of you yet." She turned and pulled her way back into the interior of the chamber.

Rees felt his shoulders slump. "Hollerbach, I'm too young to be a Captain. And I've no desire for the job."

Hollerbach smiled gently. "That last alone probably qualifies you as well as anyone. Rees, I fear you must face it; you're the only man on board with first-hand experience of the Belt, the Raft, the Bone world . . . and so you're the only leader figure remotely acceptable to all the ship's disparate factions. And after all it has been your drive, your determination, that has brought us so far. Now you're stuck with this responsibility, I fear.

"And there are some hard decisions ahead. Assuming we round the Core successfully we will face rationing, extremes of temperature in the unknown regions outside the Nebula—even boredom will be a life-threatening hazard! You will have to keep us functioning in extraordinary circumstances. If I can assist you in any way, of course, I will."

"Thanks. I don't much like the idea, but I guess you are right. And to help me you could start," he said sharply, "by sorting out your differences with Jaen yourself."

Hollerbach smiled ruefully. "That young woman is rather forceful."

"Hollerbach, what do you expect to see down there anyway? I guess a close view of a black hole is going to be spectacular enough . . ."

A flush of animation touched Hollerbach's papery cheeks. "Far more than that. Have I ever discussed with you my ideas on gravitic chemistry? I have?" Hollerbach looked disappointed at the curtailing of his lecture, but Rees encouraged him to continue; for a few minutes, he realized gratefully, he could return to his apprenticeship, when Hollerbach and the rest would lecture him each shift on the mysteries of the many universes.

"You will recall my speculation on a new type of 'atom,' " Hollerbach began. "Its component particles—perhaps singularities themselves—will be bonded by gravity rather than the other fundamental forces. Given the right conditions, the right temperature and pressure, the right gravitational gradients, a new 'gravitic chemistry' will be possible."

"In the Core," Rees said.

"Yes!" Hollerbach declared. "As we skirt the

Core we will observe a new realm, my friend, a new phase of creation in which—"

Over Hollerbach's shoulder there loomed a wide, bloodstained face. Rees frowned. "What do you want, Roch?"

The huge miner grinned. "I only wanted to point out what you're missing. Look." He pointed.

Rees turned. At first he could see nothing unusual—and then, squinting, he made out a faint patch of dull brown amid the upward shower of stars. It was too far away to make out any detail, but memory supplied the rest; and he saw again a surface of skin streched over bone, white faces turning to a distant speck in the air—

"The Boneys," he said.

Roch opened his corrupt mouth and laughed; Hollerbach flinched, disgusted. "Your home from home, Rees," Roch said coarsely. "Don't you feel like dropping in and visiting old friends?"

"Roch, get back to your work."

Roch did so, still laughing.

Rees stayed for some minutes at the hull, watching until the Boneys' worldlet was lost in the haze far above. Yet another piece of his life gone, beyond recall . . .

With a shudder he turned from the window and, with Hollerbach, immersed himself once more in the bustle and warmth of the Bridge.

Almost powerless, its soft human cargo swarming through its interior, the battered old ship plunged toward the black hole.

The sky outside darkened and filled up with the fantastic, twisted star sculptures observed by Rees on his first journey to these depths. The Scientists left the hull transparent; Rees gambled that this would distract the helpless passengers from their steadily worsening plight. And so it turned out; as the shifts passed a growing number spent time at the great windows, and the mood of the ship became one of calm, almost of awe.

Now, with closest approach to the Core barely a shift away, the Bridge was approaching a school of whales; and the windows were coated with human faces. Rees discreetly made room for Hollerbach; side by side they stared out.

At this depth each whale was a slender missile, its deflated flesh an aerodynamic casing around its internal organs. Even the great eyes had closed now, so that the whales plummeted blind into the Core—and there were row upon row of them, above, below and all around the Bridge, so many that at infinity the air was a wall of pale flesh.

Rees murmured, "If I'd known it would be as spectacular as this I wouldn't have got off last time."

"You'd never have survived," Hollerbach said. "Look closely." He pointed at the nearest whale. "See how it glows?"

Rees made out a pinkish glow around the whale's leading end. "Air resistance?"

"Obviously." Hollerbach said impatiently. "The atmosphere is like soup at these depths. Now, keep watching."

Rees kept his eyes fixed on the whale's nose— and was rewarded with the sight of a six-foot patch of whale skin flaring into flame and tumbling away from the speeding animal. Rees looked around the school with new eyes; throughout the hail of motion he could see similar tiny flares of burning flesh, sparks of discarded fire. "It looks as if the whales are disintegrating, as if air resistance is too great . . . Perhaps they have misjudged their path around the Core; maybe our presence has disturbed them—"

Hollerbach snorted in disgust. "Sentimental tosh. Rees, those whales know what they're doing far better than we do."

"Then why the burning?"

"I'm surprised at you, boy; you should have worked it out as soon as you climbed aboard that whale and studied its spongy outer flesh."

"At the time I was more interested in finding out whether I could eat it," Rees said drily. "But . . ." He thought it through. "You're saying the purpose of the outer flesh is ablation?"

"Precisely. The outer layer burns up and falls away. One of the simplest but most efficient ways of dispersing the heat generated by excessive air resistance . . . a method used on man's earliest spacecraft, as I recall from the Ship's records—records which are, of course, now lost forever—"

Suddenly fire blazed over the hull's exterior; the watching passengers recoiled from a sheet of flame mere inches from their faces.

As soon as it had begun it was over.

"Well, that was no planned ablation," Rees said grimly. "That was one of our steam jets. So much for our attitude control."

"Ah." Hollerbach nodded slowly, his brow furrowed. "That's rather earlier than I expected. I had entertained hopes of retaining some control even at closest approach—when, of course, the ship's trajectory may most easily be modified."

"I'm afraid we're stuck with what we've got, from this point in. We're flying without smoke, as Pallis might say . . . We just have to hope we're on an acceptable course. Come on; let's talk to the navigators. But keep your voice down. Whatever the verdict there's no point in starting a panic."

* * *

The members of the navigation team responded to Rees's questions according to their inclinations. Raft Scientists pored over diagrams which showed orbits sprouting from the Core like unruly hair, while the Boneys threw bits of shaped metal into the air and watched how they drifted.

After some minutes of this, Rees snapped, "Well?"

Quid turned to him and shrugged cheerfully. "We're still too far out. Who knows? We'll have to wait and see."

Jaen scratched her head, a pen tucked behind her ear. "Rees, we're in an almost chaotic situation here. Because of the distance at which we lost control, our final trajectory remains indeterminately sensitive to initial conditions . . ."

"In other words," Rees said, irritated, "we have to wait and see. Terrific."

Jaen made to protest, then thought better of it.

Quid slapped his shoulder. "Look, there's not a bloody thing we can do. You've done your best . . . and if nothing else you've given old Quid a damn interesting ride."

Hollerbach said briskly, "And you're not alone in those sentiments, my Boney friend. Jaen! I presume your use of the Telescope is now at an end?"

Jaen grinned.

It took thirty minutes to adjust the instrument's orientation and focus. At last Rees, Jaen, Hollerbach and Nead crowded around the small monitor plate.

At first Rees was disappointed; the screen filled with the thick black cloud of star debris which surrounded the Core itself, images familiar from observations from the Raft. But as the minutes passed and the Bridge entered the outermost layers of the material, the sombre cloud parted before them and the debris began to show a depth and structure. A pale, pinkish light shone upwards at them. Soon veils of shattered star stuff were arching over the hull, making the Bridge seem a fragile container indeed.

Then, abruptly, the clouds cleared; and they were sailing over the Core itself.

"My god," Jaen breathed. "It's ... it's like a planet ..."

The Core was a compact mass clustered about its black hole, a flattened sphere fifty miles wide. And, indeed, it was a world rendered in shades of red and pink. Its surface layers—subjected, Rees estimated, to many hundreds of gravities—were well-defined and showed almost topographical features. There were oceans of some quasi-liquid material, thick and red as blood; they lapped at lands that thrust above the general spherical surface. There were even small mountain ranges, like wrinkles in the skin of a soured fruit, and clouds like smoke which sped across the face of the seas. There was continual motion: waves miles wide crisscrossed the seas, the mountain sheets seemed to evolve endlessly, and even the coasts of the strange continents writhed. It was as if some great heat source were causing the Core's epidermis to wrinkle and blister constantly.

It was like Earth taken to Hell, Rees thought.

Hollerbach was ecstatic. He peered into the monitor as if he wished he could climb through it. "Gravitic chemistry!" he croaked. "I am vindicated. The structure of that fantastic surface can be maintained solely by the influence of gravitic chemistry; only gravitic bonds could battle against the attraction of the black hole."

"But it all changes so rapidly," Rees said.

"Metamorphoses on a scale of miles, happening in seconds."

Hollerbach nodded eagerly. "Such speed will be a characteristic of the gravitic realm. Remember that changing gravity fields propagate at the speed of light, and—"

Jaen cried out, pointing at the monitor plate.

At the center of one of the amorphous continents, etched into the surface like a mile-wide chessboard, was a rectangular grid of pink-white light.

Ideas crowded into Rees's mind. "Life," he whispered.

"And intelligence," Hollerbach said. "Two staggering discoveries in a single glance . . ."

Jaen asked, "But how is this possible?"

"We should rather ask, 'why should it not be so?' " Hollerbach said. "The essential condition for life is the existence of sharp energy gradients . . . The gravitic realm is one of fast-evolving patterns; the universal principles of self-organization, like the Feigenbaum series which govern the blossoming of structure out of chaos, almost demand that organization should arise."

Now they saw more gridworks. Some covered whole continents and seemed to be trying to buttress the "land" against the huge waves. Road-like lines of light arrowed around the globe. And—at the highest magnification—Rees was even able to make out individual structures: pyramids, tetrahedra and cubes.

"And why should intelligence not arise?" Hollerbach went on dreamily. "On a world of such violent change, selection in favor of organizing principles would be a powerful factor. Look how the gravitic peoples are struggling to preserve their ordered environments against the depredations of chaos!"

Hollerbach fell silent, but Rees's mind raced on. Perhaps these creatures would build ships of their own which could travel to other hole-based "planets," and meet with their unimaginable cousins. At present this strange biosphere was fueled by the influx of material from the Nebular debris cloud— a steady rain of star wrecks arcing on hyperbolic trajectories into the Core—and from within by the X-radiating accretion disc around the black hole, deep within the Core itself; but eventually the Nebula would be depleted and the gravitic world would be exposed, naked to space, fueled only by the heat of the Core and, ultimately, the slow evaporation of the black hole itself.

Long after all the nebulae had expired, he realized, the gravitic people would walk their roiling worlds. With a sense of dislocation he realized that these creatures were the true denizens of this cosmos; humans, soft, dirty and flabby, were mere transient interlopers.

Closest approach neared.

The Core world turned into a landscape; passengers screamed or sighed as the Bridge soared mere tens of miles above a boiling ocean. Whales drifted over the seas, pale and imperturbable as ghosts.

Something was tugging at Rees's feet. Irritated, he grabbed a Telescope strut and hauled himself back to the monitor; but the pull increased remorselessly, at last growing uncomfortable . . .

He began to worry. The Bridge should be in virtual free fall. Was something impeding it? He peered around the transparent hull, half-expecting—what? That the Bridge had run into some glutinous cloud, some impossible spout from the strange seas below?

But there was nothing.

He returned his attention to the Telescope—to find that Hollerbach was now upside down; arms outstretched he clung to the monitor and was gamely trying to haul his face level with the picture in the plate. Bizarrely, he and Rees seemed to be being pulled toward opposite ends of the ship. Nead and Jaen were similarly arrayed around the Telescope mount, clinging on in the presence of this strange new field.

Screams arose around the chamber. The flimsy structure of ropes and sheets began to collapse; clothes, cutlery, people went sliding toward the walls.

"What the hell's happening, Hollerbach?"

The old Scientist clenched and unclenched his hands. "Damn it, this isn't helping my arthritis—"

"Hollerbach . . . !"

"It's the tide!" Hollerbach snapped. "By the Bones, boy, didn't you learn anything in my orbital dynamics classes? We're so close to the Core that its gravity field is varying significantly on a scale of a few yards."

"Damn it, Hollerbach, if you knew all about this why didn't you warn us?"

Hollerbach refused to look abashed. "Because it was obvious, boy . . . ! And any minute now we'll get the really spectacular stuff. As soon as the gravitational gradient exceeds the moment imposed by air friction—ah, here we go . . ."

The image in the monitor blurred as the Telescope lost its lock. The churning ocean wheeled over Rees's head. Now the shanty construction collapsed completely and bewildered passengers were hurled about; spatters of blood appeared on flesh, clothes, walls.

The ship was turning.

"Nose down!" Hollerbach, hands still clamped

to the Telescope, screamed to make himself heard. "The ship will come to equilibrium nose down to the Core—"

The prow of the ship swung to the Core, ran past it, hauled itself back, as if the Bridge were a huge magnetized needle close to a lump of iron. With each swing the devastation within the Chamber worsened; now Rees could see limp bodies among the thrashing passengers. Absurdly, he was reminded of the dance he had watched in the Theater of Light; like dancers Bridge and Core were going through an aerial ballet, with the ship waltzing in the black hole's arms of gravity.

At last the ship stabilized, its axis pointing at the Core. The passengers and their effects had been wadded into the ends of the cylindrical chamber, where the tidal effects were most strong; Rees and the other Scientists, still clinging to the Telescope mount, were close to the ship's center of gravity, and were, Rees realized, escaping comparatively lightly.

Blood-red oceans swept past the windows.

"We must be near closest approach," Rees shouted. "If we can just survive the next few minutes, if the ship holds together against this tide—"

Nead, arms twined around the shaft of the Telescope, was staring at the Core ocean. "I think we might have to survive more than that," he said.

"What?"

"Look!" Nead pointed—and, his grip loosened, he slipped away from the Telescope. He scrabbled against the sheer surface of the instrument, hands trying to regain their purchase; then his grasp failed completely. Still staring at the window he fell thirty yards into the squirming mass of humanity crushed into one end of the cylindrical chamber.

He hit with a cracking sound, a cry of pain. Rees closed his eyes.

Hollerbach shouted urgently, "Rees. Look at what he was telling us."

Rees turned.

The sea of blood continued to churn; but now, Rees saw, there was a distinct whirlpool, a tight knot gathered beneath the Bridge. Shadows moved in that maelstrom, vast and purposeful. And—the whirlpool was moving with the hurtling ship, tracking its progress ...

The whirlpool burst like a blister and a disc a hundred yards wide came looming out of the ocean. Its jet black surface thrashed; with bewildering frequency vast limbs pulsed out, as if fists were straining through a sheet of rubber. The disc hovered for long seconds; then, its rotation slowing, it fell back into the pounding ocean.

Almost immediately the whirlpool began to collect once more.

The old Scientist's face was gray. "That's the second such eruption. Evidently not all the life here is as civilized as us."

"It's alive? But what does it want?"

"Damn it, boy, think for yourself!"

At the heart of this gale of noise Rees tried to concentrate. "How does it sense us? Compared to gravitic creatures we are things of gossamer, barely substantial. Why should it be interested in us ... ?"

"The supply machines!" Jaen shouted.

"What?"

"They're powered by mini black holes ... gravitic material. Perhaps that's all the gravitic creature can see, as if we're a ship of ghosts surrounding crumbs of ..."

"Of food," Hollerbach finished wearily.

Again the creature roared up from its ocean, scattering whales like leaves. This time a limb, a cable as thick as Rees's waist, came close enough to make the ship shudder in its flight. Rees made out detail on the creature's surface; it was like a sculpture rendered in black on black. Tiny forms—independent animals, like parasites?—raced with eye-bewildering speed across the pulsing surface, colliding, melding, rebounding.

Again the disc fell away, colliding with its spawning sea with a fantastic, slow-motion splash; and again the whirlpool began to gather.

"Hunger," Hollerbach said. "The universal imperative. The damn thing will keep trying until it swallows us whole. And there's nothing we can do about it." He closed his rheumy eyes.

"We're not dead yet," Rees muttered. "If baby wants feeding, we'll feed baby." An angry determination flooded his thoughts. He hadn't come so far, achieved so much, merely to see it brushed aside by some nameless horror . . . even if its very atoms were composed of black holes.

He scanned the chamber. The rope network had collapsed, leaving the interior of the chamber scoured clear of people; but some ropes still clung where they had been fixed to the walls and ceilings. One such led from the Telescope mount directly to the exit to the Bridge's corridor. Rees eyed its track. It lay almost exclusively within feet of the ship's waist, so that when he followed it he could stay close to the weightless zone.

Cautiously, one hand at a time, he loosened his grip on the Telescope mount. As the rope took his mass he drifted slowly toward one end of the chamber . . . but too slowly to matter. Rapidly he worked his way hand over hand along the rope.

With the port only feet away the rope came loose of its mountings and began to snake through the air.

He scrambled over the wall surface with the palms of his hands and lunged at the port. When he had reached its solid security he paused for a few breaths, hands and feet aching.

Once more the animal erupted from its ocean; once more its wriggling face loomed over the Bridge.

Rees shouted over the moans of the passengers. "Roch! Roch, can you hear me? Miner Roch . . . !"

At last Roch's broad, battered face thrust out of the mass of crushed humanity at one end of the cylindrical chamber.

"Roch, can you get up here?"

Roch looked about, studying the ropes clinging to the walls. Then he grinned. He stepped over the people around him, pushing heads and limbs deeper into the mêlée; then, with animal grace, he scrambled up the ropes plastered against the great windows. As one rope collapsed and fell away he leapt to another, then another; until at last he had joined Rees at the port. "See?" he told Rees. "All that hard work in five gees pays off in the end—"

"Roch, I need your help. Listen to me—"

One of the food machines had been mounted just inside the Bridge's port, and Rees found himself giving thanks for the fortuitous narrowness of the Bridge's access paths. A little more room and the thing would have been taken down to one of the Bridge's end chambers—and Rees doubted even Roch's ability to raise tons through the multiple-gee climb to the ship's mid point.

The ship shuddered again.

When Rees explained his idea Roch grinned, his

eyes wide and demonic—damn it, the man was even enjoying this—and, before Rees could stop him, he slapped a broad palm against the port's control panel.

The port slid aside. The air outside was hot, thick and rushed past at enormous speed; the pressure difference hauled at Rees like an invisible hand, slamming him into the side of the supply machine.

The open port was a three-yard square slice of chaos, completely filled by the writhing face of the gravitic animal. A tentacle a mile long lashed through the air; Rees felt the Bridge quiver at its approach. One touch of that stuff and the old ship would implode like a crushed skitter—

Roch crawled around the supply machine away from the port, so that he was lodged between the machine and the outer wall of the Observatory.

Rees looked at the base of the machine; it had been fixed to the Bridge's deck with crude, fist-sized iron rivets. "Damn it," he shouted over the roar of the wind. "Roch, help me find tools, something to use as levers . . ."

"No time for that, Raft man." Roch's voice was strained, as Rees remembered it once sounding as the big man had got to his feet under the five gees of the star kernel. Rees looked up, startled.

Roch had braced his back against the supply machine, his feet against the wall of the Observatory; and he was shoving back against the machine. The muscles of his legs bulged and sweat stood out in beads over his brow and chest.

"Roch, you're crazy! That's impossible . . ."

One of the rivets creaked; shards of rusty iron flew through the turbulent air.

Roch kept his swelling eyes fixed on Rees. The muscles of his neck seemed to bunch around his widening grin, and his tongue protruded, purple, from broken lips.

Now another rivet gave way with a crack like a small explosion.

Belatedly Rees placed his hands on the machine, braced his feet against the angle of floor and wall, and shoved with Roch until the veins of his arms stood out like rope.

Another rivet broke. The machine tilted noticeably. Roch adjusted his position and continued to shove. The miner's face was purple, his bloody eyes fixed on Rees. Small popping sounds came from within that vast body, and Rees imagined discs and vertebrae cracking and fusing along Roch's spine.

At last, with a series of small explosions, the remaining rivets collapsed and the machine tumbled through the port. Rees fell onto his chest amid the stumps of shattered rivets, his lungs pump oxygen from the depleted air. He lifted his head. "Roch . . . ?"

The miner was gone.

Rees scrambled up from the deck and grabbed the rim of the port. The gravitic beast covered the sky, a huge, ugly panorama of motion—and suspended before it was the ragged bulk of the supply machine. Roch was spreadeagled against the machine, his back to the battered metal wall. The miner stared across a few feet into Rees's eyes.

Now a cable-like limb lashed out of the animal and swatted at the supply machine. The device was knocked, spinning, towards the writhing black mass. Then the predator folded around its morsel and, apparently satiated, sank back into the dark ocean for the last time.

With the last of his strength Rees closed the port.

16

As the flight through space wore on, again and again Rees was drawn to the hull's small window space.

He pressed his face to the warm wall. He was close to the waist of the Bridge here: to his left the Nebula, the home they had discarded, was a crimson barrier that cut the sky in half; to his right the destination nebula was a bluish patch he could still cover with one hand.

As the ship had soared away from the Core the navigation team had spent long hours with their various sextants, charts and bits of carved bone; but at last they had announced that the Bridge was, after all, on course. There had been a mood of elation among the passengers. Despite the deaths, the injuries, the loss of the food machine, their mission seemed bound for success, its greatest trial behind it. Rees had found himself caught up in the prevailing mood.

But then the Bridge had left behind the familar warm light of the Nebula.

Most of the hull had been opaqued to shut out the oppressive darkness of the internebular void. Bathed in artificial light, the reconstructed shanty town had become once more a mass of homely warmth and scents, and most of the passengers had been glad to turn inwards and forget the emptiness beyond the ancient walls of the ship.

But despite this the mood of the people grew more subdued—contemplative, even somber.

And then the loss of one of their two supply machines had started to work through, and rationing had begun to bite.

The sky outside was a rich, deep blue, broken only by the diffuse pallor of distant nebulae. The Scientists had puzzled over their ancient instruments and assured Rees that the internebular spaces were far from airless, although the gases were far too thin to sustain human life. "It is as if," Jaen had told him excitedly, "the nebulae are patches of high density within a far greater cloud, which perhaps has its own internal structure, its own Core. Perhaps all the nebulae are falling like stars into this greater Core."

"And why stop there?" Rees had grinned. "The structure could be recursive. Maybe this greater nebula is itself a mere satellite of another, mightier Core; which in turn is a satellite of another, and so on, without limit."

Jaen's eyes sparkled. "I wonder what the inhabitants of those greater Cores would look like, what gravitic chemistry could do under such conditions . . ."

Rees shrugged. "Maybe one day we'll send up a ship to find out. Travel to the Core of Cores . . . but there may be more subtle ways to probe these questions."

"Like what?"

"Well, if our new nebula really is falling into a greater Core there should be measurable effects. Tides, perhaps—we could build up hypotheses

292

about the mass and nature of the greater Core without ever seeing it."

"And knowing that, we could go on to validate whole families of theories about the structure of this universe . . ."

Rees smiled now, something of that surge of intellectual confidence returning briefly to warm him.

But if they couldn't feed themselves all these dreams counted for nothing.

The ship had picked up enormous velocity by its slingshot maneuver around the Core, climbing into internebular space within hours. They'd traveled for five shifts since then . . . but there were still twenty shifts to go. Could the ship's fragile social structure last so long?

There was a bony hand on his shoulder. Hollerbach thrust forward his gaunt face and peered through the window. "Wonderful," he murmured.

Rees said nothing.

Hollerbach let his hand rest. "I know what you're feeling."

"The worst of it is," Rees said quietly, "that the passengers still blame me for the difficulties we face. Mothers hold out their hungry children accusingly as I go past."

Hollerbach laughed. "Rees, you mustn't let it bother you. You have not lost the brave idealism of your recent youth—the idealism which, untempered by maturity," he said drily, "drove you to endanger your own skin by associating yourself with the Scientists at the time of the rebellion. But you have grown into a man who has learned that the first priority is the survival of the species . . . and you have learned to impose that discipline on others. You showed that with your defeat of Gover."

"My murder of him, you mean."

"If you felt anything other than remorse for the actions you have been forced to take, I would respect you less." The old Scientist squeezed his shoulder.

"If only I could be sure I have been right," Rees said. "Maybe I've seduced these people to their deaths with false hope."

"Well, the signs are good. The navigators assure me our maneuver around the Core was successful, and that we are on course for our new home ... And, if you want a further symbol of good fortune—" He pointed above his head. "Look up there."

Rees peered upwards. The migrating school of whales was a sheet of slender, ghostly forms crossing the sky from left to right. On the fringes of that river of life he caught glimpses of plate creatures, of sky wolves with firmly closed mouths, and other, even more exotic creatures, all gliding smoothly to their next home.

Throughout the Nebula there must be more of these vast schools: rank on rank of them, all abandoning the dying gas cloud, scattering silhouettes against the Nebula's somber glow. Soon, Rees mused, the Nebula would be drained of life ... save for a few tethered trees, and the trapped remnants of humanity.

Now there was a slow stirring in the whale stream. Three of the great beasts drifted together, flukes turning, until they were moving over and around each other in a vast, stately dance. At last they came so close that their flukes interlocked and their bodies touched; it was as if they had merged into a single creature. The rest of the school drifted respectfully around the triad.

"What are they doing?"

Hollerbach smiled. "Of course I'm speculating—and, at my age, mostly from memory—but I believe they're mating."

Rees gasped.

"Well, why not? What better circumstances to do so, than surrounded by one's fellows and so far from the stresses and dangers of nebular life? Even the sky wolves are hardly in a position to attack, are they? You know, it wouldn't surprise me—given these long, enclosed hours with nothing much to do—if we too didn't enjoy a population explosion."

Rees laughed. "That's all we need."

"Yes, it is," Hollerbach murmured seriously. "Anyway, my point, my friend, is that perhaps we should emulate those whales. Self-doubt is part of being human ... but the main thing is to get on with the business of survival, as best one can. And that is what you have done."

"Thanks, Hollerbach," Rees said. "I understand what you're trying to do. But maybe you need to tell all that to the passengers' empty bellies."

"Perhaps. I ... I—" Hollerbach collapsed into a bout of deep, rasping coughing. "I'm sorry," he said at last.

Rees studied the old Scientist with some concern; in the blue internebular light it seemed he saw the lines of Hollerbach's skull.

The Bridge entered the outermost layers of the new nebula. Thin air whistled around the stumps of the control jets.

Rees and Gord manhandled Nead into the corridor close to the port. The young Scientist's legs—rendered useless by the smashing of his spine during his fall at closest approach—had been strapped together and stiffened with a length of wood. Nead insisted that he felt nothing below his waist, but Rees saw how his face twisted at each jarring motion.

Studying Nead he felt a deep, sick guilt. The lad was still barely eighteen thousand shifts old, and yet by following Rees he had already been maimed; and now he was volunteering for still more peril. The stumps of snapped rivets at the supply machine's vacant mount reminded Rees of the sacrifice Roch had made at this place. He was, he found, deeply reluctant to witness another.

"Listen to me, Nead," he said seriously. "I appreciate the way you've volunteered for this mission—"

Nead looked at him in sudden concern. "You have to let me go," he insisted.

Rees placed a hand on Nead's shoulder. "Of course. What I'm trying to tell you is that I want to see you fix the new steam jets out there . . . and then return, safely. We need those jets, if we're not to fall straight into the Core of this new nebula. We don't need another dead hero."

"I understand, Rees." Nead smiled. "But what can happen? The air out there is desperately thin, but it contains oxygen, and I won't be out for long."

"Take nothing for granted. Remember our sensor instruments were constructed ages ago and in another universe, for god's sake . . . Even if we knew precisely what they were telling us we wouldn't know if we could rely on them working here."

Gord frowned. "Yes, but our theories back up the instrument readings. Because of the diffusion of oxygen-based life we expect most of the nebulae to consist of oxygen-nitrogen air."

"I know that." Rees sighed. "And theories are fine. All I'm saying is that we don't know, here and

296

now, what Nead will find on the other side of that door."

Nead dropped his eyes. "Look, Rees, I know I'm crippled. But my arms and shoulders are as strong as they ever were. I know what I'm doing, and I can do this job."

"I know you can . . . Just come back safely."

Nead smiled and nodded, the characteristic streak of gray in his hair catching the corridor light.

Now Rees and Gord fixed two steam jets to Nead's waist by a length of rope. The bulky jets were awkward but manageable in the micro-gravity conditions. Another rope was fixed to Nead's waist and would be anchored to the ship.

Gord checked that the inner door to the Observatory was sealed, so that the passengers were in no danger; then they exchanged final, wordless handshakes, and Gord palmed the opening panel.

The outer door slid out of sight. The air was sucked from Rees's chest. Sound died to a muffled whisper and he tasted blood running from his nose. A warmth in his popping ears led him to suspect he was bleeding there too.

The door revealed a sea of blue light far below. They had already passed through the nebula's outer halo of star-spawning hydrogen and it was possible to make out stars above and below them. Far above Rees's head a small, compact knot of redness marked the position of the Nebula from which he had flown. It was strange to think that he could raise a hand and block out his world, all the places he had seen and the people he had known: Pallis, Sheen, Jame the barman, Decker . . . He knew that Pallis and Sheen had decided to live out their remaining shifts together; now, eyes fixed on that distant blur, Rees sent out a silent prayer that they—and all the others who had sacrificed so much to get him this far—were safe and well.

Rees and Gord lifted Nead bodily through the open Port. His legs swinging as if carved from wood, the injured Scientist shoved himself off in the direction of a jet mounting. Rees and Gord waited in the open doorway, the securing rope in their hands.

Nead slowed a few feet short of the jet mount. Rees watched anxiously as Nead scrabbled at the frictionless surface of the hull. Then the mount came within reach and he grabbed at it gratefully, locking his fingers around small irregularities in the iron surface.

He hauled on his ropes. Gord and Rees bundled the first steam jet out of the port and shoved it toward the young Scientist. They judged it well, the package of machinery stopping a few feet short of Nead. With fast but precise motions Nead dragged at his rope and fielded the machine. Now the Scientist had to align the jet, at least roughly, with the Bridge's axis, and he spent long seconds struggling with the old device's bulk.

At last it was correct. From a chest pocket Nead dragged out adhesive pads and slapped them against the mount; then, the strain showing on his face, he hauled the machine into place over the pads. Finally he untied the rope from the secured jet and cast it free.

Nead had worked fast and well, but already some thirty seconds had passed. The bulk of the work had still to be performed, and the pain in Rees's chest was reaching a hollow crescendo.

Now Nead scrambled toward the next mount, over the curve of the hull and out of sight. After unbearably long seconds there was a tugging on one rope. Rees and the mine engineer threw the second steam jet through the hatch. The bulky machine bumped around the hull.

It was impossible to gauge the passage of time. Had only seconds passed since they had launched the machine?

Without reference points time was an elastic thing ... Blackness closed around Rees's vision.

There was a flurry of motion to his right. He turned, his chest burning. Gord had begun to haul on the rope, his face blue now and his eyes protruding. Rees joined him. The rope moved disturbingly easily, sliding unimpeded over the frictionless surface.

A sense of dread blossomed alongside Rees's pain.

The end of the rope came rushing around the curve of the hull. The line had been neatly cut.

Gord fell back, eyes closing, the effort he had expended apparently pushing him over the brink into unconsciousness. Rees, his vision failing, placed his palm over the door's control panel.

And waited.

Gord slumped against the door frame. Rees's lungs were a jelly of pain, and his throat tore at the empty air ...

A blur before him, hands gripping the rim of the door frame, a face contorted around blue lips, a stiff body with strapped legs ... Nead, he realized dully; Nead had returned, and there was something he had to do.

His arm, as if independent of his will, spasmed against the port's control panel. The port slid shut. Then the inner door opened and he was pulled backwards into the thickening air.

Later Nead explained, his voice a rasp: "I could feel I was running out of time, and I still wasn't finished. So I cut the rope and kept going. I'm sorry."

"You're a bloody fool," Rees whispered. He struggled for a while to raise his head from his pallet; then he gave up, slumped back, and drifted back to sleep.

With Nead's jets they guided the ship into a wide, elliptical orbit around a hot yellow star deeper inside the new nebula. The great doors were hurled open and men crawled around the hull attaching climbing ropes and fixing fresh steam jets. Thin, bright air suffused the musty interior of the ship; the stink of recycled and tanked air was dispelled at last and a mood of celebration spread among the passengers.

Even the ration queues seemed good-humored.

The bodies of those who had not survived the crossing were lifted from the ship, wrapped in rags and dropped into the air. Rees glanced around the knot of mourners gathered at the port. He observed suddenly what a mix of people they were now: there were Raft folk like Jaen and Grye, alongside Gord and other miners; and there was Quid and his party of Boneys. They all mingled quite unselfconsciously, united by grief and pride. The old divisions meant nothing, Rees realized; in this new place there were only humans . . .

Eventually the Bridge would move on from this star but these bodies would remain here in orbit for many shifts, marking man's arrival in the new world, before air friction finally carried them into the flames of the star.

Despite the influx of fresh air Hollerbach continued to weaken steadily. At length he took to a pallet fixed before the Bridge's window-like hull. Rees joined the old Scientist; together they gazed out into the new starlight.

Hollerbach fell into a fit of coughing. Rees rested his hand on the old man's head, and at last Hollerbach's breathing steadied. "I told you you should have left me behind," he wheezed.

Rees ignored that and leant forward. "You should have seen the release of the young trees," he said. "We just opened the cages and out they flew ... They've spread out around this star as if they were born here."

"Perhaps they were," Hollerbach observed drily. "Pallis would have liked that."

"I don't think any of us younger folk realized how green leaves could be. And the trees seem to be growing already. Soon we'll have a forest big enough to harvest, and we'll be able to move out: find whales, perhaps, fresh sources of food ..."

Now Hollerbach began to fumble beneath his pallet; with Rees's help he retrieved a small package wrapped in grubby cloth.

"What's this?"

"Take it."

Rees unwrapped the cloth to expose a finely tooled machine the size of his cupped hands; at its heart a silver orb gleamed, and around the orb multicolored beads followed wire circles. "Your orrery," Rees said.

"I brought it in my personal effects."

Rees fingered the familiar gadget. Embarrassed, he said: "Do you want me to have it when you're gone?"

"No, damn it!" Hollerbach coughed indignantly. "Rees, your streak of sentimentality disturbs me. No, I wish now I'd left the bloody thing behind. Lad, I want you to destroy it. When you throw me out of that door send it after me."

Rees was shocked. "But why? It's the only orrery in the universe . . . literally irreplaceable."

"It means nothing!" The old eyes glittered. "Rees, the thing is a symbol of a lost past, a past we must disregard. We have clung to such tokens for far too long. Now we are creatures of this universe."

With sudden intensity the old man grabbed Rees's sleeve and seemed to be trying to pull himself upright. Rees, frowning, laid a hand on his shoulder and gently pressed him back. "Try to rest—"

"Bugger that," Hollerbach rasped. "I haven't time to waste on resting . . . You have to tell them—"

"What?"

"To spread. Fan out through this nebula. We've got to fill every niche we can find here; we can't rely on relics of an alien past any more. If we're to prosper we must become natives of this place, find ways to live here, using our own ingenuity and resources . . ." Another coughing jag broke up his words. "I want that population explosion we spoke of. We can't ever again risk the future of the race in a single ship, or even a single nebula. We have to fill this damn cloud, and go on to the other nebulae and fill them as well. I want not just thousands but millions of humans in this damn place, talking and squabbling and learning.

"And ships . . . we'll need new ships. I see trade between the inhabited nebulae, as if they were the legendary cities of old Earth. I see us finding a way even to visit the realms of the gravitic creatures. . . .

"And I see us one day building a ship that will fly us back through Bolder's Ring, the gateway to man's home universe. We'll return and tell our cousins there what became of us . . ." At last Hollerbach's energy was exhausted; the gray head slumped back against its rag pillow, eyes closing slowly.

When it was over Rees carried him to the port, the orrery wrapped in the stilled fingers. Silently he launched the body into the crisp air and watched it drift away until it was lost against the background of the falling stars; then, as Hollerbach had wished, he hurled the orrery into the sky. Within seconds it had vanished.

There was a warm mass at his side—Jaen, standing quietly with him. He took her hand, squeezing it gently, and his thoughts began to run along new, unexplored tracks. Now that the adventure was over perhaps he and Jaen might think about a new kind of life, of a home of their own—

Jaen gasped. She pointed. "My god . . . look."

Something came lunging out of the sky. It was a compact, pale green wheel of wood, like a tree six feet wide. It snapped to a halt mere yards from Rees's face and hovered there, maintaining its position with rapid flicks of rotation. Short, fat limbs snaked out of the trunk, and what looked like tools of wood and iron were fixed at various points to the rim. Rees searched in vain for the tree's tiny pilots.

"By the Bones, Rees," Jaen snapped, "what the hell is it?"

Four eyes, blue and shockingly human, snapped open in the upper surface of the trunk and fixed them with a stern gaze.

Rees grinned. The adventure, he realized, was far from over.

In fact, it might barely have begun.